THE PHOENIX KEEPER AND THE CITY OF THE SUN

MARGARITA ARTISTA

MARGARITA ARTISTA

PUBLISHED BY AZALA PRESS
COVER DESIGN BY RACHEL MCEWAN DESIGNS

© *MARGARITA ARTISTA*

"The two most important days in your life are the day you were born and the day you find out why."
Mark Twain

"As individuals express their life, so they are."
Karl Marx

"A ship is safe in harbour, but that's not what ships are for."
William G. T. Shedd

"What good are wings without the courage to fly?"
Atticus

For
Mom, Dad, and Adam

&

In loving memory of
Mema

THE
PHOENIX KEEPER
—AND THE—
CITY OF THE SUN

A Note From The Author:

This novel and its affiliates are a work of fiction. The ideas, discourse, and actions presented throughout the development of this story are not meant to be taken as historically accurate. The way people, places, and institutions are named and described throughout this story are not intended to be whole representations.

This work is not intended to encourage, discourage, idealize, or romanticize any thoughts or actions. This work is intended to make you think.

A conscious effort to maintain equal representation of different genders, sexualities, ethnicities, religions, lifestyles, and other significant markers of individuality has been made in the creation of these books. No representation throughout this story is meant to be taken as a whole representation of the entire group to which that person belongs.

This work is intended to act as an acknowledgement that we all have differences and similarities, endure hardships and celebrate accomplishments, and can be good or bad, no matter our walks of life. We are not defined by our skin tone, who we choose to love, the religion that we follow, or any singular detail in itself. Rather, these things become small ingredients that are mixed into the recipe of who we are. They are not us; they are parts of us.

PROLOGUE

WHEN TELLING a story as complex as ours, it is often difficult to determine the true beginning.

One could argue our story began when I'd misplaced my keepsake, never thinking I'd see it again. But that was many, many years ago – long before we reconnected, and long before everything else began. So perhaps that is the contextual beginning to one part of our story, but this story contains many moving parts that form a puzzle we couldn't even piece as we were living it. And arguably, that little bit is only a very small piece of a very big puzzle.

Upon further consideration, I concur that the more relevant commencement of our story was that night when I ran.

As I had for most of my life, I continued running as fast as I could, towards something I couldn't explain but away from anything I understood. There was no joy in the things I knew well. My only hope for satisfaction was to run towards the future.

My feet hit the grass along the cliffs harder with each galloping step, my breath coming in short and raspy waves that contrasted the deep, blue ones of the ocean below. I felt a shadow suddenly appear above me and glanced up at the darkened sky to see him flying a few feet above. My partner in stride for as long as I'd been running. The only accompaniment I both tolerated and hadn't yet pushed away. The single most resounding lesson I'd learned was that you could not be abandoned if you abandoned them first. But the accompanying truth is that whether you are the abandoner or the abandonee, the bottom line is that you still end up alone. I suppose I was lucky that he stuck around, then, but maybe it was because he didn't really have another choice. It's impossible to break that kind of bond – except, of course, with death.

I ran the same route I'd run countless times before, until the predictable lookout at the top of the hill, where I gathered myself and sat in the grass. He came and landed beside me, as he always did. Together, we gazed out at the darkness before us, in both the sky and in the water.

It took a moment for my uneven breathing to settle and for my eyes to focus on the night. The stars began twinkling into view, one by one. It reminded me of when I was a young boy. She would sit me in her lap and hold me carefully, pointing to the constellations, teaching me their names.

I swallowed, burying the memory away as I reached into my pocket and pulled out a cigarette. I produced a flame with my fingertip and lit it before breathing it in slowly. The smoking didn't help much anymore. But it didn't make things worse, either. There were other escapist routes I'd taken that were far more dangerous.

A blinking light in the sky caught my eyes, and I focused on it. A plane, most likely bound for Los Angeles. Each time the light shone, I could just barely make out the bright red maple leaf on its fin. An Air Canada flight. I stared at it as it flew through the sky, pondering who might be on it. The concept of several hundred people all flying from one city to the other intrigued me, just the same as several thousand of us all convening at the university in the next few days for the start of a new semester. Thousands of different people with thousands of different destinies – who knows how they might intersect?

The blinking light slowly vanished behind some trees, and I supposed that would be the last of the flight's impact on me. Just a thought-provoking plane in the night, carrying a bunch of passengers who made no real difference in my life.

I was incredibly wrong. Foolishly wrong. But it's sometimes difficult to recognize your fate – especially if you are a dying flame, and that fate is a beacon of light.

PART 1: THE REBIRTH

CHAPTER 1

- S -

EVEN THOUGH MY lids were shut, the sudden flicker of light was bright enough to jolt me from my sleep.

My eyes popped open, bringing into focus the dorm room I hadn't quite become accustomed to yet. The desk and chair at the opposite side of the room came into view, and beside them was the bookshelf – a perfectly cozy study nook. Everything seemed clean and befitting to the space; the suitcase I'd not yet unpacked was the only part of the room that seemed out of place – that is, if you ignored the slender girl who stood in the open doorway to the bathroom.

"Oh!" she exclaimed as I blinked at her. "I didn't think anyone was in here!"

I yawned and sat up in bed, rubbing the sleep out of my big, brown eyes. "*Oui,* the university gave me an early move-in because I'm from out of town."

She looked down at a collection of papers she held in her hand. I assumed they must have been the same welcome forms

I'd received, because the next words out of her mouth were, "So, you must be Seraphine?"

I nodded. "And you must be Emmanuella."

"That's me," she replied, and she pointed to her chest where a nametag that read *Emmanuella Rosa* was stuck; the university was handing them out to all dorm residents. "You can call me Em."

"Nice to meet you, Em."

"You, too. Do people ever call you Sera?"

"Not really. But you're welcome to call me that if you want."

"Sweet. Nicknames are the best." She nodded towards me. "Sorry, by the way. I didn't mean to wake you up."

"It's all good," I said, looking at the clock on my night-stand. It read nine in the morning. "It's about time I got up, anyways. I have a bunch of eight-thirty lectures I'll have to start getting into routine for."

"Same here," she said, approaching the windows over which the curtains were drawn. "You want the curtains open?"

"Sure."

She parted the drapes. The space was lively and airy with the presence of the natural light, which had no trouble streaming in thanks to the size of the massive window and the strength of the sun that sat high over San Diego. There was a screen door, too, that led out on to the small terrace over-looking one of the campus courtyards. The little palm plant that sat on the corner of my balcony seemed to be as cheerful about the sunlight as I was.

"Well, I've definitely seen worse views!" she exclaimed.

I agreed as I stood from the bed and stretched, pushing my dark brown curls away from my face. "Did you just arrive?" I asked her.

She turned back to face me – in the light, I could see that her long, tousled hair was jet black, and her eyes were a deep brown that complimented her medium skin tone. "Yeah.

Maybe about an hour ago, but there was a huge line to get the keys at reception, so it took way longer than it should have." She rolled her eyes at me. "Like, they've got two people working the UC San Diego's residence services on move-in day. Whose bright idea was that?"

"Mhm. Sounds like how hectic it was getting my luggage at the airport yesterday," I said, eyeing my suitcase. "I should probably unpack."

"So should I," she replied. "And then I definitely need some food."

"I second that. The cafeteria's in the next building over, I think."

She gave me some finger guns. "You and me, Sera. Cafeteria date." I gave her a finger gun and a wink back.

It took the two of us a couple of hours to unpack our things and make the dorms our own. When we were both satisfied, I stuck my own nametag on my chest, and we walked down four flights of stairs and over to the cafeteria.

The cafeteria was large and full of new students bustling to and fro in a flurry to grab some lunch. Emmanuella and I each got a sandwich and a salad before sitting down at a table.

"You said you were from out of town?" she asked me.

"*Oui*, I'm from Montreal."

"Ah. That explains it."

I smiled slightly. "Is my accent strong?"

"No. You don't really have much of an accent when you're speaking English, actually. But you keep saying '*oui*,' so I figured something was up."

I laughed. "I see."

"What brings you all the way from Canada, then?" she then asked.

"None of the universities over there had a convincing marine biology program, and I kind of wanted an excuse to get out anyways."

"Makes sense. I hear it's cold up there."

"It is." I nodded towards her. "What about yourself? Where are you from?"

Her story was melancholy, but inspiring. Her mother was a hardworking, undocumented immigrant who had risked everything to birth and raise Emmanuella in California. Unfortunately, her mother was later discovered and sent back to Mexico when Emmanuella was eleven; Em had remained in California with close family friends that she described as her second family – she even referred to their daughter as her own sister. After studying hard all throughout high school, she earned a generous scholarship and was looking to get a degree in education, dreaming of helping children who faced similar struggles as she did within the system. I personally could see young students taking quite a liking to her, and I could feel the passion as she spoke, so I had no doubts she was on the right track.

When we had finished eating, we decided to go to the campus bookstore to purchase our textbooks and lab materials. I found the books for all my other classes before I eventually stumbled upon the biology text I needed – the last one on the shelf.

As I reached for it, another hand did as well. I looked up and realized it belonged to a tall, handsome individual with fair skin and bright, hazel eyes. His nametag read *Elijah King*.

I retracted my hand. "Oh, sorry," I muttered.

Elijah held up one finger as a symbol for me to wait. I watched as he brushed his brown hair to the side and fiddled with a small device in his ear.

"Sorry," he then said with a small smile. "I have hearing aids, but it was super noisy in here, so I turned them down. What was it you said?"

I returned his smile. "I said I was sorry – about the book. You can have it."

He shook his head with a small laugh. "No, no, it's all good," he said. "You were here first. Take it. It's yours."

I glanced around. "You sure? The bookstore might not get any until after classes start."

"Yeah, it's no big deal." He stopped for a second, then grinned at me. "If you're worried about my grades, though, maybe you and I could share until they do."

I studied him, my own lips curling a bit. "Aren't your grades your own responsibility?"

"I was hoping to pin them on you, actually."

I crossed my arms, my smirk widening as I lowered my gaze. "Why? So you have an excuse for your parents when you fail out?"

He leaned against the bookshelf. "I plan on telling them I was too distracted by this witty girl with the prettiest eyes I've ever seen." He looked me up and down, his own gaze bright. "Maybe they'll forgive me when I bring you home and finally get them off my case about finding a nice girlfriend."

I bit my lip to hide my amusement. "Not that I'm opposed to it, but it will be difficult if we aren't in the same section."

"What's your section?"

"Wednesdays and Fridays from eight-thirty to nine-fifty. Building three, hall sixty-four," I replied.

He pulled out his phone and began tapping away. "Nothing a little rearranging can't fix." He then showed me his screen proudly, which was open to the site where we could register for classes and adjust our schedules. "I just made it my section, too."

I raised an eyebrow. "You must really want to get to know me."

"Am I that transparent?"

It was my turn to scan him up and down. "Hmph. Well, the worst you could be is just another disappointment to me."

"Oof. Harsh."

"Not harsh. Just the truth."

He sighed, then placed his hand over his chest as his eyes softened a bit. "I swear I will do anything in my power not to disappoint you." He blinked. "I can't help the fact that I am a guy, though, so take that with a grain of salt, I guess."

I swirled my tongue around my cheek as my smile widened, extending my hand towards him. "Honest, yet charming. I'm Seraphine."

He shook it. "I'm Elijah. That's a lovely name," he remarked. "I look forward to sharing a textbook with you, Seraphine. I'll keep an eye out for you in class." He paused, then added with a sly smile, "Though I really don't think I'll have much trouble spotting you in a crowd."

I tucked a strand of my curls behind my ear. It was an automatic response to flattery that I'd developed over the years for reasons I didn't really understand.

Elijah then returned to his book search, and I picked up the last biology textbook. When I'd also found the text I needed for my elective, Greek Mythology, I made my way back to Emmanuella and we both paid our dues.

We returned to our dorm building, arms piled high with our mountain of materials. Upon reaching the fourth floor, we were met with three other boys in the hall.

"Sheesh, that's a lot of books," said the palest one with a big, goofy grin. His nametag read *Keiffer Traugott.*

"You girls need some help there?" asked another with skin and eyes of ebony. *Roscoe Manning* was written on his nametag.

"How chivalrous," Emmanuella replied, sneaking me a crafty look to which I rolled my eyes. "That would be lovely, boys."

She plopped some of her books into Keiffer's hands as I placed some of mine in Roscoe's. "Where's your dorm?" questioned the third, whose nametag read *Sajan Kapoor.* His eyes were a stunning, silvery-blue against his warm skin.

"Just right down the hall there," I replied, nodding with my chin.

Roscoe and Sajan helped me to my dorm, while Keiffer went with Emmanuella. "You two probably know where the bookstore is, by the looks of things," Roscoe noted as I was putting my books away on the shelf.

I let out an amused breath. "Either that, or the library."

"Nah. Anybody who went to the library would definitely have found something more tolerable than − " he grabbed one of the textbooks at random " − *Introductory Mechanics, Volume Three.*"

I laughed. "Like what?"

He grinned, leaning against the wall as his long dreadlocks fell over his shoulders. "Hell would I know? All my books are written by dead, old, white guys."

I raised my eyebrows in confusion, throwing an inquisitive glance at Sajan. "He's a political science major," he explained simply.

"Got it," I said. "And you?"

"Computer science. And Keiffer's in mechanical engineering." He shifted his eyes. "…Somehow."

"Wow. Smart bunch." I nodded towards Roscoe. "How do you all know each other?"

"We were all on our high school basketball team, and now we're on the university's," Roscoe answered. "Managed to get a full ride that way."

"Even Keiffer," Sajan added, glancing around the room. "…Somehow."

My lips twitched at him. "What's up with Keiffer?"

Sajan and Roscoe exchanged glances. "Keiffer is…something else," Roscoe remarked.

Just then, I heard Emmanuella yelling from the other room. "Hey! What the hell do you think you're doing, moron?"

Roscoe and Sajan looked at me. I frowned before heading through the bathroom and into her dorm, where I came face to face with Keiffer running Em's hair straightener through his hair. Emmanuella was at her bookshelf, a hand on her hip and a disgruntled expression on her face.

I frowned at Keiffer, to which he just smiled innocently. "I've always wanted to try one of these things," he explained.

I glanced at the cord of the straightener, which was unplugged. "Well, you might want to plug it in first," I noted.

"You have to plug these things in?" he exclaimed in disbelief, pulling the straightener away from his hair to study it more closely. "I thought they just flattened the hairs by crushing them! You know, like a pancake." He paused. "Or, like, a million tiny pancakes. A million tiny hair-shaped pancakes." He grinned, chuckling to himself. "On a head."

I blinked, glancing at Emmanuella. She rolled her eyes and let out a sigh of exasperation before turning back to her bookshelf.

"We told you," I heard Roscoe whisper from behind me.

I gave my head a quick shake and turned back to him and Sajan. "The bookstore is just on the other side of the cafeteria."

"Swell." He turned to look at Sajan. "We should swing by before dinner, hey?"

Keiffer made a face. "Books before dinner? What are you guys, animals?"

Roscoe rolled his eyes. "We're here to study, you know."

"Yeah, but I don't have to starve at the same time!"

"It'll be, like, five minutes. Stop being a little bitch."

Keiffer huffed. "Fine." He put the hair straightener down and turned to Em. "We'll catch you guys later – if we survive."

She snorted as she shot him a look. "I'd wish you luck, but that would be stupid."

"She gets it," Sajan remarked.

I smiled at Roscoe. "Thanks again for the help."

He gave me a salute. "Don't mention it. We're on this floor, too – might check out the lounge later, if you want to meet us there."

"Sounds like a plan."

The floor's lounge was way at the end of the hall. The room was a fair size, with a TV and accompanying sofas, a small kitchen, and two tables with four chairs each. When Emmanuella and I walked in later that evening, the TV was on, and the boys were already in the room along with two girls we hadn't met yet.

"There they are!" Roscoe announced. "Emmanuella and Seraphine, come meet our other floormates!"

The girls introduced themselves to us. Everly Trotman had a striking mocha complexion and a physique that complimented her kinesiology major. She shared her dorm with her childhood best friend, Chenoa Bernhard, who had Cherokee heritage and a passion for indigenous law, which she was hoping to get into after completing a criminology degree. There was fire in her hazel-green eyes and great length to her raven hair.

"Make sure you two keep your hair straighteners away from this one," Emmanuella warned Everly and Chenoa as she sat down, motioning towards Keiffer. He stuck his tongue out at her as Roscoe and Sajan snickered.

Chenoa glanced between us all. "What?"

"It's a long story," I replied. "But the warning is relevant."

Everly smirked. "You some kind of troublemaker or what, blondie?" she asked Keiffer.

"More like a trouble finder," Roscoe answered for him.

Everly looked Keiffer up and down — I could recognize that sort of look from a mile away. "What kind of trouble do you like finding?" she asked him in a voice that was also very telling. I found myself raising my eyebrows in surprise at her forwardness.

Somehow, it went right over his head. "I like finding food," was his clueless reply. I threw a glance at Emmanuella, who had to suck in her lips to keep from laughing. Sajan hit his face with his palm while Roscoe shook his head slowly.

In an effort to spare Everly any embarrassment, I nodded towards the TV and chimed, "What are we watching?"

"I wanted to catch up on the news," Roscoe said. "President Klein was supposed to be making an announcement this afternoon."

"Please tell me it's that he's resigning," Chenoa sighed hopefully. I had a similar opinion about the American president, but I didn't voice it.

Roscoe rolled his eyes. "I wish. No, it's probably got to do with a trade deal or something."

"Republicans and their money-hungry ways," Chenoa said with a click of her teeth.

"Must be a great time to be a political science student, what with all the contention," Sajan remarked.

"You certainly never run out of material," Roscoe replied. "For better or for worse."

He ended up being right about the trade deal. We watched the president's obnoxious announcement about it until none of us could take anymore, and then switched to a football game, which was considerably more bearable.

At one point, Keiffer went over to the fridge and opened it. "Aw, damn," he said. "There's nothing in here."

"What, did you expect the university to provide milk and eggs?" Emmanuella teased him.

"Well, no," Keiffer replied. "I was kind of hoping there'd be cheese, though."

"Cheese?" we all repeated in unison.

Keiffer looked at us all blankly. "I like cheese," he explained quietly.

Chenoa shook her head. "If they gave us anything, we wouldn't be forced to buy that overpriced crap they call food in the cafeteria."

I studied the kitchen. "I mean, they gave us a microwave,

an oven, and a stovetop," I observed. "There's a lot we can do with that, still. We just need ingredients."

"Like cheese?" Keiffer suggested.

We all shot him a look. "We also need a coffee maker," Everly piped up.

"Can't believe they left that out, honestly," Roscoe noted. "Coffee's more important than blood to students."

"Seraphine's got a point, though," Sajan remarked. "If we all pitch in, we could probably save some money stocking this fridge and making meals in here, when we can."

"And we could get cheese!" Keiffer enthused.

Em rolled her eyes at him. "Keiffer's cheese obsession aside, I think it's a good idea."

"Me, too," I said.

"All right, then. Shall we do a floormate grocery run?" Roscoe proposed.

Everly did a quick search in her phone. "There's a Trader Joe's about a ten-minute bus ride from here. And a Wal-Mart that's walking distance from it. We can get a kettle from there."

"Let's go!" Sajan said.

And so, we all embarked on the voyage to the stores, gathering the various ingredients we needed from Trader Joe's – including cheese – and the ever-so valuable coffee maker and cutlery from Wal-Mart before returning to UC San Diego. We packed all the things away in the fridge and cabinets, and then set up a small mason jar where we could each contribute some weekly funds for our groceries. By then, it was dinnertime, so we prepared some of the pasta and meatballs we'd just bought and ate it all together at the table and chairs.

"This was a genius idea," Keiffer said as he practically swallowed the spaghetti without a chew.

"Agreed," said Chenoa.

"What time is everyone waking up for class tomorrow?" Sajan asked. "We should try to have breakfast together if we can."

"I've got an eight-thirty one, so I've got to be up at seven at the latest," Everly said after swallowing a bite of her vegan version of dinner.

"Same here," I chimed.

Everyone agreed that we could meet in the lounge the next morning just before eight, and with the plans solidified, we all headed to our dorms for bed.

The next morning, we prepared ourselves a pancake breakfast and copious amounts of coffee for the first day of classes. It was encouraging to see familiar faces before heading off to my first lecture – biology.

The lecture hall was large, and I arrived relatively early, so after I had found myself a seat at the back, I watched as more and more bodies began to fill up the room. Closer to eight-thirty, I saw Elijah walk in. He paused and glanced around the hall, spotted me, and then gave me a small wave and a smile. I smiled back, and he made his way up towards me.

"Told you it wouldn't be hard to find you," he said with a wink as he sat down beside me.

I let out a humoured breath, pushing my open textbook so that it was between us. "Here you are, as promised."

"Much appreciated," he said, and the professor walked in then – a short, old man who introduced himself as Dr. Johnson. He zoomed through the course syllabus, assured us more textbooks would be arriving in the bookstore soon, and then sent us away earlier than the class should have ended.

"You know, my floormates and I all decided to cook food and eat together, instead of depending on cafeteria food. You could join us, if you'd like," I offered to Elijah as we left the lecture hall.

"I like the sound of that," he replied. "Which residence are you in?"

"It's the brand new one, just across from the main cafeteria," I said. "We're on the fourth floor."

"Sweet. Mind if my roommate joins? He could use some friends as well."

"By all means."

He agreed to swing by for dinner, and we parted ways. I had my first physics lecture that afternoon, and right after it was my first laboratory for the same subject. I was a little nervous as physics was not my strength, but I also needed it to go further in marine biology and thus was determined to pass.

I walked into the room, which consisted of large steel counters all facing a long whiteboard and teaching bench. It looked as though it could fit about thirty people, and most students in the room when I arrived were male. I found an empty stool at one of the counters at the back of the room and plopped myself down.

A teaching assistant ran the laboratory − a graduate student. He was short, lanky, and wore big, black-rimmed square glasses.

"Good morning, and welcome to your Mechanics lab," he said in a bit of a shaky voice. "My name is Lucah. I must apologize as this is my first time ever assisting with a lab course, so please forgive my nervousness."

He cleared his throat. "This lab runs adjacent to your PHYS 1A lectures. What you study each week in your lectures, you will then apply that same week in this lab. You are allotted three hours in this lab to complete your weekly task alongside your lab partner. I have randomly selected and assigned you each to a partner whom you will remain with for the entire semester. Are there any questions so far?"

Nobody had any questions, so he nodded and gave us all a little smile. "Excellent. I will now show you your assigned partners up on the screen here."

He turned on a projector with a little remote, which brought up a list of pairs. A low murmur spread throughout the classroom as everyone searched for their names. I scanned the list quickly and found my name at the very end, unpaired. I crinkled my brows a bit – did I not have a partner? This was the one lab class where I really felt like a partner would be necessary for me, and I became a little anxious.

Lucah was gazing over the list as the class did, and he suddenly turned to face us. "Oh, yes! That's right! Is there a, uh – " he paused and checked the list again " – a Seraphine Pierre, here?"

I raised my hand. "That's me."

"Oh, perfect. I apologize, the class was originally odd-numbered, which is why you see your name alone here. I was going to make an exception and have one group of three, but I was notified by the department head shortly before class that a student was interested in transferring into this section due to a scheduling conflict. They'll just be stopping at the main office first to do some quick paperwork, but they should be here within the first hour."

I smiled, relaxing a bit. "That works for me. Thanks so much."

"Wonderful. All right, now I'll take attendance, starting from the top."

He went through the list of names, and people paired up as he went down the list. When everyone had paired up and shuffled around the room accordingly, Lucah put up a different document on the projector. It looked like an assignment briefing.

"This is your first task. This one is quite simple and shouldn't take you the full three hours by any means. You will be using the tools provided and following this guide – " he motioned to the screen " – to laser a circle of a particular diameter into sheet metal. You will then complete a lab report following the format and answering the questions provided in your assignment guide. The lab report is always due the day after your lab. You will be turning them in the paper slot with your section number just outside this room before the building closes at nine o'clock in the evening. Everyone will be given a different diameter they need to achieve, so don't look at the other groups at your bench! I'll hand out this guide so you have it at your counters. Otherwise, feel free to start grabbing the supplies you need from around the classroom and begin!"

Everyone quickly launched into action. I gathered everything the assignment guide stated I would need and then headed back to my counter, opening my notebook. I thought I would prepare the report first before undertaking any of the actual task, just so that my partner wouldn't miss too much of the physical work.

About ten or so minutes after I began writing, Lucah's voice came from behind me. "Um, sorry to disturb you, Seraphine, but your lab partner has arrived now."

I immediately stopped writing and turned to face him. "Oh, that's all – "

The sight before me caught me off guard, ending my sentence prematurely. Lucah stood behind me, a shy smile on his face. Next to him towered an unsmiling, frigid man; his obvious unapproachability surprised me, but not enough to surpass the astonishment I felt from the fact that I recognized him.

"This is Felix Clarkson," Lucah said.

CHAPTER 2

THE NAME CLARKSON rang with wealth, chimed with success, and boasted of dispensation. It ran synonymous to business, to industry, to capitalism and consumerism as concepts. It was iconic in its own field; a hard name to forget, and an even harder name not to know.

Clarkson Corporations was a global conglomerate power-house, founded in the mid-twentieth century by Felix's grandfather. After he passed away, Felix's father, Luther, took over the company as its owner and president. The only reason I knew any of this was because the corporation was constantly in the public eye. They partnered with numerous brands, public figures, and endorsed major events, like the Olympics and the Super Bowl. They had an astounding number of connections with politicians and world leaders, so much so that I could practically hear the whispers of potential for bias and corruption. Their name was plastered on hotels and resorts, office buildings and towers, even golf courses and bottles of liquor. And Felix's brother, the infamous Julius Clarkson, had earned himself quite the reputation as a bit of a trouble-making ladies' man, dating famous names one right after another as if he had these women fired towards him through a revolver. The name was hard to escape; it seemed many things in our world were somehow linked to the Clarksons in some sort of tangled web. And as a result, they were one of the richest families in the world.

Felix seemed to keep himself under wraps much more than his brother and father did. If you didn't pay much attention to the news, he'd probably slip past your radar, as the only time he seemed visible was when he accompanied his family for a grand opening of some sort. But he was striking enough that I remembered him, even if his presence was seldom captured on camera.

Looking at Felix Clarkson, I could clearly see the evidence of his family's work, success, and name; it all fit into place nicely, like the pieces of a privileged puzzle. He had stylish brown hair that bordered his intensely featured, fair-skinned face, complete with a smooth jawline, high cheekbones, and a sculpted chin. Stubble groomed his jaw neatly, and his neck sat perfectly between his broad and sturdy shoulders. He had to have been well over six feet tall, and he was fit – not lanky, but not too muscular, either. He had a gold-lined Rolex on his left wrist, and his entire outfit was a pretentious mixture of blacks and dark greys – I could make out the Givenchy logo that was etched on the bottom of his suit-like jacket and an unmistakable Gucci print on his belt. On his left hand, I could see a small, black tattoo – a star, which sat on the patch of skin above where his thumb met his hand.

This all could have been distracting on its own if it weren't for his eyes, which won the contest that was his appearance. They were a striking lavender colour, with specks of blue and gold swirled in like a whirlpool; I'd never seen eyes like them before. They caught the rays of the sun through the windows and glowed radiantly like a field of the slender flowers would under such a golden spotlight – I could nearly see the small, delicate petals dancing in his irises. I hadn't even known eyes like them were possible, but they perfectly embodied him. I discovered through him a truth to the statement that the eyes were the window to the soul. They said everything about Felix Clarkson, and at the same time, they said nothing at all.

I didn't usually find myself cowering to men, especially the rich and powerful, but there was something about his demeanour that almost made him intimidating. Maybe it was the alluring mischief to his being – the air about him, besides the pompous one, was dark and enigmatic. Some of his facial features seemed to hint quietly at an Eastern European background, but they also appeared to teeter in balance with his Western ones. I couldn't really stop myself from staring at him. It was hard to pinpoint, but he seemed off in some way.

He appeared to have a story. I wasn't sure if I wanted to read it or not.

Uncertain of how to feel about the situation I was suddenly thrust into, I nodded once at Lucah, who turned to Felix. "Felix, this is Seraphine Pierre. She'll be your lab partner for this semester," he told him.

Felix's gaze shifted to him. It looked to be disapproving. This evidently unsettled Lucah, so much so that he looked back at me and gave off that awkward chuckle people did when they didn't know what else to do with themselves.

"Ah, well then, good luck to you both," he said quickly, and then hurriedly bustled away, leaving me with the man made of marble.

Felix's eyes then travelled back to me. There were a few tense seconds as we held each other's gazes. He looked me up and down several times, slowly, searching, but there was no change to the expression on his face. I didn't quite understand why he was giving me such a sullen look, since all I'd really done was exist.

- F -

In retrospect, my instincts knew then.

Perhaps my senses could pinpoint it, too, but upon reflection, the attraction was more human than magic...as embarrassing as that may be to admit. I was drawn to her like a moth to a flickering light in the creepy shadows of an abandoned room.

She carried herself differently than the women I was used to. Her curls were a deep, umber brown made caramel by the daylight, and they fell from her scalp in delicate ringlets, starkly framing the warm skin of her softly edged face. Her features were easy on the eyes, yet anything but gentle – her eyes were hickory-smoked and shaped liked almonds; she carried prowess in them, along with a light that gave them a glaze of honey when the sun kissed them. She was much shorter than me, but stood with the confidence of a tigress. Her curves were accentuated by her dark jeans and a red blouse that hugged wherever it touched. She was not thin, nor large; she was beautifully balanced, perfectly full of a curvaceous figure so becoming to her that it was thrilling. It was hard to imagine such an exotic flower existed until you stumbled upon her, blooming in a pool of light that sifted through the trees of a dark and tangled woodland.

She did not stall me because she was beautiful, although that certainly did make it difficult to pull my gaze away. But her energy was more than just prettiness – it was almost as if the light came to her, surrounded her, bowed to her, as if it knew the command she'd have with it. She was her own premonition of the greatness she would become. That glint in her eyes came from deep within her, a lightning strike down her spine and back up again.

She was something I wasn't accustomed to, something I didn't expect, a light at the end of the tunnel I hadn't realized I'd been running towards. But the stars knew, then, even if I hadn't read that far ahead. She was the sun and its rays, light and fire and stardom fused into the body and soul of a goddess. It was as if the reflection of everything I craved shimmered in her eyes, looking at me, forcing me to bear witness to my deepest desires. Everything I dreamt of, everything I longed for – there she was, personifying it all with grace and glory.

And it scared me to death.

It took every ounce of my being to keep my composure as I internally fought every emotion that flew at me, desperate to ensure she didn't see the storm she had caused. I was a fool to try and push fate away. But again, it was instinct. Immediately upon seeing her, I retreated inwards, as I always did.

No – this time was different.

The only way to guarantee the survival of a city is to not let anyone inside its walls. When something made me feel this way, it had the capacity to kill me from within like a Trojan horse. So I built my walls, and I built them feverishly, taller than mountains and carved from the strongest slabs of stone. I shielded the pieces of any heart I had left, cowering behind a mask no one would care to unravel. That was what I had learned, what the resounding lesson had been ever since I'd been left behind. It was all I'd ever known.

I didn't like anyone seeing inside my head, where the room was dark save for the one, whispering candle that was bound to take its last breath any day. Nobody would like me, so nobody got the chance to try.

Even if they were the most divine woman to ever shine in all the dullness of the world.

- S -

I motioned to the materials on the bench. "Well…shall we?"

His face didn't shift in the slightest. "I suppose there isn't much of a choice," was his stoic reply, his voice drowning in an English accent.

I tried not to take the lack of enthusiasm personally – maybe this wasn't his favourite class, either. "I've just begun the lab report here, if you want to take a look," I said, shuffling over.

He shook his head, reaching for some of the supplies. "That's all right, Miss Pierre."

I blinked. I was surprised he didn't want to see what I'd written, and I couldn't remember the last time I'd been addressed so formally. "Oh, you can just call me Seraphine."

"I'd prefer that I call you Miss Pierre," he answered without missing a beat.

I stared at him. I was dumbfounded – generally, I got along well with most people. And when I didn't, there was usually a good reason for it. But here I was, unaware of a problem that had clearly been created. From where or why, I did not know.

I decided against saying anything further and instead turned back to the report I'd started. I heard scratching metal and shifting paper as he prepared the experiment, setting the metal brace to suspend the laser and aligning the sheet of metal we were to test on. Then there was quiet; a glance showed me that he was inputting some things in the device attached to the brace and writing them down.

As I was scribbling some more things into my notebook, the sound of the laser startled me, and I watched as the programmed tool followed the path Felix had set. It completed a full circle, and then he shut the laser off and inspected his work.

After a moment, he nodded once – I suppose to himself – and picked up his pencil. "We achieved a diameter of four point six inches with a height of eleven inches above the table, and the laser was set to move at a speed of twenty-four miles per hour. That will answer your first few questions." He removed the sheet metal and looked at me for the first time in a long time. "I'll just finish up my lab report, and then you can use this for the rest of the calculations."

I looked at the circle, then at him. "Wait – so you finished the experiment?"

He didn't seem amused by my confusion. "Well, yes."

I glanced around at the other groups – partners talking amongst one another, exchanging ideas, some even laughing. "I thought we were supposed to do it together," I replied, turning back to him. "That's why we're partners."

He frowned at me. "This experiment certainly doesn't require two people."

"*Oui*, but I require being a part of the work in order to learn from it," I countered, irritated.

He shrugged. "If you'd like to repeat the experiment with another sheet, be my guest."

I cleared my throat, crossing my hands over my chest. "Look, I'm not normally one to start a fire, but I don't think this is fair."

He motioned to his page. "I gave you the answers you needed. Like I said, you're free to reconfirm them, if you wish." He then turned back to his own lab report, as if I wasn't still there staring at him in disbelief.

I took a deep breath in before I decidedly got up and went to gather another metal sheet. I returned to our bench and dismantled the brace, studying the experiment instructions and fitting the pieces together as best as I could as I restarted the experiment. I struggled with even the setup alone, questioning how Felix could have done it with such ease. Once I finally had the brace secured, I turned to the computer that was to program the laser. Step-by-step, I tried to recreate what the instructions wanted me to do. But most of the inputting was formulaic or numerical, and I'd never dealt with any sort of device with functions like I was met with. It seemed every time I punched something in, I received an error.

"Um, so for this..." I trailed off as I was met with the

fourth or fifth malfunction, not even sure what my exact question was.

"The instructions outline everything you need to do quite clearly," was the unhelpful answer I received. I subsequently decided against asking him anything else, turning back instead to the instructions and reading them repeatedly. I'd figure it out myself.

After several minutes, nothing had become clearer to me with rereading. I still hadn't successfully programmed the laser when Felix began packing up his things. I watched him leave the lab in my peripheral without so much as a glance back at me.

I sucked in my lips and stared at the equipment before me, my fingers trembling a bit with annoyance as I tried once again to punch in some numbers. It was going to be a very long semester.

My last class of the day was Greek Mythology. I'd chosen it at random – it did seem interesting, but it was mainly just to fill part of the humanities requirement I needed for my degree. I arrived at the lecture hall and sat down in an empty row near the back. It was a smaller space than the biology hall, and when it was full, a young woman walked in, set a briefcase down on the front desk, and then shut the lecture hall doors.

"All right, good afternoon, folks," she said. "Welcome to An Introduction to Greek Mythology. I am your professor for this semester, Dr. Ellerbeck. Let's begin with a syllabus of the course."

As she ended her overview and announced that we would begin looking at our first mythical creature next class, the fifty-minute mark hit, and everyone exited the room.

I headed promptly for my dorm and found Elijah and a

boy I didn't recognize were nearing the entrance. Elijah spotted me and smiled as I approached.

"Oh, there she is," he said, and he motioned to the other boy, who had tanned skin, dark brown eyes, and curly black hair. "This is my roommate, Hakeem Abadi. He's an information technology student."

"Nice to meet you," Hakeem said – his accent was slight, but spoke of Middle Eastern descent. It reminded me a lot of my mother's.

I smiled and shook his hand. "Nice to meet you, too. I'm Seraphine."

"It's very kind of you to invite us for dinner," Hakeem said. "We really appreciate it."

"Agreed. Thank you," Elijah added.

"It's no trouble at all," I said, reaching for the door. "Follow me."

We made our way to the lounge and found everyone else had already arrived.

"Hey everyone – this is Elijah and Hakeem," I said as we walked in. They were met with a resounding chorus of various greetings.

As Elijah went to go chat with the other boys, Hakeem followed me into the kitchen, where Everly was grabbing ingredients from the fridge. "What are we making?" I asked her.

"Stir-fry?" she suggested as she faced us, a whole bunch of vegetables in hand.

I could feel the surprise stun Hakeem's body next to me as soon as he made eye contact with her. "Whoa," he breathed.

I looked over at him, then back at Everly. She glanced at me in confusion before she laughed a bit awkwardly. "Everything okay?" she asked.

Hakeem cleared his throat and ran a hand through his hair. "Yeah, just…um…just a big fan of stir-fry." He looked her up and down as he stepped closer, extending his hands. "Let me help you with that…uh…"

"Everly," she answered, slowly giving him some of the vegetables.

"Everly. I'm Hakeem." He smiled. "I know a great recipe. I can show you, if you like."

She eyed him, then smiled in return. "Sure, Hakeem. I'd like that."

I saw that as my cue to leave them be, and I returned to the rest of my friends with a smirk on my face.

Hakeem and Everly put together a fabulous stir-fry. While we ate, we all learned that Elijah was majoring in physics and Hakeem in information technology, and everyone shared their day's events. We all then decided to work on our homework in the room together while exchanging casual conversation.

A couple hours went by before we all decided to turn in for the night, but before they left, everyone on my floor assured Elijah and Hakeem that they were welcome to come over whenever they wished.

I slept well that night, and the following day seemed similar in terms of routine. In the late afternoon, I once again had Greek Mythology. Dr. Ellerbeck waited until the hall was full before shutting the doors.

On the screen behind the professor was a picture of the first mythical creature in Greek Mythology that we would be studying. It was a gorgeous drawing of a huge, elegant bird. The beak was finely pointed, the neck was elongated, the body was strongly built, and the legs were long and came to sharp claws at the feet. The wings were covered in intricately woven orange feathers and stretched far over the body, giving it a large wingspan. Its eyes were big, bright, and beautifully blue, and in the picture, it stood tall and proud on the top of what looked like a palm tree, its wings covering most of the width of the picture and its prowess emitting strength and grace all at the same time.

"The Phoenix," Dr. Ellerbeck began her lecture, "is one of the most highly regarded creatures in Greek Mythology. A symbol of rebirth and regeneration, it was said that they never died, but simply decomposed or burst into flames before being reborn again. Because of this, it became one of the first symbols of Christianity."

I inspected the picture closely as Dr. Ellerbeck continued. I had heard of Phoenixes before, but I'd never given them much thought, nevertheless been forced to consider them. But it was striking to me that the idea of Phoenixes was so well developed. Dr. Ellerbeck spoke of them so compellingly, so passionately, that I felt there *had* to be something that set the foundations for the idea. Rationally, it was the only way I thought an entire population could envision something on such a large scale. There were birds around the same size or larger than them long before the Ancient Greeks – in fact, there were ostriches and emus only several miles away in the San Diego Zoo. So who was to say Phoenixes, or something like them, didn't ever exist, and that the civilization attached phenomena to them to explain the unexplainable?

I found it perplexing at first to grapple with that feeling – after all, I was in a mythology course and everything in it was supposed to be mythical. But Dr. Ellerbeck spoke of them as if they were fact, and every detail had method, rhyme, and reason. I found logic to the meaning the Ancient Greeks gave them, and to the information Dr. Ellerbeck was teaching us – too much logic and too much information for it all to have been brought out of nowhere.

Ancient populations had different minds than the modern world did. I envied the ability to believe like a civilization of centuries past without judgment. And, in the quiet of my own mind, I found myself doing just that.

When the class ended, I felt a little melancholy – I had

gotten so invested that I wanted to hear more. But nevertheless, Dr. Ellerbeck shut the textbook she had been referring to before she addressed the class again. "Tomorrow, we continue looking at the Phoenix and examining how the Greeks thought it would have lived from birth to rebirth. Have a good rest of your day."

I left the class feeling refreshed, and I kept thinking about the lecture for the rest of the day. Even after I'd eaten dinner with all my friends and returned to my dorm, I found myself prying open my Greek Mythology textbook and glancing over the Phoenix section in bed. Something about them had me mesmerized. The photo Dr. Ellerbeck had put up on the screen was on one of the pages in my text, and I ran my finger over its outline, pondering what I'd learned.

The textbook was easy to get lost in, enchanting my mind to drift away like a lullaby…

The song was haunting and persistent, lulling me towards the little, yellow light in the distance.

I pushed away the darkness, pushed against the void that continued pressing against me. It felt as heavy as water and came at me as hard as a vendetta. But I was unshakeable, and the hypnotic song continued calling me, beckoning me like a siren.

The light was getting closer and closer, the darkness growing weaker and weaker. I could feel heat on my face, warming my skin, reeling me in like a fish on a line. I was panting, desperate, as if the light was salvation.

It was so close I could touch it. I reached out, but then it burst into rays of light so blinding that I gasped at the sudden change in brightness, hurriedly shielding my eyes. I could feel the song dance around me as the rays softened, and when I lowered my arm, I saw the yellow light.

But it was not a yellow light at all. Not anymore.

It was graceful, and elegant, and built from a sovereignty that could bring you to your knees. Its eyes were bursting with an entrancing grace as they shone like two lemons on a tree in the heat of the sun. A creature of light, emitting a halo of radiance that had lured me like the promise of a thousand lifetimes.

And then suddenly, the light burst once more, and the Phoenix shrieked.

I shot up straight in bed with a panicked gasp, startled from the dream in which I'd been so hypnotized. My breathing came in heavy pants as I took in my surroundings. I realized I was in my bed, the Greek Mythology textbook open in my lap and my bedside light still on.

Slowly, I began to relax. Everything appeared ordinary.

I sighed and laid back down in bed. With a bit of trepidation, I shut my textbook, flicked off my light, and let my eyes fall shut. The bizarreness of the dream made it difficult to fall asleep, but eventually, the dread of a looming seven o'clock alarm convinced my mind to drift into a light slumber.

CHAPTER 3

I DID NOT SLEEP well that night at all, and when I awoke the next morning, I didn't feel rested in the slightest. I found Emmanuella pouring some coffee in the lounge.

"Morning, Sera!" she said cheerily. "Coffee?"

"The way I feel, I'll need the whole kettle," I said, yawning.

"Didn't sleep well last night, huh?" Em asked.

I shook my head.

"Oh, that sucks," she said, handing me a mug of coffee. "University anxiety, maybe?"

I took a sip of the coffee. "Well, I had this weird dream that just – " I shook my head. "It woke me up."

Emmanuella nodded. "Oh, yeah. I know what you mean. I get those all the time."

"You do?"

"Totally. Most of them are nightmares that I'm back in high school." She shuddered. "God forbid I ever go through that again."

I smiled, amused. "I hated high school, too."

"Well, we made it out alive," Emmanuella told me, patting me on the shoulder. "Let's just hope none of my nightmares come true."

"Cheers to that," I said, clinking my coffee mug with hers as Keiffer walked in.

"Oh, hell yeah! Are we doing drinks already? Count me in!" he exclaimed cheerily.

Emmanuella frowned at him. "Dude, it's like, eight in the morning."

He threw his hands up and grinned. "But it's five o'clock somewhere, right?"

Em sighed, rubbing her forehead. "It's just coffee, you dingus."

"Lame," Keiffer mumbled.

I rolled my eyes as I asked him, "Want some French toast?"

His eyes grew to twice their size. "You bet your donkey's ass I do! You must make the best French toast," he replied.

"Donkey's ass?" Emmanuella repeated in bewildered confusion as I frowned. "Why would I make the best French toast?" I added.

He motioned to me. "Uh, hello? French Canadian!"

Em scoffed. "That's one of the lamest puns I've ever heard."

Keiffer shook his head slowly and leaned in towards me. "I think someone's a little bitter that there's no such thing as Mexican toast," he whispered with a wink. I couldn't help but laugh.

After a brief conversation and some delicious French toast, we all parted ways to head to our classes, and the day continued as normal.

My first class of the day was chemistry, followed by my chemistry lab. The lab was small − there didn't seem to be more than about twenty people in it − and the benches were chock-full of all sorts of chemistry supplies: beakers, test tubes, funnels, burettes and burette clamps, and tons of containers filled with various compounds, liquid and solid. There was even a cupboard filled with heavily protected chemicals that were quite dangerous, like sulphuric acid.

I was paired up by the teaching assistant with Myra Nakaoka, a fair, Japanese student who had dyed her hair blonde to make her small, brown eyes pop. It turned out chemistry was her major, and although shy, she did appear to understand the premise of a lab partner, so I was in better shape than I was in my physics lab.

Our experiment was to test the solubility of sodium chloride in three different liquids – water, oil, and ethanol. "I can record the start weight of the powder before I put it in the test tube, and the percentage yield after I've let all of it get absorbed and filtered it out of the liquid," Myra explained quietly to me. "Then, you calculate the difference between the two, and that'll give us our measurements to work with."

"Sounds easy enough," I replied. "I'll grab the liquids, you grab the solute."

We got what we needed for the solute test in water before getting straight to work. Once we had a rhythm going, the two of us made a great team, flowing through the experiment and collecting the data we needed.

We finished the water test and moved on to the oil. I had just begun the set of measurements prior to mixing in the sodium chloride when he walked in.

The lab was quiet with focus, so quiet that Felix Clarkson's movement was enough to break my concentration. He had a Fendi monogram shirt on and black jeans to match. I watched as he approached the teaching assistant and spoke to her in a hush; the teaching assistant simply nodded at him before he turned to scan the room.

His eyes fell on mine, left for a moment, and then returned. I couldn't read the expression on his face, nor did I really want to. Instead, I hurriedly turned back to my calculations.

"Do you know him?" Myra whispered to me, taking me by surprise. I didn't realize she had noticed.

"*Oui*, he's my physics lab partner for the semester." I

paused, before mumbling bluntly, "The whole fucking semester."

She cracked a small smile at me. "I can tell just how well that's going from your enthusiasm."

"Oh, it's been an absolute delight so far."

"What makes it so delightful?"

I sighed. "He's – " I stopped as I searched for the right wording. "He's just…bizarre."

She laughed. "Yeah, sometimes you get stuck with some weird people as partners, but I'm sure you can manage. It's just one semester, after all."

"I guess you're right," I said with a sigh, glancing upwards at the subject in question. He was still probing the room as if he were looking for something.

Eventually, his eyes found their way back to mine. I watched as his brows furrowed and he faced his palm up towards him, an icy emotion washing over his face like a windshield wiper swipes away the rain on a car. He stared at his hand for a second, and then looked back up at me. Even from a distance, I could see the lavender in his eyes swirl.

The unexplained staring was making me uncomfortable, so I forced myself to turn back to the experiment and tried my best to ignore him. But moments later, I felt a presence beside me. And when I looked over, there he was, sitting down at the stool at the other end of our bench.

I exchanged a glance with Myra, and judging by her expression, she also thought his uninvited arrival was strange. But Felix didn't say anything, nor acknowledge either of us. He simply placed his materials on the bench and grabbed a few test tubes from the cupboard as he went about setting up what I could only assume was his own experiment.

I shook my head, forcing the distraction away with it. We completed the solubility test in oil and had one more test to run – the solute in ethanol. "We need more sodium chloride," I noted, nodding to our now empty beaker. "You grab that, I'll grab the ethanol."

"Got it," Myra said. We both left the bench and returned with the required materials.

I conducted all the calculations prior to mixing the solute with the solvent. Myra and I looked them over and confirmed they were accurate before she gave me a nod. Then, I poured the sodium chloride into the ethanol.

Immediately, it burst into flames.

I gasped as Myra screamed, and we both shielded our eyes as we hurtled ourselves away from the bench. The lab erupted with a series of panicked outbursts, and I felt two hands grab me and pull me backwards as the sound of a fire extinguisher exploded in front of us. The chemicals flooded my mouth and nostrils, and I coughed harshly as it slowly began dissipating in the air.

The chaos eventually settled, and I turned back to see that the lab assistant had put out the unexpected fire, leaving the bench covered in foam. "Let's keep the fires to a minimum, shall we?" she suggested with a bit of irritation.

A low murmur travelled throughout the lab, and I could feel everyone staring at Myra and me. I didn't really care. My thoughts were wild with confusion and astonishment.

"That's not possible," I breathed. "Sodium chloride bubbles in ethanol. It doesn't ignite like that."

The lab assistant gave me a tired expression. "You must have grabbed the wrong solution," was her disillusioned response.

I didn't even bother addressing her, because I knew I hadn't grabbed the wrong solution. It was ethanol – I was sure of it. I just couldn't wrap my head around what had happened.

I turned in bewilderment to look at Myra, only to discover that she was focusing on something behind me. It was then that I realized I was still being held tightly, fingers digging into my arms so hard I thought they would leave bruises.

I turned and looked up at Felix. As soon as we made eye contact, he hastily released me, his passive expression remarkably unphased by the incident that had just occurred.

I studied him, my mouth parting soundlessly. I didn't know what exactly to say. Nothing that had happened in the last few moments made any sense to me.

I suppose he decided the silence needed filling. "Perhaps you are one to start a fire, after all," he told me quietly, his lips barely parting. And blazing in those striking lavender eyes, I saw flames so astute and cunning that I could only reason they had been lit by the unthinkable fire themselves.

After Myra and I cleaned up the mess left by the accident, we completed our experiment – successfully, this time – and were the last to turn in our lab report. I was relieved to finally be getting out of there as everyone else, including Felix, had left long ago. As I was packing up, I invited Myra to join my friends and I for dinner at our lounge. She agreed, thanking me for the invite, and we parted ways.

I put my headphones in and listened to some of my favourite music as I walked around campus, exploring aimlessly. The campus was beautiful, but there was something about the music that made it even more pleasurable to walk around. I enjoyed the little things that reminded me I was living.

As I was walking, my phone buzzed with a text message.

Elijah King
Hey, Seraphine. Do you have a class right now?

. . .

I sucked in my lips to hide my smile.

Me

No, I don't, actually! Do you?

Elijah King

Nope! I was wondering if maybe you wanted to grab some coffee and go over some biology notes together.

I gave up on trying to hide the smile.

Me

Sure, that sounds like a plan! Where should I meet you?

Elijah King

There's a little café just outside the Arts building. Do you know where that is?

Me

I think I can find my way there.

Elijah King

Great! I'll wait for you here. See you in a few. :)

I put my phone away giddily and quickly found a sign that directed me towards the Arts building. Within ten minutes, I had found my way to the café Elijah had mentioned and spotted him just outside it.

He waved me down as soon as we made eye contact. "Hey! How's your day going?" he asked with a smile.

"Good, thanks!" I answered. "And yours?"

"Just swell, thank you," he replied, opening the door. "After you."

I beamed, heading inside and up to the counter. Elijah followed me in.

The barista behind the counter grinned at us both. "Hey, there! What can I get for you?"

"Two coffees, please," Elijah said.

"All right, and how would you like them?"

"Mine will just be black," Elijah answered, turning to me. "And hers will be…?"

"Two sugars, two creams," I finished for him. She nodded and wrote the two orders down on paper cups she'd pulled from a stack.

"You get all your sweetness from your coffee?" Elijah noted.

I giggled. "I suppose. I like my coffee and tea as sweet as can be."

He laughed and turned back to the barista. "That'll be all, thanks," he noted, pulling out his wallet. She nodded at the two of us and quickly made our coffees before handing them to us.

"Shall we sit outside? It's nice out," Elijah suggested.

"Sounds good to me," I said.

We found a picnic table out by the greenery beside the café. "So, is San Diego treating you well so far?" he asked me as we were setting our things down.

I smiled, more to myself than anything. "Very well," I replied.

"That's good to hear. Hey, I've lived here all my life, so if you ever want to find your way around town or something, don't be afraid to give me a shout, okay?" he offered.

I beamed at him, tucking a strand of hair behind my ear. "I appreciate that. Thank you," I responded. "I'd love to get to know the city more."

"I'll have to take you on a little tour one day, then," he said with a grin, and I nodded enthusiastically before we both pulled out our notes and I opened my textbook.

- F -

I stared at my palm, listening to it, feeling the power rumble through me.

It was her. There was no denying a fact that was as profoundly chiseled in stone as the Ten Commandments. My senses had heaved me to her in the chemistry lab, had cried out when I had touched her. And now, they had drawn me to this café, where I watched her drone on and on with the unexciting boy as she sipped that ridiculously sweet coffee. She had no idea I lurked at a table nearby, pondering how in the world it could be her, but more importantly, what to do about it.

The first one I'd sensed since my parents. Was that significant enough to approach her about it, to abandon my original plan of evasion and cowardice? Logic indicated that the answer to that question was crystal clear. But I had emotional construct of a hurricane, slapped with harsh winds and flooded with stormed rains that destroyed any ability to make a purely rational decision if there was any sort of feeling swimming around it. And these feelings were circling me so vigorously that I was drowning in my own tempest.

I glanced around the café, at all the students gathered at tables of two, or four, or six. The room was alive with chatter, so lively and so loud that my reflexes were begging me to leave. But when my eyes fell to her again, my being began rooting itself in place.

I thought about what I'd done in the lab, how quickly the scene had played. Grabbing her to confirm my senses was part of the plan, but the paralysis that overcame me the moment she was in my arms was not. It was as if I'd been struck by lightning, thwarting me as I tried to be her hero and her villain all at the same time.

I sighed, studying my thrumming palm again as I retreated further into my thoughts. What I needed was a way to keep her close without growing too close to her. I'd sworn off love in any of its forms. I couldn't risk getting wounded so deeply again.

But though I feared agony, I also feared being a fool. The question I had to answer was which I feared more.

- S -

That night, I set up a video call with my parents. I had agreed to call them once or twice a week before I'd left.

"Hi, sweetheart!" my mom chimed as her bright eyes came into view on my laptop. "How was your first week?"

"Busy, but good," I said. "How are you guys?"

"We're missing you a lot and counting down the days until you're home for Christmas," my dad, who was sitting beside my mom, replied.

I watched my mom roll her eyes before clapping her hands together. "So, tell us everything!"

And I did. I told them about my classes, about our group collaborating on dinners, and how much more I liked the weather in San Diego. When my physics lab came up, though, I told them it was going well, and I consciously skipped telling them who my lab partner was and the struggles I was having with them. I didn't want my parents to worry any more than they already were. I'd grown to appreciate how much they worried about me, because I knew now that it meant they cared. It would be a lie to say I didn't miss them, but it was also a bit freeing to have my independence in San Diego.

When I'd caught them up on everything, we ended our call, and I went to bed.

The light was vivid and dazzling, stronger than a thousand men combined. I stumbled towards it in a desperate flurry, its core expanding as I neared, the winds around me swirling with a heat of which I could not determine the source.

I heard a voice in the tails of the breeze that wrung through my hair. "Seraphine," she called, her voice as sweet as molasses. "Seraphine."

I tried to respond, but my voice was hidden in my breath as I ran, faster and faster. The light was in reach, and it ruptured as my fingers tried to grab it. I gasped and fell to my knees as the light swallowed me whole.

"Seraphine," she breathed on the nape of my neck, a tingling sensation trailing down the hairs of my body. "Seraphine."

I pulled my head upwards, squinting through the bright light. I could barely make out the Phoenix's shadow towering over me.

"Keeper," whispered the voice, before a deafening scream.

I started awake, jostling my sheets about. When I realized it had just been a dream, I huffed to myself and lay back down in bed. I stared at the ceiling as I recounted how strange it had been, how weirdly similar it was to the other I'd been startled by the previous night. I was much too old to be having nightmares like this.

Sighing my thoughts away, I eventually turned on my side and tucked myself back into a deep sleep.

CHAPTER 4

THE NEXT MORNING WAS SATURDAY, and there were no classes I had to get ready for, so I slept in to make up for the interruption. When I eventually woke later in the morning, I lazily made my way to the lounge.

I ended up walking in on Sajan and Roscoe, sitting on the sofa, enveloped in each other's arms as they kissed.

I blinked. My sudden entrance startled them as much as the unexpected sight had startled me, and they pulled away from one another in a hurry. We all stared at each other in a bit of embarrassed perplexity.

In the second it took me to clear my throat, I managed to race through all my thoughts – the conditioning of society to expect heteronormativity, the unrealistic nature of that expectation, and the conclusion that it was just as probable and natural for Sajan and Roscoe to be gay as it was for them to be straight.

I gave them both an apologetic smile as I said quietly, "Sorry to interrupt. I didn't know you guys were in here."

They both seemed a bit flustered, but also relieved. "No, it's okay," Roscoe replied, waving me off. "We probably should have gone somewhere more private."

"It's no big deal," I replied. "How long have you guys been together?"

They looked at each other, then back at me. "Just after high school," Roscoe said. "A couple months now."

Sajan shifted uncomfortably as he tugged at his shirt. "But the thing is, uh…that nobody knows."

I frowned. "Nobody knows?"

Sajan shook his head. "Not my family, not his. Not even Keiffer," he replied. "So, um…do you think you could maybe keep this between us three?"

I shrugged. "Sure, but…there's nothing to be ashamed of."

"That's not exactly true," Roscoe noted, and him and Sajan exchanged glances again. "Sajan's family is a little…uh…"

"They're very traditional," Sajan continued. "If they knew, they wouldn't really accept the relationship. Or the fact that I'm…well…"

I understood precisely what they were trying to say. "Don't worry," I told them. "Secret's safe with me."

Sajan smiled bashfully. "Thanks," he said.

"Don't mention it," I told him, approaching the kitchen. "You guys want scrambled eggs?"

"Would love some," Roscoe said, standing. "We're famished from basketball practice."

"I'm sure you are," I replied. "Give me a few minutes."

I whipped up some scrambled eggs and served them alongside some coffee. As we ate, the air in the room became less awkward and more status quo.

"What are you guys up to for the rest of the day?" I asked as I finished eating.

"Not much, to be honest. Hey, we should get everyone together and do something," Roscoe responded.

"Sure," I replied. "What were you guys thinking?"

"How does bowling sound?" Sajan suggested as he brought his plate to the sink. "There are lanes not too far from here."

"Sounds fun to me," Roscoe noted, looking at me. "You down for that?"

"I'd love to," I said.

"Sweet. Let's invite everyone else," Sajan chimed.

And so, after texting everyone and formulating a quick plan, our group of friends agreed to meet at two o'clock in front of the university's entrance so we could all take the bus down to the bowling alley together.

We all hopped on the bus, and in no time, we were at the bowling alley. The ten of us took two lanes, with Elijah, Hakeem, Keiffer, Emmanuella and me on one while everyone else remained on the other. The lanes were beside each other, though, so it didn't separate much in terms of conversation — in fact, we ended up getting a little competition going between us, quickly becoming teams and trying to earn the most points because the losers had to pay for the other team's dinners. Luckily, my team won, and when we all decided to eat at The Cheesecake Factory, everyone on the other team split the bill equally for all ten meals.

After dinner, we returned to the bus stop. Somewhere along the bus ride, it had somehow been decided that we were going to go clubbing. I wasn't particularly a party person, but I did love to dance, so I didn't object when we all headed downtown.

We ended up at a nightclub called Spin. It was packed with people our age and loud enough that my ears started ringing almost immediately upon entering. But the music was good, making my body move with it in as much automation as my breathing. Soon after we arrived, I found myself on the dance floor with my friends, drinks in hand.

The DJ started playing a Latin song that I instantly recognized. "Oh, I love this song!" I exclaimed.

"Bitch, me too!" Emmanuella screamed in my ear.

I burst out laughing as we all started dancing to it. Roscoe and Chenoa were pretty good dancers. Keiffer and Sajan were not. Everyone else could at least move with the rhythm, but

Sajan seemed a bit shy, opting to just sway back and forth while sipping his drink. Keiffer, however, was off in his own universe. I suppose that shouldn't have been much of a surprise, considering what I knew of him. But he didn't seem to care, and it made it that more fun.

After the song ended, Hakeem and Everly ventured off to get more drinks. The rest of us continued dancing to the next song, our smiles as bright as the flashing lights. There was so much chatter and laughter amongst us all that I almost didn't notice the pair of lavender eyes lurking from the bar.

I barely caught sight of him when I went to get a shot with Emmanuella. He was leaning his shoulder against the wall, slowly and methodically running the tip of his finger around the rim of his glass as he stared at me with a narrow gaze. The wisps of smoke from the club's fog machines billowed around him as if to try and conceal him further.

I had no idea what business he had staring at me as I enjoyed my Saturday night. I ignored him as best as I could as Emmanuella thanked the bartender and we returned to my friends. But admittedly, knowing he had somehow ended up here made me feel like I'd come down with a fever I just couldn't sweat out.

"Seraphine!"

I turned my attention to Elijah. He was approaching me with outstretched arms, stumbling between bodies with a grin on his chipper face.

"Dance with me, Seraphine!" he shouted as he neared. And I was about three drinks in, so naturally, I started grinding on him.

We danced like teenagers in the corner of a high school gym before we began making out in the middle of the dance floor. I could hear Keiffer and Roscoe hooting at us, but I didn't care. As immature as it was, it was also another one of those times I was made to remember that I was alive.

And then suddenly, an alarm started blaring.

The jostling sound was a rude interruption in the club's atmosphere, startling Elijah and I as we jerked apart from one another. The music came to an abrupt halt as the flashing lights dissolved, replaced by normal, fluorescent ones that illuminated the previously darkened space. As soon as the room was bright, I could see the clouds of smoke in the air had thickened, and the smell of something burning hit me soon after.

"Fire!" I heard someone shout. "Fire!"

"Everyone out!" came another voice. "Get out!"

The panic was instantaneous. The crowd moved in pandemonium, sweeping me away from Elijah before I could even process what was happening. I looked around frenziedly, trying to spot any of my friends, before I realized I was surrounded by strangers and would have better luck finding them outside the building than within.

I spotted an exit sign and quickly began following the movement of the crowd towards it, feeling the heat of more bodies than I could count suffocating me. I was pushed and shoved in every which way as people desperately fought to get out first. Sweat and skin pressed against my own, and the smell of the fire was rapidly growing stronger.

Eventually, I reached the doorframe and shoved my way out of the building, nearly toppling on to the pavement of the parking lot. As soon as I righted myself, I tried my best to separate from the swarm of people that had enveloped me like locusts, glancing at the faces and hoping to recognize any.

I found myself stumbling up a small incline in the lot, a good distance from the exit and from anybody else. I stood on top of a concrete barrier, trying to get a better view of the sea of heads and faces. It was a futile effort; I couldn't seem to spot any of my friends. What I could see were bright flames bursting from the roof of the club, swallowing it more quickly than I thought possible as a stampede of people exploded from its doors. In the distance, I could hear sirens, and the fact that they didn't sound close enough to me made my heart beat a little faster with fright.

"I suppose you must be kindling."

I jumped at the sound of the English accent and whipped around to face him. He was standing underneath a lamppost just behind me, wearing that cold, oddly composed expression. Between his two fingers, a stream of smoke slowly danced from a cigarette into the air, like a belly dancer in a curtained lounge. Where he had come from, I had no idea. He hadn't been there mere seconds ago.

"What?" was all I could muster in my state of shock.

"Perhaps instead of starting fires, you fuel them on." He nodded towards the club. "Or play within them."

I gave him a look of disbelief and disdain. "Are you suggesting I might have had anything to do with this?"

He brought the cigarette to his mouth before exhaling slowly, a gray cloud of smoke billowing in front of him. It shadowed his face, slipping through the air as he eyed me narrowly. Even from such a distance, I could see his lavender eyes had become smoky.

"I'm not suggesting. I'm explaining." He looked me up and down as the smoke caressed his features, darkening the little lift at the corner of his lips. "Have you ever considered that you may not know what you're capable of?"

"What the hell are you talking about?" I snapped, scoffing as I realized with frustration that he was distracting me with absolute nonsense. "I don't have time for this. I need to find my friends."

I hopped off the barrier before he could interject, heading for the crowd. The sound of the sirens had drawn closer now, and I could see flashing lights making their way from down the road.

I hadn't taken more than a few steps before I heard him say, "Wait, Miss Pierre."

I rolled my eyes and turned back around. "What now?"

He took a step away from the lamppost before he reached into his pocket and pulled out a set of keys.

My keys.

My eyes widened, and I fumbled around in my pocket. I hadn't even realized I'd dropped them – they must have fallen out in the flurry of escaping the building.

"Oh," was all I managed to say as I approached him.

Felix outstretched the keys to me in his palm, and as he did, something about them seemed to catch his attention. I didn't understand why – it wasn't anything special. I didn't have many keys, and the keychain itself just had a small, mundane charm of the Eiffel Tower with an "F" for "France" inscribed in a little plaque. I had found it on the ground at a café in Paris while on vacation with my family many years ago. It was battered and needed some glue to reinforce it, but with all things considered, the charm was still intact, so I didn't feel the need to replace it.

Felix ran his finger over the charm slowly as he frowned, seeming to forget entirely that I stood before him or that they belonged to me. Eventually, I cleared my throat. "Could I have those back?"

As quickly as he'd become distracted by it, his eyes darted up to mine. Then, he hastily plopped the keys in my hand.

"There she is – Sera!"

The sound of Emmanuella's voice sent a shot of relief through my veins. I turned and saw her running towards me – behind her, I could see the rest of my friends gathered in a small circle by the firetrucks that had just arrived.

"Until the next fire, kindling," I heard Felix say. But when I turned to respond, I saw he had already begun vanishing into the shadows and smoulders of an alleyway.

The bus ride back to the university was alight with conversation about the night's events. Thankfully, none of my friends seemed injured or frazzled beyond repair. I, however, was befuddled and exhausted. I sat quietly and listened to my friends theorize about what had happened in the club, sharing their wild stories about how crazy it had been trying to get out of the burning building. I had no interest in adding my experience to the conversation. All I wanted was to get home safe and go to bed.

The minutes seemed to drag on and on as the bus meandered down the road. Eventually, we arrived back at the university. I hurriedly wished my friends good night before I locked myself in my dorm, gratefully clambering into the comfort of my bed.

"Seraphine."

That voice as smooth as honey beckoned me again, drawing me in like a melody. The light shone so bright that I thought it might be the sun. All around me were hues of yellow and gold, of a brightness that worked in harmony with her calls.

"Keeper," she sang. "Seraphine."

I stared up at the light all around me, at the Phoenix that was circling above, flying with grace and purity. Even if I tried to shut my eyes, the light invaded me. There was no escaping such a glorious and free entity.

Perhaps this was heaven I had fallen into, so yellowed with dreams of everlasting peace and bright with the promises of an endless sleep. I breathed slowly and deeply, savoring the liberty of such a splendid place.

I felt her next words fall on my skin. "Wake me up, Seraphine," she cooed. "Wake me up, Keeper."

Fire erupted around me, licking me with its tongue of flames. I gasped as the inferno danced around me, the yellow tones of heaven now drowned in the heat of hell.

"Seraphine," she repeated. "Wake up."

I swallowed the fire as I screamed an endless scream.

I woke up with terror, my brain scrambling to comprehend how real it had all felt. I tried to remind myself that it was just a dream, that the fire wasn't real, that I had left any semblance of kindling behind at the club.

But the sound of her voice still resounded all around me.

"*Wake me up, Keeper,*" came her whispers through the air.

I frantically glanced around as I scrambled out of bed. "Who are you? Who's there?"

"*Wake me up, Keeper.*"

I hurried for the bathroom door, checking Emmanuella's room through it. She was fast asleep. I burst back into my room and opened the door to my dorm. No one was outside.

"*Wake me up, Keeper.*"

"Who are you?" I repeated, my voice shaking. "What do you want?"

Out of nowhere, a flurry of lights began fluttering about in the middle of the room. The illuminations stemmed from a central orb, glowing in numerous beams of whites and yellows. I thought I could see sparkles fall from the light like glitter from a child's craft as it enveloped my dorm with its radiance. My eyes stung so badly from its power that I had to cover my eyes in the crook of my elbow, my breathing heavy with my bewilderment and fright.

And then, it all stopped.

It took several breaths for me to slowly pull my arm away from my face. My eyes grew even wider with bafflement and my lungs, out of a combination of exasperation and surprise, let out a huge gasp of air.

I didn't really know what I was anticipating to see. Nevertheless, it was exactly where the orb had been. It was relatively large, ovate, and metallic, catching the glimmer of faint moonlight that peeked through a small gap in my curtains.

I stared at the egg for a very long time before I could fully comprehend that it was, indeed, an egg that had appeared from the light. My mind did a few cartwheels and mental backflips. I don't think anyone had ever adequately prepared me for this scenario. But there it was, a magic egg, somehow present right before my eyes.

I shook my head and shut my eyes for a long time before reopening them. The egg was still there.

I rubbed my eyes harshly with my hands and then blinked several times upon parting them. The egg was still there.

I looked down at my arm, pinching it painfully. Then I looked back at the center of the room. The egg was still there.

I let out a deep breath as I accepted the reality before me. Slowly, I then approached the egg, reaching for it with a trembling hand. As I got nearer, it got harder to inch my hand forward.

Taking one sharp inhalation, I clasped my eyes shut and forced my hand on to the egg's surface in one swift motion. I felt the surface beneath my fingers. It was smooth and warm, like a candle that's just been lit. I reopened my eyes and watched as each of my fingers slowly caressed it, rubbing it gently from side to side.

Well, it was definitely real, and not blowing up or disappearing, which I guessed was a good sign. But what was I supposed to do with it?

I retracted my fingers, and the instant I did, I heard a crack.

My eyes widened again. I wanted my ears to be deceiving

me so badly, and just as I started to believe they were, I heard another one.

I looked around for any other source of the sound. Nothing. Nobody around, nothing that could make a noise. *Crack.*

I turned my attention back to the egg in horror and could see a very fine line slowly drawing itself across the egg's surface, like Da Vinci tempting his paper with a pencil. *Crack.*

More lines began to appear, like veins across the surface of a wrist. My heart felt as though it would go into cardiac arrest. *Crack.*

There was one final cracking sound, and suddenly, the edges of the shell burst open like French doors, letting off a little flurry of light. The light dimmed, and the eggshells began rustling as a little bird's head poked its way out of the residue. It looked at me with bright, yellow eyes, and then wiggled itself out from the shells, knocking them carelessly out of the way. It stood no taller than a mug and was as wide as the palm of my hand. Plumage the colour of sunflowers lined its entire body, and a little yellow tail sprouted from its behind as a small beak did the same from its head. It looked like a miniature, juvenile replication of the pictures of Phoenixes I had seen in class, except it was much smaller and covered in feathers that must have been dipped in the sun's bright yellow rays.

My eyes were about to pop out of my head. I was looking at a Phoenix chick.

I was looking at a Phoenix chick?

How the hell was any of this happening?

I leaned back against the wall in exasperation and rubbed my head. There were two very prominent thoughts swirling in my swamp of a brain. The first, obviously, was an exclamation of excitement. *A baby Phoenix?* How lucky was I to be able to witness such a thing right in front of me? I wanted to hold it, befriend it, snuggle its little, feathery body…and, of course, the heart-thumping adrenaline that caused these emotions then also caused the second thought process to roll its film. Yeah, sure, I could do those things for a little while…but then what? What exactly am I supposed to do with a baby Phoenix? I can't really bring it to an animal shelter or sell it anywhere, and how am I supposed to explain to my roommate that I have a baby mythical creature living in my dorm?

The Phoenix chick made a slight peeping noise, and I snapped my attention back to it. It cocked its head to the side and then turned its head and dug it into the broken eggshells. I watched as it then pulled out a small object attached to a thin, golden chain. It then approached me, made another peeping noise, and looked at me expectantly.

I frowned, looking at the bird, and then at the object that was strung around the chain. It was a pendant that held a beautiful, yellow stone lined with gold that glinted like stars. I tentatively held out my hand towards the baby Phoenix, attempting to take the object without scaring it. It plopped it into my palm willingly, almost as if it was offering it to me.

I examined the necklace in my hand for a long time. Slowly, I undid the clip and snapped it around my neck, letting it dangle in the center of my chest as my mind raced. What was this thing? What did this all mean?

Suddenly, there was a knock − not on my door, but on my window. In retrospect, I should have taken that mere fact alone as a sign that things were about to get even weirder.

I gripped the necklace in my hand as I straightened, approaching the window slowly. With careful fingers, I grabbed hold of one of the curtains, pulling it to the side.

And even in the dark of the night, there was no mistaking the colour of the eyes that met mine.

CHAPTER 5

"IT'S ABOUT TIME, MISS PIERRE," Felix said, his voice muffled by the window.

I simply stared back at him in shock. My mind had reached its capacity for bewilderment, unable to process even the most basic response. He looked the same as when I'd last seen him in the parking lot of the club, his eyes alight with a churning, lavender flame – perhaps the fire had wandered into them and gotten encased within.

Felix raised his eyebrows slightly. "May I come in?"

I blinked, shaking my head quickly. "How did you – "

"I got a ride," he answered plainly before I could finish, nodding towards the doorknob. "I think it's time you and I had a little chat."

The thought of letting a man as strange as him into my dorm in the middle of the night was beyond unsettling. I took a few steps backwards, never letting my eyes part from his, as I grabbed a pair of scissors from my desk.

"What do you want?" I asked him as I held up the makeshift weapon.

Felix sighed. "Miss Pierre, the scissors are much too blunt to do any significant damage. You should choose something sharper." He nodded towards my desk. "Perhaps a knife or a letter opener."

I gaped at him. "You're helping me choose a weapon to stab you with?"

He shrugged. "If I'm going to be stabbed, I should be stabbed well, no?"

My eyes flickered between my desk and him.

He held his hands up defensively. "I swear on my life that I won't hurt you."

"Why should I trust you?" I challenged.

He held my gaze with conviction. "Miss Pierre, you have no reason to hide it from me. I already know."

I squinted at him. "Know what?"

"That you're a Keeper," he replied.

I straightened. That was the word I'd heard in my recurring dreams, and just now, before the Phoenix had hatched.

Slowly, I lowered the scissors back on to the desk.

Felix dropped his eyes, the lavender in them whirling like the ocean tides. "Just let me in so we can talk."

I didn't move right away. But when my brain finally spoke to my feet, it had them move towards the balcony door. I stepped back as soon as it was unlocked to allow for some space between us.

Felix came inside, gingerly closing the door behind him, as if he were taking extra care not to startle me. He nodded once at me, then turned his attention to the baby Phoenix on the floor. The little yellow bird stared back at him with wide eyes.

"A Light Phoenix," he murmured. "Hmph. I thought for sure you'd be a Fire Keeper."

I couldn't hold my curiosity back any longer, especially since he seemed to have the answer. "Keeper – what is a Keeper?" I asked.

He immediately frowned at me. "You don't know?"

I shook my head.

His frown deepened. "How can that be?" he pondered.

"Someone must have provoked the belief within you in order for the Phoenix to hatch to you."

I fluttered my eyes in confusion. "Belief? Belief in what?"

He motioned to the Phoenix. "Belief in Phoenixes, of course. They don't choose a person whose mind is too small to be their Keeper. They can't form a bond with a human who doesn't believe in them."

I was beyond perplexed. "A bond?"

He nodded intently. "The bond founded upon belief, granting you access to the Phoenix's sixth sense. Your magic."

"Magic?" I repeated, my eyes widening.

Felix stared at me for a few long seconds. Finally, he sighed and rubbed his forehead with his palm.

"I'm beginning to think that you have no knowledge of what you've become," he murmured.

I crossed my arms. "Just beginning, eh?"

He gave me a look. "Well, I originally had different plans for this conversation. But I suppose, based on circumstances, that I should readjust."

He took a deep breath and looked at my Phoenix once again. "This Phoenix hatched to you because you are its designated Keeper – a Phoenix Keeper – and it is your responsibility now to nurture it, train with it, and fulfill your duties as its bonded partner. You will continue to foster and develop this bond with it over the course of both of your lifetimes, which has already begun developing in the form of your belief in what others think to be myth, shortly before it hatched."

He frowned slightly at me. "I don't understand, though, where you got that from. It doesn't seem like you were aware of Phoenixes or Phoenix Keepers before now."

I considered this for a moment. "Would learning about them in a Mythology class count?"

He cocked his head to the side. "Do you take a Mythology class?"

"*Oui.* Greek Mythology. My professor got me really

invested in Phoenixes from her lesson. She talked about them as if they were real – " I shifted a bit, feeling a little vulnerable " – well, to me at least. I don't know anything about Phoenix Keepers…but I do know a lot about Phoenixes now. And, well, I felt a little convinced that they had to exist for the Greeks to come up with such a creature."

Felix looked upwards in thought. "Well, I suppose that could do the trick, and it does make sense in your case. And this belief you formed is also why it hatched to you – it sensed the foundation of a beginning bond." He looked back at me. "Your Phoenix would have tried to reach you through this bond in your dreams."

I broke eye contact, a little uncomfortable that he somehow knew this. "I have had some…weird dreams lately."

He nodded. "Every Phoenix Keeper does. It's how our Phoenixes first appear to us before they materialize. It's a way to let us know they're coming."

I considered all the information I'd absorbed as I looked at the little yellow Phoenix. "I'm a little confused – I became a Phoenix Keeper from my Greek Mythology class, but the rest of the students didn't. How is that possible? We all heard the same lecture."

Felix shrugged. "Didn't form a strong enough belief, or a belief at all. It's as simple as that. The effect the lessons had on you most likely was not the same as the effect they had on your colleagues."

"Okay." I eyed him. "So how did *you* know I was a Phoenix Keeper?"

"Phoenix Keepers are able to utilize their Phoenix's skills, and we acquire various forms of magic from the bond we share with them. Honed senses and the ability to sense things that others cannot are one of these perks. Phoenixes can sense the presence of other Phoenixes, and Phoenix Keepers can sense the presence of other Phoenix Keepers. I could sense a Phoenix Keeper in you from even before you hatched the egg, and I could use the increasing and decreasing strength of the same sense to find you."

I raised an eyebrow. *That* explained a few things.

"So, you're – "

"A Phoenix Keeper? Yes. I have been since I was a small boy."

Somehow, that seemed to explain some more things.

"Where's your Phoenix?" I inquired.

He jerked his head towards the window. "Out in the night. Hiding."

"Hiding?"

He nodded once at me. "That brings me to the reason I wanted to talk to you."

I raised my eyebrows expectantly. "Go on."

Felix motioned to my Phoenix again. "Phoenixes grow at an incredible rate due to their magic enhancements, and generally, we like to keep mortals and Phoenixes separated from each other – makes things a lot less complicated, believe me. By tomorrow, your Phoenix will be twice its size. And it will certainly be too big to hide in your dorm by the end of the week."

I looked at my Phoenix. *Really?* That tiny thing was going to be too big for my dorm in seven days? It was hard to believe, but then again, so was its mere existence. Since I was apparently very good at believing in my Phoenix itself, I sort of shrugged off whatever doubts I had about its growth and turned back to Felix.

"So, what do I do?" I prodded him.

He pursed his lips, his eyes tracing my face. "You don't know of anywhere else you can hide it, do you?"

"No," I answered.

"You know of absolutely no hideaways or infrequently visited places that aren't easily accessible to the general public?"

I gave him an unimpressed look. "I moved here four days ago, Felix. I barely know my way around the campus."

He frowned at me. "You moved into the dorm four days ago, you mean?"

"I mean I moved into the *country* four days ago."

"The *country?*" he repeated in what seemed like mild shock.

"*Oui.* I'm from Montreal."

"Montreal? As in Montreal, Canada?"

I narrowed my gaze at him. I found it impossible to bite my tongue. "No. As in Montreal, Japan," I said flippantly.

He furrowed his brows at me. "There's no Montreal in Japan."

I rolled my eyes. "Of course not. I was being sarcastic."

"Oh," he said, his frown deepening. "There's no need to be sarcastic with me."

I scoffed. "I can do whatever I want," I shot back boldly.

He crinkled his nose slightly in distaste. There was a tense moment of silence.

"Is there a reason you're being so...?" he finally asked, drifting off as he read my changing face.

"So what?" I pressed.

"So..."

I raised an eyebrow. "*Oui?*"

I could tell he was struggling to commit to his observation by the strained look on his face, a mix of both frustration and regret. "So...hostile?" he then blurted in a bit of exasperation.

I crossed my arms. "It's the middle of the fucking night, and I woke up from a nightmare that led to me hatching a Phoenix after a fire blazed through the club I was at. Then you decided to pop in through my balcony and explain a bunch of shit I'm still trying to comprehend, so please tell me how, exactly, you'd like me to react instead?"

He studied me for a moment. "I was going to suggest that you have your Phoenix stay hidden with mine at my estate. As of right now, it does not look like you have many other options." He lowered his gaze. "And, since that is an offer of assistance, perhaps you can react a bit more agreeably."

I snorted. "Really? *You're* trying to help *me?*"

His narrowed gaze was both muddled and irritated.

I threw a hand on my hip, pointing the other one at him as I noted, "You didn't want to help me at all in the physics lab. You left me completely to my own devices. And now you want to do something nice for me?"

Felix's eyebrows shook as his face morphed into a shattered mask, struggling to hide any remnants of his alarm to my blatant remarks. I could tell I had caught him completely off guard.

I raised my eyebrows with smugness. "Care to explain?"

He cleared his throat as he looked me up and down. "I've had…an epiphany."

"An epiphany, huh?" I repeated with scepticism.

He swallowed, shrugging. "That's the best way to describe it." His lavender eyes were unstill as they met mine.

I could tell by the way the muscles sat in my face that my expression was tired and dubious. Somehow, that didn't deter him from going on. "What do you say?" he asked as he motioned to my Phoenix.

Felix's words hung in the air as I stared at him, swirling my tongue around my mouth. His explanation wasn't much of an explanation at all. I was exhausted, and dazed, and cranky, and the last thing I wanted to do was make myself vulnerable to him.

After a while, I let out a huff as I approached my Phoenix and took it in my arms protectively. "No, thank you," I told him firmly.

Felix blinked. "No?" he repeated.

I shook my head. "No."

He frowned at me. "But you need – "

"I'm perfectly capable of finding a solution on my own," I told him bluntly.

His frown seemed to have etched itself into his face, and he stared at me for a very long time. He opened his mouth to speak, but my words came out before his did.

"I think it's best if you go now," I said simply.

He cleared his throat again. "All right," he said, and he made his way to the doorway. His steps were hesitant and reluctant, and when he was underneath the doorframe, he stopped and turned to look at me again.

I held his gaze robustly. I could see distaste and frustration swirling slowly around the irises of his eyes and flickering in luminosity, like two small tsunamis he was trying desperately to push back into the sea.

Eventually he shook his head and looked away as he stepped out into the hallway. "I'll see you in the lab, Miss Pierre," I heard him say.

And it was that exact moment in which Felix Clarkson became the thorn in my side.

CHAPTER 6

IF MY EYES were made of metal, they would have creaked as I parted them the next morning, besieged with deciding whether to welcome me to Sunday or send me back to my dreams.

The late morning sunlight was streaming through the parted curtains, illuminating the feathers of my Phoenix, who sat curled in a fluffed-up ball beside me on my bed. It gave me a single chirp as I blinked at it, as if it had been waiting for me to wake up.

I smiled, a bit humoured. "Hello, little friend."

The Phoenix cheeped again.

I reached for it slowly, gauging its reaction. There was no sign of fear, so I placed my hand on its little body and began rustling its feathers. It was then that I realized it had, indeed, grown significantly – where one hand had sufficed for picking it up yesterday, I would now definitely need two.

My brows shook a bit as I recalled everything Felix had told me, and I sat up in bed to study the Phoenix further. He hadn't been kidding about their growth rate – it had been less than twelve hours, and the Phoenix had already doubled in size. I needed to get a move on finding it a good hiding spot.

"All right, then," I said to the Phoenix as I sat up. "Let me get some breakfast, and then we're off to find you a little hideaway."

The Phoenix cocked its head to the side as it made a peep.

My face softened. "You must be hungry too, huh?"

It chirped, stretching its wings and fluffing them.

I let out an amused breath. "I'll bring you back some fruit," I told it before making for the door and heading to the lounge.

The door to the common area was closed. As soon as I swung it open, I was greeted with a regrettably familiar English accent.

"Good morning, kindling."

I jumped, bracing myself against the wall. "For fuck's sake," I muttered under my breath, scowling at the source of the sound.

Felix was sitting on the sofa, one leg crossed over the other, a half-eaten apple in his hand. He was dressed in the same outfit he'd been wearing when he'd invaded my dorm, which I could now see was a Dolce & Gabbana shirt and black Armani jeans, but his eyes seemed a bit dull with tiredness.

"What the hell are you doing in here?" I snapped at him. "How the fuck did you even get in?"

Felix shrugged, taking a bite of his apple and chewing it with an infuriating slowness, as if he knew every second he delayed his answer frustrated me even more. "You let me."

"What?"

"You let me out through your door." He motioned to the hallway. "I came in through the hall."

My mouth fell open. "You've been here the whole night?"

He patted the sofa. "It's not so bad to sleep on."

"Are you out of your fucking mind?"

He took another bite of the apple. "Seemed pointless to travel back and forth to the same place. Thought I would save myself the time."

I motioned in frustration with my hands. "Do you not

realize how incredibly fucking weird this is?" I asked with incredulity.

He swallowed, nodding towards me. "You should really look into acquiring some new vocabulary for your little hissy fits."

I gaped at him. "Excuse me?"

He stood, and I thought I saw the corner of his mouth twitch as he brushed off a small piece of apple that had fallen on to his pants. "Relax, Miss Pierre. You're overreacting."

"Don't you tell me – "

"How's your Phoenix?" he interrupted.

My nose crumpled with irascibility. "Don't change the subject."

"A lot of orders this morning, hm?" he noted, his eyebrow rising with his audacity. "Have you found a hiding spot for it?"

"How the fuck would I have found anything if I've been – " I shook my head violently " – you know what? I'm not engaging in this."

I turned on my heel and made for the kitchen, flinging cupboard doors open a little too harshly as I searched for the things I needed to make a bowl of oatmeal.

Felix didn't make a sound the entire time I had my back to him, but knowing he was still there irked me. I found my actions rough and erratic as I struggled to keep my frustration at bay. My sporadic fingers were so fueled by annoyance that I ended up dropping the glass bowl as I went to fill it with oats.

"Shit!" I hissed as the bowl shattered into a bunch of shards all around me. I hurriedly scrambled to try and pick them up, pricking a finger on an edge and drawing a drop of blood before I abandoned that idea. I glanced around the room for a different solution as I felt Felix approach the catastrophe I'd created.

"You know the interesting thing about glass?" he then asked rhetorically, and I shifted my eyes to see that he was in the process of picking up a large shard carefully between his forefinger and thumb. "It's something we are so familiar with, and yet, everybody seems to conveniently forget where it comes from."

I watched as Felix held the glass up against a ray of sun that had sifted through the window, making it shimmer and glint in the warm light. "Isn't it incredulous that glass is made from sand? Something so fine, so minute, so insignificant…it can be turned into this completely dissimilar substance that has so many uses, so long as it is manipulated the right way. You know how it's made, yes? You heat up the sand until it becomes a liquid, and then you cool it in the desired shape. Marvelous, really, but even more striking is that if you don't touch or meddle with sand in any way, that's all it will ever be. It will remain as sand and never resemble anything remotely close to glass. Two completely unrelated states, connected only by the proper handling of its origin. Isn't that wondrous? I don't think we give things like this enough credit."

He sighed and brought the shard close to his face, squinting at it. "But I suppose people just don't have an interest in the wonders of our world. The masses tend to have trivial minds when it comes to things that are handed to them, and they shy away from things that go beyond simplicity. Everyone seems to be frightened by such big ideas. It's a shame. I think big ideas are what makes this world such a fascinating place."

I stared at the shard. What the hell was he going on about?

"It's remarkable that one thing can be turned into some-thing almost entirely different with the precise treatment and processing," Felix went on. "It makes you wonder what else in this world could be changed so drastically when handled just the right way."

He gently plopped the shard of glass into his palm and held it between us, his eyes flickering up to me, the lavender hue that encased his irises sparkling like the waves of an unfathomable lavender lake in the early evening sun. "You strike me as the kind of person whose mind is adventurous enough to agree," he said, so quietly it was almost a whisper.

I held his gaze, studying his features. It was the closest we'd ever been, and for the first time, I was able to see what looked like a weariness to the lines in his skin and the darkness under his eyes. There was no denying he was handsomely made, but an exhaustion had seeped into his being. Whether it was from lack of sleep or something else, I couldn't determine. But something was draining Felix Clarkson, and given you could only really tell if you got close enough, I reckoned he was conscious of what it was, and of who could see it. It was like looking at the smoke and ashes of a fire that should be burning way brighter than it was.

When I didn't say anything, he chose to instead. "My offer still stands."

Not this again. "I haven't even tried to find a place for it yet," I countered.

"Miss Pierre, there's no way to guarantee your Phoenix remains hidden and safe unless it's on private property." He motioned out the window. "You expect to find a place no one will ever stumble across on campus? If you can locate it, surely anyone else can. And if this hideaway is not on campus, it'll indisputably be a bit of a journey for you."

I looked him up and down. "I'm a little confused as to why you insist on having my Phoenix reside with yours," I told him after a while.

He took a few seconds to respond. "It would be very wrong of me to deny you any assistance when I can see that you and your Phoenix could benefit from it."

"I never asked for your assistance," I replied swiftly, eyeing him. "Denial of assistance is not the real issue here, now is it?"

"I would say that's digging a little too deep into the dirt."

"You handed me the shovel."

I could see a slight falter of luminosity in those lavender stars. "Do you always bite the hand that feeds you?"

I scoffed, crossing my arms. "I feed myself, thank you very much."

He rolled his eyes and huffed, but before he could say anything else, Emmanuella walked into the lounge.

"You're in here?" Em exclaimed in surprise before she caught sight of Felix. "Oh – hi."

Felix cleared his throat, straightening a bit. "Hello."

An awkward quiet fell over the room as Em's eyes bounced back and forth between Felix and me. She then seemed to notice the shattered glass on the floor, a deep frown crawling its way into her brows.

"What happened?" she asked.

I looked down at the shards myself. "Butter fingers," I muttered in a bit of defeat.

"You need help?"

"No, it's fine, I got it."

I grabbed some paper towel and began sweeping the glass into a pile. Nobody said a word to each other as I gathered the last bits and began transferring them to the trash. I could feel both of them eyeing me. The tension in the room was as tightly wound as a music box.

I finished cleaning up and stood. "Were you looking for me?" I asked her, slicing the stroppiness in the space.

Emmanuella seemed to remember something. "Oh, yeah. There are some weird noises coming from your room."

My heart jumped a bit. "Weird noises?"

"Yeah, almost like knocking or bonking sounds." She shrugged. "I called over to you to ask if you were okay, but you didn't say anything back, and your bathroom door is locked."

"Oh." I laughed awkwardly. "Probably just some books toppled over on my shelf or something. I'll go have a look."

"Want me to go with you?"

I began to panic. "Well, uh – "

"Actually," Felix suddenly cut in, stepping between Em and me. "Miss Pierre and I – "

"Miss Pierre?" Emmanuella snorted. "What is this, Pride and Prejudice?"

I couldn't help but smirk. Felix gave her a look, but went on. "We were just about to go and work on a report for our physics lab in there, so no need to trouble yourself."

He threw an expectant expression at me. "Right?"

I faked a smile. "Right." I turned back to Emmanuella. "Thanks for letting me know."

"Yeah, no biggie." She threw a curious glance at Felix. "Good luck on your report."

"Much appreciated. We'll need it," I replied, before I motioned to Felix. "Come on."

He followed me out of the lounge and back to my dorm. Upon entering the room, I found my Phoenix at the foot of my desk, knocking its beak against the wood. There were chunks of it strewn all around the little feathered creature, and clear gnawing marks up and down the desk's leg.

"Hey, quit it!" I exclaimed as I hurried towards the bird.

My Phoenix squabbled a bit, burying itself further underneath the desk and finding a new piece of wood to chew on.

"Shit, stop it! I won't get my damage deposit back like this!" I hissed, falling to my hands and knees as I reached for the little troublemaker. The Phoenix squealed and nipped at me, but eventually submitted to my grasp as I yanked it out from under the desk.

I smoothed the ruffled feathers on the little curmudgeon to calm it down as I surveyed the damage to the furniture. "Fuck," I muttered under my breath.

"They do that to keep their beaks nice and trim."

My glance over at Felix was a scowl. He was leaning against the shut doorway nonchalantly, watching me.

He nodded towards my Phoenix. "They love to play with wood, too. Destroying is fun for them." He shrugged. "Most birds love the taste of it. It's in their nature."

"Great. Thanks for the unwanted science lesson," I snarled

at him as I threw myself down on the desk chair. The Phoenix looked up at me curiously, and to that, I simply stroked its feathers some more as I sunk into the seat of my own downfall.

I had been wrong.

I was so caught up in my own stubbornness that I was failing the nature of the creature I held through no fault of its own. Whether I fully understood how I'd ended up here, or wanted to engage with Felix or not, should not have been the crux of my focus. The heart of the matter was that I now had a responsibility, and I was too busy meandering in a selfish quest to avoid unpleasantry that I'd neglected that very duty. I'd denied a safe space for it not once, but twice, nearly leading to its discovery and landing me in the middle of a financial debacle. And it had only been twelve hours.

My eyes fell to a photo of my family on my desk. I thought about how many sacrifices my parents had made for my brother and I throughout our lives. When they received bonuses, it went to our college funds – not to a well-deserved vacation for the two of them. Countless soccer games for my brother and dance recitals for me, field trips they had to miss work for, extra hours they had to put in so that the Christmas tree would be brimming with gifts…they didn't do these things because it was always enjoyable, but because they had a job to do as nurturers. And they wanted to do it well.

The feelings of guilt could not be swallowed away as I glanced back down at my Phoenix. It had nestled into my arms, watching me with big, inquisitive eyes. If those eyes truly belonged to a companion I was bonded to, then it deserved a companion that acted as such.

With a sigh, I turned to look at Felix, who was monitoring me with a careful expression. "I'll take you up on your offer," I said.

There was a flash of wickedness in those lavender eyes that dissipated as quickly as it came. It was that very mischief I had dreaded and longed to avoid, the same one that made my blood rise with a boiling indignation.

"You aren't going to retaliate any further?" he asked me with a bit of doubtfulness, his eyebrows rising, taunting.

I struggled to keep my voice steady and unangered. "No promises," I murmured.

There was no response for a long while. I watched as his expression hardened, ice creeping into the features of his face and freezing any remnants of a fiery malice to stillness. A muscle feathered in his jaw. The slight frown that began to crease his features was rigid, the lavender in his irises dense and darkened.

Finally, he looked at my Phoenix and said quietly, "Let's go."

CHAPTER 7

I FOLLOWED Felix in an obstinate quiet down one of the walkways on campus, my Phoenix tucked under one half of my jacket to hide from prying eyes. He led me to the parking lot, towards a bright yellow Lamborghini Aventador. My eyes shifted when he pulled out a set of keys and unlocked it, the ostentatious machinery practically singing its own praises as its lights flashed on.

For the first time in a long time, Felix threw a glance back at me. "Make yourself comfortable," he instructed before he made for the driver's side.

I huffed a bit to myself as I opened the passenger door, feeling ridiculously out of place in the car worth more than everything I'd ever owned combined. I parted the jacket and brought my Phoenix on to my lap before I buckled myself in. Nearly as soon as Felix had sat down, he'd started the car and was pulling out of the parking lot.

There was a very long and uncomfortable silence as Felix drove the exquisite car smoothly. I wasn't sure what to do with myself.

"What's its name?"

His question caught me off guard. "What?"

"Your Phoenix," he said. "What is its name?"

I stopped and thought about this for a moment. I hadn't really thought of a name for it yet.

"Well, I mean, it depends on if it's a female or a male. I really like – "

"No, Miss Pierre. The pendant it gave you – the one around your neck. It's a locket. Inside it has your Phoenix's name inscribed. You don't get to choose a name. It already has been given one," he explained.

"Oh," I muttered before I opened the locket with my fingers and pried it apart gently.

In the center of the golden metal, written beautifully in elegant handwriting, was the name *Aurora*.

"Aurora," I said with a little bit of a glow. It was a lovely girl's name.

"Aurora…" Felix repeated it slowly. "Hm. Suits a Light Phoenix."

"It does?" I asked.

"Well, yes. It's another word for 'the dawn,'" Felix said matter-of-factly. "In addition, it's part of the full name *Aurora Borealis*, which is another name for the Northern Lights, a scientific phenomenon that describes the display of lights caused by gaseous particles colliding in the atmosphere. It mainly occurs in Northern Canada and Europe."

"Ah, *oui*, I've heard of that," I said. I saw Felix nod out of the corner of my eye.

"Keep that pendant on you at all times," he instructed plainly. "You can show it atop your clothing or not, that's up to you. But it's the most important possession of a Phoenix Keeper, and it's crucial that you don't take it off."

"Right, okay," I said.

There was another long silence.

"What's your Phoenix's name?" I asked.

"Fuego," he answered.

"Fuego? That's Spanish for fire."

"That's correct."

"So, I'm guessing she's a – "

"He is a Fire Phoenix, yes," Felix finished for me.

"Oh, nice." I glanced out the opposite window. "And you thought I was going to have a Fire Phoenix?"

Felix didn't reply right away, which confused me at first, because I'd learned the information from him. "I did, yes."

"And why's that?"

I heard him clear his throat. "No particular reason."

I turned to stare at him. "You expect me to believe that?"

He took a deep breath in. "You have this…" he sucked in his lips as he thought. "…fiery disposition."

"Fiery disposition?"

"…Yes."

"Are you saying I have a temper?" I accused.

We came to a stop at a red light, where he hesitantly made eye contact with me. "Not so much of a temper as a temperament."

I squinted at him. "And that temperament is fiery?"

From the look on his face, I could tell he regretted opening the can of worms before him. "Fiery may not be a negative thing."

"You're implying I'm hot-headed."

"That's an inference from my words that you've made, Miss Pierre."

"But that's what you mean."

He sighed. "I can neither confirm nor deny that."

I rolled my eyes. "So, Phoenixes pick Keepers like themselves?"

He turned back to focus on the road as the light turned green. "Not necessarily."

I frowned. "Then why would you think – "

"I don't know. It was a stupid thought," he blurted before I could finish. "A Light Phoenix seems just fine for you."

"Well, I'm glad to hear that," I said with a bit of an edge.

There was a pause as tension began to crawl into the vehicle.

"So, your parents never told you about Phoenixes?" Felix then inquired quickly, almost as if to prevent the car from getting anymore frigid.

"No." I looked at him. "Should they have told me?"

He ran a hand through his hair, his other lightly gripping the steering wheel. "Well, it's possible they were not Phoenix Keepers. It's uncommon, though. Generally, Phoenix Keepers bear children who also become Phoenix Keepers, as they pass on their knowledge through education and stories to further the lineage. That's what my father did, anyways – hence the reason I'm now a Phoenix Keeper."

"Oh," I said. "That makes sense."

"It also makes sense now why you're so misinformed about the situation – you were never informed in the first place," Felix thought aloud. "No matter, though. I suppose I gave you a bit of a crash course."

"That you did. In the middle of the night."

I could see his features go a little sheepish. "All right, we're here," was the convenient announcement that followed, and I had no doubt it was to serve as a distraction from my bitter recollection.

I turned my attention to my surroundings. I noticed that we had driven up a slow incline amid the gorgeous La Jolla area of San Diego. Felix slowed the car to a stop in front of an elaborate gate which was attached to an equally extravagant fence. It spanned beyond my vision on either side and enclosed what looked like a massive area of land. He reached into a compartment inside the car and pulled out a little device, which, when he pressed a button, opened the gate slowly. He replaced the device in the compartment and continued driving down what was now a driveway.

Inside the fence, the scenery was magnificent. Beautiful gardens lined the driveway with flowers of every complimenting size, shape, and colour. Large flowering trees were placed methodically throughout the property. The lush, green grass was well-trimmed to perfection. I could see a wistful pond and small creek on the right side, leading out beyond my sight into what looked like a private forest. On the left, in the near distance, I could see more large palm trees and what looked like an orchard.

Felix drove up to a cobblestone roundabout with a huge, stunning fountain sitting prettily in the middle. There were three possible driveways we could have continued on – one that led to the right, one that led to the left, and one that led straight and ended in front of a huge mansion not too far from where we were. Felix turned left.

"If you go right, you'll end up at my brother's villa. Straight ahead was my father's mansion, and we're currently heading to mine," Felix explained.

"Wait, so you all live here?"

"Well, yes," he answered bluntly.

I frowned at him. "How big is this place?"

"About four hundred acres altogether."

"*Four hundred acres?*" I repeated in disbelief, and wished that I hadn't – I didn't want him to think that I was impressed, because I wasn't. I was just shocked that there were people who struggled to survive on a daily basis, and then there were the Clarksons and their four-hundred acre estate, who probably couldn't comprehend the very real issue of not having shirts over their chests or food in their bellies.

"Yes. Two eight-thousand square foot villas – my brother's and mine – and my father's eleven-thousand square foot mansion, along with all the shared gardens, orchard, and forests. Each of our manors comes complete with their own private gardens, home gym, pool, hot tub, tennis and basket-ball courts, bar…you name it, and it probably has it. There's a communal golf course behind my father's place, and a path that leads down to the docks on our private beach. We each have our own boats, too."

"Private beach?"

"Mhm-hmm. The property lines the Pacific Ocean. It was officially named Clarkson Beach shortly after my father purchased the property, actually," Felix stated matter-of-factly. His words were puffing out their chest – he probably was, too.

My mouth became a gaping hole, my eyes wide. *Were these people insane? How rich could a family be?*

As if to answer my question, Felix's villa came barreling into view, taking me completely by surprise. It had its own artistic fountain placed beautifully in the centre of its front courtyard and was lined by rosebushes. The enormous building itself was accented with sharp angles, a feat of modern architecture, and became larger and more magnificent the closer we got. Felix pulled out another device from the compartment in his car and pushed a button which opened the hefty garage doors. He then parked the car smoothly between a red Ferrari 458 Spider and a silver Aston Martin Rapide S. As if that wasn't enough, there were three other spots for cars in the garage – two of which were occupied by a silvery-blue Koenigsegg Regera and a dark gray Porsche Carrera GT.

"You have *five* cars?" I exclaimed in disbelief.

"For now," Felix answered frankly. "My Bugatti hasn't arrived yet."

He then casually stepped out of the car and shut the door behind him. Still in shock, I carefully held Aurora to my chest as I exited the car and followed him out of the garage in disbelief.

Felix led me up the steps to his marvelous front door and opened it, walking through it with a pompous stride. I sheepishly trailed him, trying not to feel small, but at the same time not really being able to control how I felt with the overwhelming prosperity he practically shoved in my face.

If the outside of Felix's villa didn't blow you away, the inside sure would. We stepped into a gorgeous marble-floored foyer with two glass staircases wrapping around the circular room and leading up to the second floor. A sharp, modern chandelier hung glamorously in the centre of the room, the glass accents hanging delicately from it catching the light through the marvelous windows and sparkling with a beautiful crystal gleam. Two huge archways led out of the room on either side, and the white walls were lined with a black crown moulding. The entire house sang of wealth, boasting with modernism and clean details. It was almost as ostentatious as Felix himself.

Between the two staircases was a glass table which Felix approached. His hands ran through a stack of papers which I soon realized were envelopes that seemed to have been placed carefully next to the phone that sat atop it.

"Ah, excellent. She picked up my mail," Felix said. *She?*

Almost as if on cue, a petite young woman wearing all black appeared in the left archway. I scrambled to hide Aurora from view, but she didn't seem to notice me as she looked expectantly at Felix.

"Welcome home, sir. I hope your day was well. I picked up your mail for you," she said in an almost rehearsed fashion.

"Yes, miss, I can see that," Felix said, not looking up from his fingers which were still sifting through the envelopes. "Where are the other maids and the butler?"

At this point, the fact that Felix had more than one maid *and* a butler was not all that surprising.

"Miffy is in one of the bathrooms. Gwendolen, I am not sure. Francis went to pick up some groceries. Did you need something, sir? I can see you have brought a guest," the maid asked, not looking at me as she acknowledged me.

"Tell one of the other maids that I would like my linens cleaned by tonight."

"All of the linens?" the maid inquired.

Felix turned abruptly to her, squinting. "I sleep on all my

linens, don't I? What would be the purpose of only cleaning some of them?"

She swallowed. "I just wanted to clarify, sir."

He sighed and shook his head as he turned back to the mail. "Yes, miss, all of the linens must be cleaned."

"Of course, sir," she said. "Was there anything else I could do for you?"

"No. Dismissed," Felix said with an authority that came naturally to him, as if he were molded to play the role. And with that, the maid disappeared just as quickly as she'd come.

I watched her scurry out, bewildered at how she just submitted to him and his every beck and call so dutifully. I'd never seen such a power imbalance play out so blatantly in front of me.

"I swear some people wouldn't know the difference between a potato and a peach if they tasted them both," I heard Felix mumble. I turned back to look at him and saw he was dialing a number on the phone. He then picked up the receiver and waited for a few moments.

"Hello? Yes, Father, it's me...yes, I'm fine. Listen, that girl I was telling you about...yes, her. Well, I was right...mhm-hmm...indeed. No, she had no idea...mhm ...yes, precisely... no, she doesn't think her parents were Phoenix Keepers... mhm-hmm...no, she doesn't. She's here with me now...yes... no, she's from Montreal. Where are we? Why, we're in my house...mhm...mhm-hmm...Miss Pierre. Yes. Yes, I believe so...I'm going to have it stay with Fuego...no, she lives at the university...yes...it's a Light Phoenix. Mhm...wait, *now?* Well, I *suppose* so...well, sure, yes. Has Julius returned home yet? ... Hm? No? Good...Father, I will speak about him however I please...well, whatever. When should we expect you? ... Mhm...well, all right, then. I suppose I'll see you soon...mhm-hmm. Yes. All right. Goodbye."

He placed the phone back on the receiver and threw a glance at me. "Come with me," he commanded.

He led me through the left archway that the maid had appeared in and into a living room. The showcase of wealth seemed to continue with the flow of the house, and it took me a few rooms to determine that the recurring theme was 'new money.' The rooms were large with little furniture, and they were mixtures of black and white, glass and marble. There were no stray books or papers on the tables, no jackets thrown over a chair from a morning rush. All the wall art seemed to be black and white photography. Everything was purposeful, tactful, clean, blank.

In one room, there was a huge, onyx fireplace in the center. On one side, there was a black leather sofa and a white, fluffy rug. On the other side, a sleek pool table, and that was it, despite there being much more space in the room.

I looked down at the fur as I stepped on it, a little disheartened at the fact that it may have been an animal. "Is this real?" I questioned.

"No," Felix replied instantly as he continued walking. "I do not believe in slaughtering animals for their skin."

It was the first thing he'd said that had genuinely pleased me. "I see," I said simply. At least we saw eye-to-eye on something.

He turned to meet my gaze, and I was stunned to see his lavender eyes were incredibly stern. "Wealthy is not a synonym for inhumane, Miss Pierre," he declared. "Not in my thesaurus."

The way he spoke signified that it was important to him that his point be driven home. I nodded quickly, and he turned back to face the front. I thought it was strange he could make such a statement when he had just faulted a maid for desiring clarification about his linens, but perhaps irony did not exist in his books.

He continued to lead me through a dining room that could seat twenty, a beautiful sunroom with one white sofa, and a study with a large desk in the middle and black bookshelves behind it. I noticed another interesting trend – mirrors. In most of the rooms, there seemed to be a decorative mirror that went with the theme of the space. There were big ones and small ones, rectangular ones and round ones. Most were rimmed with black or white – some had no rim at all. They seemed to be the focal décor, with other modern sculptures or large photographs sprinkled throughout as a supporting act.

Then he led me through a modern kitchen into a small room, the main purpose of which appeared to be providing a doorway to the garden. It had no mirrors, and almost no furniture. There were, in fact, only three things: a chair, a small potted plant, and a grayscale photograph of a saddened woman looking over her shoulder at a man fixated with his reflection in a pond.

I eyed the photo. "Echo and Narcissus," I said, more to myself than to him.

I saw him glance at the photograph, then back at me. "Yes," he said matter-of-factly. And there really wasn't much else I wanted to say about it, so I simply nodded in response.

Felix showed me through the door and out on to a vast, black deck. We stepped on to a stone path amidst what must have been Felix's private garden. There were a lot of rocks, and sculptures, and fountains. The flower bushes that lined the path methodically were all white. A huge pool complete with a waterfall and hot tub sat to the left of the deck, and some fruit trees stood with leaves that glowed in the sun behind it.

"I keep Fuego in what I would say resembles a cellar," Felix explained. "I've, of course, made some modifications to better suit him. Aurora should be comfortable there with him. It's far out past the garden, where none of my staff are allowed. In fact, the only people who know the cellar even exists are myself, my father, and now, you."

"Really?" I questioned. "How have you managed to keep this all a secret?"

"It's simple, really. We don't allow my staff past a certain point in my garden, we don't discuss matters involving Phoenixes around them, and we don't keep staff around for very long. I don't even think I've kept a maid around for more than a few months. That one I spoke to earlier has only been here a week or so."

It surprised me that this was the case. "Where do you find all those maids?"

"Oh, it isn't that difficult. Plenty of desperate women out there looking for money. Some men, too. But mainly women. It's a bit of a pity, really, but I'm not complaining. At least that frees them up to work for me."

I didn't respond to this statement – the sentence "well, I'm glad to hear that" didn't seem to be a fitting reply. I was more interested in the whole concept of sensing; that was beyond my brain's capability of understanding.

"That whole sensing thing…it's hard for me to comprehend. How does that work?" I asked him. It was an abrupt topic change, but I think he expected it, because his answer was quick.

"Ah, well, it might be a bit outlandish to explain. Do you know how, when you think to yourself, there's this controllable voice in your head unique to you that tells you your own thoughts?"

I thought about this. "*Oui.*"

"Well, when you sense something, it's basically like adding another uncontrollable voice to your head which tells you information about your surroundings. It's all available through your Phoenix's tune with the world. Like I said, though, you must have a strong bond with your Phoenix for it to work. As you two grow together, your bond will over time. Once you fully bond, you can even telepathically communicate with your Phoenix. And, when you fully bond with your Phoenix, it'll enable you to be able to telepathically communicate with other Phoenix Keepers, too. You can even go so far as to bond with another Phoenix Keeper."

I considered the doors my Phoenix was going to open for me. I looked down at Aurora as she sat silently cradled in my arms. The sensing was just one reward in what seemed like a bucket full of them. If that was the beginning of our powers together, how many other amazing things would become available to me?

By this time, we had made it so far away from Felix's mansion that it was disappearing in the distance, and the beginnings of what looked like a forest greeted us as the stone path said goodbye.

"The entrance to the cellar is in past these bushes here, in a clearing," Felix said. He pushed away some branches of the brush. I followed him in between the bushes.

Sure enough, not long after we had walked through the trees, we came to a clearing with a little wooden structure sitting casually in the middle. Felix took a key out of his pocket and unlocked the door to the structure, opened it wide, and motioned inside.

"Ladies first," he said simply.

CHAPTER 8

BEHIND THE DOOR was a long staircase, surrounded by wooden walls and illuminated by dim lights. Cautiously, I made my way down, and I could hear Felix follow behind me.

The staircase was deep and narrow, and about halfway down the walls became stone. Finally, I made it to the bottom, and the space opened much wider than I expected.

The cellar was huge – about two stories deep and as wide as a football field. A large skylight that was attached to a mechanism for opening brightened the room with natural daylight in the center of the ceiling. From what I gathered, it must have been concealed from view above ground in a covered clearing somewhere in Felix's private forest. The floor itself was a light wood, and a large rug was sprawled underneath the skylight. There was a bookshelf shoved against one wall and stacked to the brim with old books, and huge bags filled with what looked like feed and a water trough shoved in the other. Some hefty cushions were also sprawled in the center, along with a large blow-up ball and a few big bells – toys for the Phoenix, I assumed. In the last corner of the room were a table and two chairs, and a large sectional sofa with two matching armchairs surrounding a coffee table. All along the room's walls were soft lights that gave the room a calming presence – it seemed like somewhere you could spend some quiet time in.

I didn't have much time to get acquainted to the room, though, before something enormous unexpectedly blocked me from walking any further.

"Good grief!" I screamed, startled. I stumbled backwards but was prevented from falling by Felix's strong shove in the other direction. He pushed past me and approached the huge figure sternly.

"Easy boy! Whoa, easy!" Felix shouted, grabbing at the figure.

As I reeled back and managed to straighten myself, I realized what exactly had jumped out at me and was instantly taken aback yet again.

Currently wrestling with Felix before me was a huge, red Phoenix. It was almost twice as big as Felix himself, its wings unfurling and spanning twice its body length on both sides. The light from the skylight glistened off its mixture of blood-red, maroon, and crimson plumage, and its large, intense eyes glistened rubicund in the afternoon sun. It was screeching loudly in different pitches at Felix as it attempted to get past him and back to me, flapping its clearly strong wings and rustling its feathers threateningly.

"Fuego, boy, *stop it!*" Felix yelled at him as he grabbed him by the back of the head. Fuego resisted for a moment before allowing Felix to bring his head down to eye level and glare at him.

And just like that, the room went silent.

I watched in confusion as Felix continued to stare at Fuego, and Fuego right back at him. Their eye contact seemed deep and thoughtful as their stares scanned each other. It was almost as if some kind of silent connection were being made.

Then, something drastically changed in both pairs of eyes, as if a giant weight had been lifted off both of their minds. The bird's ruby irises lightened, as did Felix's, and he released his grip on Fuego's head and ran his fingers through his feathers all the way down his neck.

Up until this point, I hadn't seen much but an unlikeable peculiarity to Felix, but in that moment, I saw something different. As seconds passed and he continued to pet the bird, I could almost see the softness of the feathers travel through his fingers and into his body. He became less heavy and less stiff, his stature loosening as his bones and muscles freed themselves from their prisons. His expression altered itself very marginally, too. It wasn't anything I'd seen before on him – usually his face was set in apathetic stone, but now, it was almost humanized.

It became obvious to me that this creature was something that influenced Felix. I could see closeness between the two, and given what Felix had told me about bonds earlier, I could attribute theirs to what I was seeing happen before me. There was a certain level of comfort and warmth he exerted with the bird. I felt a little glow surround my heart. How ironically beautiful it was to see that a nonhuman soul was the very thing that brought out a relative humanity in his own.

"There we go. He's calm now," Felix said quietly, stroking Fuego's head softly. "I telepathically explained the situation to him. He was just a little too enthused to see someone new down here, but he should be more reasonable now."

I observed Felix as he continued to soothe the bird, his fingers tracing each feather like a pencil traces paper. He glanced at me.

"You want to pet him?" he offered.

I hesitated – the giant bird had attacked me, after all.

Felix watched me for a moment, then shrugged, a smirk pulling at the corners of his mouth. "Suit yourself," he said mockingly.

Well, I wasn't about to just let him have that one. I began approaching Fuego cautiously. The Phoenix looked at me inquisitively as I hesitantly reached out my hand towards him.

"You know, if you're that nervous, you don't have to – "

"I want to," I cut Felix off, glaring at him. He shook his head in amusement and then backed away, motioning to Fuego with both his hands as if to say, "The stage is yours."

I cleared my throat and turned back to Fuego, steadying my hand as I brought it towards him. I was just about to reach his feathers when he jerked away suddenly, causing me to retract my hand.

I could hear Felix chuckling behind me in his usual mocking way. "You seem to have a habit of getting off on the wrong foot with everyone, don't you?" I heard him say.

I grew imminently frustrated, taking a few steps backwards from the Phoenix completely. "Whatever," I muttered, turning away from Felix and looking down at Aurora, who was still tucked into my chest. She looked back up at me with her little bright eyes, and I patted her head softly. *At least she lets me pet her,* I thought.

There was suddenly movement coming towards me, and I brought my eyes up to see Fuego had approached me. His crimson irises were shining down at Aurora with a beautiful curiosity, shimmering various shades of red in the hazy light. It seemed as though he hadn't seen her before, but was now more than intrigued to observe another one of his kind.

Aurora cocked her head to the side upon meeting Fuego's gaze, scanning him curiously. Fuego studied her back for a very long time. Aurora didn't seem unsettled by his probing – in fact, she seemed to grow elated. After a minute or so, she straightened her head and let out a little squeaky chirp. Fuego's eyes widened at this, and he blinked several times before hesitantly leaning towards her with his neck. She, too, outstretched her tiny little head out forwards.

I decided to do my part and help the two Phoenixes out in getting a closer look at each other by lifting Aurora slowly up to Fuego's head. "You see, Aurora?" I asked her in a motherly voice, running my fingers through her feathers coloured by the sun. "He's like you!"

Aurora let out another chirp before placing her cutely small beak up against Fuego's. Fuego seemed a little startled, as he simply stared at my little Phoenix as she held her beak to his. When she let out another coo, however, Fuego suddenly became very open and welcoming to the action, and he responded with his own chirping as he nuzzled her excitedly.

Aurora began wiggling happily as she let out a series of joyful bird noises, and I took the opportunity to gently put her down on the floor. "There you are! Go play with your friend!" I told her between a series of giggles.

The two Phoenixes began squealing at each other blissfully. They looked happy to be with something familiar and recognizable – happy, in a sense, to see themselves. They began flapping their wings and running about in circles around each other, singing songs that seeped with exuberance.

I laughed at the two birds as they did a sort of happy dance. Fuego, who quickly got caught up in his excitement, seemed to forget that Aurora was nowhere near as big as he was. As he began playing with her quicker and more energetically, I could see she was struggling to keep up on her stubby little baby bird legs, and she tripped over herself a few times.

"Hey, hey, easy, Fuego," I cut in softly, holding my hand up and approaching him.

His ruby eyes snapped up to meet my gaze, which made me retract my hand and my steps but didn't stop me from continuing to speak. "She's little, sweetie. You have to be careful."

He cocked his head to the side, and then turned back to look down at Aurora, who had paused at Fuego's feet. Her little chest puffed in and out as she breathed quickly, and she glanced up at me, then Fuego, and back again many times in quick head motions. Finally, she settled on Fuego's gaze, widened her eyes at him, fluffed her feathers and let out one single chirp.

Fuego stared back down at her for a moment before lowering himself down to the ground in a bird-like sort of perch, folding his legs underneath him as he struck a swan-like pose. He extended one wing out towards Aurora and carefully brought her in towards the top half of his body. Curling his neck down towards her, he then rested his head against her body and snuggled her softly as she sat partly tucked underneath some of the feathers of his wing. They both let out a series of coos as they puffed themselves up into a feathery bundle of acceptance, friendship, and love.

Fuego's gaze flickered back up to mine, and his eyes were wide. He almost seemed to be asking if this was a gentle enough way to play with Aurora. I couldn't help but smile back at him and nod. I wondered, then, if he had truly understood my instructions before – it seemed like it.

Fuego seemed to recognize my support of this idea of 'play' – I swear I could see the bird smiling back at me with its eyes. They then glimmered with what could only be taken as a sort of invitation. My smile widened into a grin as he shifted his wing over, and I carefully sat down beside Aurora before he brought his wing back over the two of us. Aurora hustled over to the side of my leg and began rubbing her head against it, looking up at me gleefully and giving off beautiful, quiet sounds. Her bright yellow eyes gleamed with affection. I giggled down at her and ran my fingers atop her little head. I then seized the opportunity I had and brought my hand – no longer shaking, might I add – to the base of Fuego's neck. He seemed to hum in response, and I could feel the warmth of his bright red plumage along with his heartbeat underneath my palm as I soothingly rubbed his feathers back and forth.

It was then, as I sat nuzzled up to what I could only describe as the most extraordinary creatures to ever live, that I knew what the feeling of true contentment and inner peace was. I felt like I had won the lottery, cured cancer, and solved world hunger all at once.

"Interesting."

I turned to look at Felix, whom I had forgotten about

momentarily. He had sat himself down a good ways away from the Phoenixes and I, loosely tucking his knees into his chest as he held them in place with his forearms. The lavender in his eyes was cloudy and foggy.

"That was a curious technique, earning his trust utilizing your Phoenix," Felix noted. "Very resourceful."

I squinted at him. "You sound surprised."

He cocked his head to the side, frowning slightly. "And you sound insulted, for some reason."

"Your statement implies that you didn't expect me to manage Fuego on my own."

"I was merely giving you a compliment, Miss Pierre."

I let out an amused breath. "Well, I wasn't looking for your approval."

His eyes narrowed and widened and narrowed again. He suddenly seemed trapped within himself, my words somehow tangling him into a web of thoughts like a spider. The room became so quiet that I could have heard a pin drop.

And then, he asked, "Who did this to you?"

I only stared in response.

"Who made you this way?" were his next words.

My brows shook a bit. "What?"

His face was strained as he tried to keep his expression bland and unreadable. "I saw you with your friends at the club," he explained bluntly. "The way you smile and laugh when you're happy. But I don't get that side of you." He lowered his curious, prying eyes. "Someone must have built this animosity. Someone must have hurt you."

I felt the sudden flash of shock as it shot across my face. I did everything I could to reel it in, but there was no denying I'd let it slip.

Men had not been kind to me.

They all came to my mind in an instant – the ones who couldn't commit, the ones who disappeared without a trace, the ones who couldn't take no for an answer. There was one who had told me marine biology was a waste of time, that I would be of better use at home with children. And then there were the ones that had shamed me for my culture, my body, my brain – the ones who saw me as a threat.

I'd been lied to, betrayed, and guilted. Despite never having a physical altercation, their actions left scars – arguably deeper than any wound. I'd come to the realization long ago that my best defense was not giving them any power. Even if they saw me naked, they would never see me vulnerable. Even if I dated them, I would never let them mean more to me than myself. That was how I could guarantee my own peace.

And so, whenever a man rubbed me the wrong way, my reaction was visceral. Somehow, he'd seen right through that intuitive response.

But there was no way I would admit it to him.

I shook my head and turned away from him, towards the bookshelf. I could feel him watching me, but he didn't say anything more. Instead, I heard him shift from the floor and slowly make his way to stand beside me.

Usually, when I snapped at men, they left me alone. That was the whole point of biting at them. But for whatever reason, I just couldn't seem to shake this one. I struggled to understand why.

I tried not to give his presence any attention as I forced myself to study the contents of the shelf. The books were gothic and old, but their bindings seemed to have been kept in relatively good shape. Along their spines, I could read their titles. *A Collection of Tales from the Keepers of Athens, 1642. Phoenix Anatomy and Physiology. The Story of Kyosho, Keeper of Riletta. An Account of Keeper Malia through the 38th Week of 1200. Wielding and Understanding Magic. Bonds and How to Strengthen Them. The Tale of Judas, Keeper of Tamea. Nami, Keeper of Yomoko, and Stefan, Keeper of Beziria: A Political Affair.*

"Are these the stories you were talking about?" I asked Felix. "The ones your father would have read to you?"

The answer was delayed. "Yes," I heard him say.

I picked up a book at random and began flipping through its pages. They were old and stained, and the writing was calligraphic. Occasionally, a hand-drawn picture would pop up on a page, usually of a Phoenix and its Keeper.

The sound of footsteps stole my attention. I turned just as a familiar, older man was stepping down the staircase. He looked to be in his late fifties, and he had aged well, for his dark brown hair only had a few strands of gray, and the wrinkles on his face were only in their early stages of appearing. He was tall, but not as tall as Felix, and his build looked to have been better in his younger days, though it was quite amiable at present, too. He wore a suit, a nice suit, complete with a red tie and black dress shoes. He made eye contact with me as he entered the cellar, and I noticed his eyes were an approachable shade of greyish blue that smiled along with his thin lips.

"Ah, excellent. You're both still here," he said, and his tone was warm and inviting, as if it were coating his English accent in sweet honey.

"Hello, Father," I heard Felix say with monotony from beside me.

His father acknowledged both him and me with a single nod. "You must be Seraphine."

I returned the nod. "*Oui*, sir."

He chuckled again and held out his hand. "Oh, my dear, no need to be so formal. You may call me Luther," he assured me soothingly.

I smiled and shook his hand. "It's a pleasure to meet you, Luther."

"The pleasure's all mine, Seraphine, dear." He motioned to Felix. "My son has briefly covered the premise of your situation. I do hope he's made you comfortable."

I could feel Felix's sidelong gaze burning holes in the side of my head as I did my best to keep my smile genuine. "Absolutely," was the word I forced pleasantly out of my mouth.

"Wonderful," he remarked, and turned his attention to Aurora, who had waddled over to us. "Ah, what a gorgeous Light Phoenix you have there! Its name?"

"Aurora," I answered.

"Aurora! Oh, how delightful!" Luther exclaimed, and he outstretched his hand towards her. "May I?"

"Of course."

He soothingly stroked Aurora's little head. "My, it's been a while since I've seen a young Phoenix." He grinned at me. "You complement each other quite nicely, you know?"

"Do we?"

"Indeed. I can see the light in both of your eyes."

I glowed. "Why, thank you, sir – I mean, Luther."

He chuckled again before handing Aurora to me. "Well, dear, it would be wonderful to get to know you more, now that your precious little Aurora resides here with Fuego. I do know it's quite short notice, but would you please be so kind as to join us for supper?"

The thought of having supper with Felix turned my stomach a bit, but his father seemed kind, and I didn't want to burn that bridge. I quickly nodded with a polite smile to accept his invitation, to which Luther smiled back in return.

"Excellent. Let's make our way there now."

I turned around and carefully placed Aurora on the ground next to Fuego, patting her head slightly. A twinge of sadness came over me as I realized this would mean goodbye until I saw her next. It was amazing to me how quickly I had gotten attached to her. She looked at me with wide eyes, and I could see the reflection of my own melancholic gaze in them. I felt bad for having to leave her, but at the same time, I knew deep down it was the best – and really, the only knowingly safe – way to do this.

I leaned in and gave her a little kiss on her head before forcing myself to follow in Luther's footsteps with Felix not too far behind me.

CHAPTER 9

LUTHER LED the way as we walked along a beautiful pathway to his mansion.

If the theme of Felix's home was 'new money,' then the theme of Luther's was completely the opposite. Its massive courtyard, filled with rosebushes and magnolia trees, was followed by an impressive entryway, with astonishing dark-wood floors and one of the highest, most intricately-detailed ceilings I had ever seen. The crown moulding was ornate, the vintage décor was breathtaking, and the way the archways curved and danced made me feel like I had walked into a fairy tale. The rooms were so beautifully decorated with such fine pieces that I would dare say the place had an air of loveliness comparable to that of the Palace of Versailles.

We were greeted by two butlers at the front door. They themselves were finely dressed in their uniforms, and they played their role so well that it wasn't a role anymore. I felt as though I'd somehow been teleported to a castle of royals and their servants in England.

"Welcome back, sir," one of the butlers said to Luther while taking off his jacket. "I see you've brought company... perhaps for supper?"

"Yes indeed, George. Please have the table set for three. Thank you," Luther replied politely, to which George nodded and scurried off.

"Can I get you anything to drink, sir?" the other butler asked as he was taking off Felix's coat.

"That sounds wonderful, Benjamin. Whatever the recommendation is I will have, please and thank you. Perhaps for Seraphine, as well?" Luther answered, looking expectantly at me.

I shook my head. "I'm all right, thanks."

"Are you sure? We have one of the finest champagnes opened to compliment this evening's meal – the chef's suggestion," Benjamin persisted.

I glanced at Luther, who smiled encouragingly at me, and then I smiled back at Benjamin. "All right, sure. I'll have a glass, please."

"Very well. And for you, Felix?" Benjamin turned to him.

"Oh, God knows I could use a glass. A large one, actually," Felix muttered. I squinted at him, but he didn't seem to notice – or pretended not to, at the very least.

"As you wish. Follow me," Benjamin said, and he turned and followed in George's footsteps as we followed in his.

He led us to a huge, extravagant dining room – I counted thirty seats at the large, rectangular table – that was decorated in dark, elegant colours and filled with mahogany furniture. There were three places set at the table, one at the head and two on either side of it. Luther sat at the head of the table, Felix to his right and I to his left.

Benjamin disappeared through a door and reappeared with a bottle of champagne in his hands. He poured it into each of our glasses before assuring us that dinner would be ready at any moment and vanishing through the doorway once again.

I took a small sip of the champagne, and my taste buds did a sort of happy dance. Benjamin had not been kidding when he said this was one of the finest champagnes available. The light fizziness merged beautifully with the soft sweetness of the delicious liquid.

"Do you like it?" Luther asked as he took a sip of his own.

"Could be stronger," Felix mumbled after taking multiple sips.

I rolled my eyes at him before I turned to Luther. "It's fantastic, *oui*. Thank you!" I replied.

Luther smiled widely. I could tell he was one of those people who got satisfaction out of seeing his guests pleased.

Benjamin and George suddenly burst back into the room carrying two steaming plates covered with silver lids each. George put down his two in front of Felix and I, and Benjamin put one in front of Luther and one in the center of us three. They both lifted the lids off to reveal some of the best-looking and best-smelling food I had ever seen.

"Your meal tonight is a chicken cordon bleu sautéed in white wine and paprika, served with honey roasted red potatoes and grilled Portobello mushrooms that were also sautéed with white wine. In the center we have prepared some buttered bread and have provided vinegar and olive oil for dipping. Your dessert to be served later will be a rich tiramisu cheesecake. Can we get anything else for you?" George said.

"Oh, this is all quite fantastic! I think we're all right for now, no?" Luther said, and his gaze turned towards me.

I nodded in agreement. "This is more than enough. Thank you so much!"

"It is our pleasure, miss. Enjoy your meal, and please don't hesitate to ask us if you desire anything," Benjamin said.

"Excuse me," Felix spoke up, holding up his now empty glass — sheesh, he drank that really fast. "I'd like some more champagne, if you don't mind."

"Of course," Benjamin said, grabbing the bottle and quickly filling the glass back up. I watched as Felix took an unusually large sip — almost as if he weren't drinking an alcoholic drink — and placed the glass back down.

Luther nodded at the two butlers then with a polite smile, and they once again were gone.

I carefully took my cutlery and delicately cut a tiny piece of my chicken cordon bleu, being extremely self-conscious about every motion I made as I was eating in the presence of what I considered important company and did not want to appear like some kind of slob. I took a small bite and savoured what was probably the best piece of chicken I had ever had in my life. The rest of the meal was astoundingly good as well, and I ate it slowly and politely. I was surprised that Felix and Luther were in such good shape, considering that they had this kind of good food available to them every day.

"So, Seraphine," Luther began as we ate. "What brings you all the way from Montreal?"

I swallowed my food. "Well, I really like marine biology, and I thought I would be presented with more opportunities if I got a marine biology degree from here rather than back at home."

"Marine biology, hm? That's a very interesting topic, indeed. But I understood from Felix you gained your belief in Phoenixes from a class you are taking?"

"*Oui*, I also take a Greek Mythology course as an elective."

"Ah, yes, that makes sense. Phoenixes are a large part of that topic."

"They are. We were actually discussing them in lecture the day before and the day of Aurora's hatching," I said.

"How exciting!" Luther exclaimed. "I assume, though, that Phoenix Keepers aren't mentioned with them, as the majority of the world's population doesn't know they exist."

"You're right. I didn't know they did either, until I became one," I said.

"Ah, yes, Felix mentioned that to me as well," Luther recalled. "I could not imagine being in your shoes, Seraphine. You seem very capable for someone who's gone through so many changes in the last little while. That's a great quality for a budding Phoenix Keeper, as it can be a tough journey. It's going to be especially tough for you because you're completely blind to the things you need to learn."

I listened carefully, suddenly feeling a little worried. "Is it going to be that hard?"

"Well, I don't mean to scare you, but I definitely won't say it's easy work," Luther said. "So many things associated with being a Phoenix Keeper are far beyond the mental capacity of the average person. There are many skills you need to learn and accommodate that utilize parts of the brain which are inaccessible to regular people, not to mention physical skills, like magic and riding."

I stared blankly at him, blinking.

Luther looked back at me, his gaze apologetic. "I assure you that if I could, I would teach you everything. But it has been a long time since my Ohên has passed – much too long for me to be able to reproduce my skills to you, and I no longer have my Phoenix to demonstrate the skills as I did when Felix was just becoming a Phoenix Keeper."

Felix, who was doing a fantastic job at not being a very active part of the conversation, suddenly seemed to find some words. "Father, there's no need to worry," he said with a shake of the head. "I will teach her."

His eyes met mine. He'd primed them with some sort of bland, convincing show of generosity, but hidden in them, I could see specks of a cunning glint, sprinkled amongst the lavender like small, nuisance bugs. Slowly, I realized I'd somehow gotten myself more trapped in the trap. I was displeased, but I made no motion to object. I'd agreed to the terms without reading the fine print carefully, and I couldn't think of an alternate option.

The painted charity on Felix's face somehow fooled his father. "That's my boy, Felix Vaughn Clarkson," Luther told him, patting him firmly on the shoulder. "I'm delighted to see you share your skills."

Felix briefly met his father's gaze with a grim smile, and I noticed he'd tensed a bit.

"When do we start that?" I asked simply.

"I suggest we start tomorrow," Felix replied. "We'll have to wait until Aurora is fully grown before we can start any kind of riding or magic training. In the meantime, I will teach you anything that doesn't require your Phoenix herself – I'll introduce you to the skills you will achieve, different attributes of your Phoenix, how to care properly for her, the types of Phoenixes and magic, theories, rules…essentially all the works."

"Sounds like a plan," I said bluntly. An unenjoyable plan, but a plan nonetheless.

We finished our dinner, and soon after, we were served dessert. When my plate was empty and my stomach was more than satisfied, Felix glanced down at my plate.

"Are you finished eating?"

I nodded.

"I'll take you home, then. Come," he said. He stood and walked towards the archway, his back straight, his muscles and stance strained.

I stood and picked up my plate, turning to Luther. "Where should I put this?"

"Oh, don't worry about it, dear. The staff will take care of it," Luther said.

I nodded and set the plate back down. "It was a pleasure to meet you, sir. Thank you for the meal."

"My pleasure," he said with a grin. "Your company is most welcome here, so don't be afraid to stop by."

I returned his smile. "I'll see you soon. Have a good night."

"You too, dear."

Felix drove me home in the Ferrari, and the drive was long, silent, and extremely obstinate. The lights whirring by in a colourful blur were the only bit of respite I had in the tense automobile.

I couldn't stop thinking about my situation, how I'd waltzed right into this discomfort. He'd known all along that I'd be dependent on him for more than just housing my Phoenix – I could tell by the way he'd measured my reaction at dinner. There was no way this was out of the kindness of his heart. Nobody ties someone up in ropes that tight unless they know they don't have a knife.

"So, what exactly do I owe you for all of this?" I blurted as I stared out into the passing night.

I think my sudden words stunned him. "Hm?" was all I got in response.

"I'm assuming you want something in return for all the... favors," I explained with brusqueness.

We came to a stop at a red light, making the silence that followed even quieter than it would have been otherwise. "You think I want repayment?" he then asked with a bit of alarm.

I shrugged as I turned to look at him. "I'm familiar with the harsh reality that is the world. You usually don't get anything in life for free."

Even through the shadows, I could see something like hurt in his lavender eyes. "You don't owe me any money," he then returned simply.

"Right. But repayment doesn't have to be monetary."

The expression of offense seemed to twist into astonishment, spreading into the lines of his face as his brows creased and his eyes widened. He parted his lips slightly, but no words came out.

I gave him an expectant look. "So, what? You want me to fuck you for all of this or something?"

He let out a breath that sounded more like a cough, breaking eye contact immediately at the suggestion. The light turned green, and he began driving again, the question hanging tightly in the air.

"You don't owe me *anything*," he eventually managed to spit out.

I rolled my eyes and turned back to look out the window. "Right."

Another pause. "If I'm being honest, Miss Pierre, it almost sounds like you *want* to give me something in return."

"Of course not. If I could have provided for Aurora without you, I would have – but I didn't have a choice. And the only thing I hate more than not having a choice is being in debt." I shrugged again. "I'd prefer an agreed upon term of repayment, rather than a surprise guilt-trip down the road. Then I can get that over and done with, and never have to think about it again," I explained matter-of-factly.

He considered this. "So...if I told you I expected something in return for my kindness, that would make you feel better?"

"*Oui.*"

We were just entering the university parking lot, and as he pulled over to the curb, he turned to me. I met his gaze as he studied me, gauging my face and my reaction. He looked me up and down, scanning me in a way that made me feel as though I were naked.

And after a long while, he finally said, "All right. I want you to bake me something."

I blinked. "Huh?"

"It can be anything you like. Maybe your favourite childhood dessert," he went on. "A recipe passed on from your mother or something."

I still couldn't believe what I was hearing. "You...want me to bake – "

"It doesn't have to be right away. But when you get the chance, that will suffice nicely," he trudged his sentence through my stammering. "As for tomorrow, text me after your last class is finished. I'll pick you up as soon as I can. Oh, and one more thing. Do not reveal anything about who you are to anyone – not even your parents. I'll explain more about why not tomorrow."

I felt as though I'd been punked on television, but I managed to collect myself slowly as I unlocked the door. "Okay," I said as I got out.

And with nothing more than a brief, returning nod, Felix Vaughn Clarkson drove off.

- F -

I scanned the spines of the books on the bookshelf, thinking.

I had never considered any of these books in a manner other than absorption. I had only ever read them to learn. But now, I would need to teach from them. Somehow, that changed the way I perceived them.

"*I think you should start with Origins,*" Fuego suggested to me, his familiar voice flooding my brain as he spoke not aloud, but through our bond.

My eyes fell to the book he had suggested, and I sighed. "*I think I'll have to. She knows nothing,*" I replied to him telepathically, turning away from the bookshelf and sitting down on the sofa. "*It's going to be a long process.*"

Fuego was staring at me, his bright red eyes contemptuous. "*May I kindly remind you that you forfeited your right to complain when you signed yourself up for this?*" he reminded me. "*You could have just let her go on her merry way and figure it out on her own. Nobody told you to do this but yourself.*"

I glanced at her Phoenix. The little yellow bundle of fluff was currently fascinated with her own feathers, preening vivaciously.

"*I'm not so sure how successful she would have been without some guidance,*" I noted as I watched Aurora.

Fuego snorted in my head. "*And how does that become your problem?*"

I frowned at him. "*You think it was a bad idea to help her?*"

Fuego fluffed himself up, stretching his neck lazily. "*Oh, absolutely not. She seems like a sweet girl with the potential to be a great Keeper. In fact, I think it's great you're helping her where no one else can. The thing is, it's completely unlike you to be nice for no reason.*"

I glared at him. "*Wow. Thanks.*"

He gave me a defensive look. "*Am I wrong?*"

I huffed and rolled my eyes, folding my arms across my chest. I didn't respond.

"*Look, you and I go way back. We've been through a lot together,*" Fuego went on. "*All I'm saying is that I know you, and because I know you, I also know you don't usually do stuff like this. It's not that it's a bad thing. It's just that I don't understand why you're doing it.*"

My eyes fell back to Aurora. She'd finished preening and was waddling around, seemingly trying out those little legs of hers and how far she could push them. No matter how many times she stumbled, she didn't seem phased. She just picked right up and carried on.

Something told me that Miss Pierre was very much the same way. Not once in our interactions had I felt her surrender willingly. She bit like a rattlesnake and kept her chin higher than heaven. Her attitude had clearly been fostered – someone had taught her to stand her ground and hold her own. And though her attitude could be frustrating, something about it was also…admirable. My opinions of her were entirely conflicted, as were my reactions to her.

"*Do you even know why you're doing it?*" I heard Fuego ask, and the sound of his voice in my mind made me realize I hadn't acknowledged his previous statement. I'd gotten lost in my thoughts, buried in a swirling sea of divergence about everything that occurred.

One thing stood out to me in the whirlpool of events, so clear in my mind that I replayed it over and over on an endless loop. The look she'd had on her face when she finally agreed to keep Aurora with Fuego could only be described as one of indignance. An act of selflessness, born from compassion – and truly against her own internal wishes. There could be differing opinions on the matter, but some may argue that it was the moral thing to do. The right thing to do.

I cleared my throat, my eyes fixated on the little yellow Phoenix. *"I'm still trying to figure that out,"* I answered.

PART 11: THE REDEFINITION

CHAPTER 10

- S -

IT WAS ABOUT two in the afternoon the next day when I had
finished my last class.

I stared at my iPhone for a long time as I sat on my bed,
hesitating to text Felix. Eventually, I did.

Me

Hey, Felix. It's Seraphine. I'm done now.

I expected that he would keep me waiting before responding,
but to my surprise, I had a response within seconds.

Felix Clarkson

*All right, Miss Pierre. I will be in the main parking lot in fifteen
minutes. Wait for me outside.*

Me
Okay.

I grabbed my purse and keys before leaving my dorm. Then I stopped outside my door. I looked down at my jeans, then went back inside and changed into a skirt. I stared at myself in the mirror, then huffed and changed into a dress and heels. Then I left.

I made it to the parking lot, and I could see Felix's Aston Martin parked straight ahead in plain sight. I approached the passenger door and opened it, causing Felix to look up from his iPhone.

He didn't say anything as he watched me get in and buckle my seatbelt. I turned to look at him when I was done, and he simply pursed his lips, scanning me up and down with curious eyes.

I raised my eyebrows impatiently. "Is there a problem?"

His eyes found mine, and the lavender was dyed with a mystified glaze. "Why have you dressed up?"

I was shocked that he would notice such a thing. I glanced outside the front window, then back at him. "This was just the outfit I was wearing today," I lied.

He studied me. "Why are you lying?" he then questioned.

I turned away. I wanted him to start the car and get us to the cellar, but for some reason he kept talking.

"I know what it's like to say something you don't mean, Miss Pierre," he continued, his words slowing. "And to pretend to be something you are not."

I made very brief, awkward eye contact with him. His lavender eyes were shady.

"I am very familiar with the art of acting," he went on. "I have been acting for a very long time."

I blinked. What the hell was he talking about? He wasn't in any movies that I could think of.

I looked out my window. "I wasn't lying," I told him quickly, clearing my throat.

There was another brief pause. Then I heard him chuckle as he started the car.

"Tell that to your eyes, kindling," he said, and he pulled out of the parking lot and on to the road.

———

We arrived at Felix's villa shortly after. He parked the Aston Martin in the garage in line with his other four luxurious cars, and we exited it quietly, walking up to his front door and into his home in silence.

"Butler!" he called out as he entered, breaking the long noiselessness we had been in. His voice boomed off the walls, ceilings, and floors.

Francis came bounding into the foyer. "Yes, sir?"

He turned directly to me. "Fancy a snack?"

I blinked. "Oh, um, well, sure."

He turned back to Francis. "Prepare something for Miss Pierre to eat," he demanded.

"Yes, of course, sir. What would she like?"

He glanced at me, and I thought he would ask my opinion, but instead he just looked me up and down before turning back. "Bring her an assortment of the freshest fruits I have. Perhaps some pastries as well. Oh, and a cup of my finest tea."

Freshest fruits? *Finest* tea? Huh. Given that I'd been nothing but snarky with him, I thought I would've been given the rejects of the Felix Clarkson Snack Stash. I guess I was wrong.

"Understood. How would she like her tea?"

I opened my mouth to respond, but before I could, Felix

spoke. "Sweet. As sweet as can be," he said swiftly. "Go, now, and don't keep us waiting."

He nodded and ran off. I turned to look at Felix curiously.

"How did you know I like my tea sweet?" I asked him.

He made eye contact with me, and surprisingly, he seemed caught off guard. "I just assumed," he eventually said with a shrug.

I squinted at him. "Why wouldn't you just ask?"

We both studied each other. Eventually, he muttered something I couldn't make out as he turned to look away.

I frowned. "Sorry, I didn't quite catch that."

He shook his head. "Nothing. Talking to myself."

I stared at him for a moment before giving out a quiet huff. He was such a mystery.

It was not very long before the butler reappeared with a plate of fruit and a mug full of what looked like a lovely cup of tea. He handed it to me with a polite smile.

"Here you are, Miss Pierre," he said.

I took the plate and smiled back at him. "This is wonderful. Thank you very much."

He nodded at me and turned back to Felix. "Anything else, sir?"

"Go find the new maid and tell her I'd like to speak with her right away. Dismissed."

He nodded and began scurrying off. Moments later, the maid that had greeted us yesterday appeared from the archway where Francis had left.

She looked at Felix, her wide smile obviously exaggerated. "You asked for me, sir?"

Felix raised his chin at her. "I need all the mirrors to be cleaned by tonight. Properly."

The maid frowned at him, her smile vanishing. "But sir...I cleaned them all just yesterday."

Felix kissed his teeth. "Right. Well, there was a reason I included 'properly' in my instructions. Whatever you did to my mirrors yesterday can be classified as a lot of things, but 'properly cleaned' is not one of them."

"Oh," the maid replied to his comment, becoming profoundly discomfited. "I'm sorry, sir."

"While the apology is a nice sentiment, it doesn't really solve the problem at hand," Felix replied.

"Of course, sir. I will gladly redo the mirrors."

"Good. And I would like you to let me know when you are finished. I will be inspecting your work."

The entire fuss about mirrors seemed like a mountain out of a molehill to me. I glanced around the room and spotted one to my left. The surface seemed clean – maybe there was the odd speck of dust, but that was to be expected on any surface. What else could have possibly been wrong with them?

"Sheesh – all this over *that?*" I blurted, motioning to the mirror. "It looks fine to me."

Both Felix and the maid flinched, and then slowly turned to look at me. The maid looked surprised. Felix looked...cold.

I folded my arms across my chest and stared back at him. "Problem?"

He inhaled sharply. "Dismissed," he then said bluntly to the maid without ever taking his eyes off me.

The maid looked at him in confusion, her mouth opening and closing very quickly but not a word being spoken. He then turned to look at her, and she promptly scurried out of the room.

Time suddenly seemed to slow. Quiet enveloped the walls. Everything about the moment dragged itself on – especially Felix, whose head turned slower than a tortoise when he finally tore his gaze away from where the maid had been and met mine.

He didn't reply for several minutes. "Miss Pierre," he then said slowly, his voice eerily composed. "Have a look in that mirror for me."

I unfolded my arms, confused. "What?"

Felix nodded towards the mirror. "Go on."

Seeing no better option, I turned to face the mirror. Obviously, I saw my reflection.

"Is what you see in that mirror the same image you'd like others to see?" Felix asked me.

I studied the reflection before me closely. "I suppose, *oui.*"

"It is not a supposition. It is a yes, or it is a no."

"*Oui,*" I replied instantaneously.

"All right. Now answer this…"

He approached the spot beside where I stood, which I watched him do in the mirror. "Is it truly the quality of the *reflection* that is reflected in the mirror? Or is it, perhaps, the quality of the *mirror?*"

My brows quivered as I considered this. Through the mirror, which was relatively clean, I could see my reflection clearly. But if there were smudges or a crack in the mirror, it would indeed affect the quality of my image.

"The quality of the mirror," I answered him.

"Indeed, it is," Felix responded. "The cleaner the mirror, the better the reflection. And therefore, if we would like others to see the best image of ourselves, we must first provide them a clear image to perceive."

He walked up to the mirror, standing in front of it as he stared at himself. "This is why it is important that the mirrors remain the cleanest surfaces in any home. If your mirror is a monstrosity…"

His eyes flickered over to mine. "…then so are you."

I held his reflected gaze steadily for a long while.

"Now then," he said. "I must do something quickly before we head to the cellar. You can wait for me in the gardens."

I nodded slowly. Without another word, I went into the gardens as he disappeared elsewhere into the villa.

I found two outdoor chairs with cushions. I sat on one, eating the fruit and sipping the tea slowly as I looked around the gardens. Singing birds flitted about the waterfall at the pool, their cheeriness providing an appropriate soundtrack to the warmth of the sun overhead, and a stark contrast to the rigidity within the walls of the building I'd just left. The building was modern, yes, and sleek, sure – but it was strange. Empty. Uninviting. Much like its occupant.

Movement in a window attracted my attention, and I turned to see Felix by a cabinet in the kitchen. He had a bottle in one hand – was that whiskey? – and was pulling a small glass out of the cupboard. He slowly poured the whiskey into the glass until it was about half-full, held it up for a closer look, and then put it back down on the counter. After decidedly pushing it away, he took a long swig from the bottle he still held, shut his eyes as he swallowed, and took in a deep breath.

I frowned. He reopened his eyes and looked back down at the bottle. Then he shook his head quickly, and he and the whiskey disappeared from view.

Several minutes later, he appeared at the doorway. He spotted me sitting and approached me, reaching into his pocket and pulling out a cigarette.

"Mind if I have a quick smoke?" he said as he sat down in the other chair.

I gave out a humoured breath. "Do I have much of a say in the matter?"

He didn't even crack a smile. "Of course. It's my poison. Not yours."

I was surprised by his reaction, so much so that I forgot to answer the question. He raised his eyebrows expectantly at me, which triggered me to wave my hand dismissively and say, "Go for it."

He lit the cigarette with his finger. I watched him bring it to his mouth, inhale the toxins, lower his hand, and puff them out. Then I watched him do the same thing again, and again, and again. Each time he smoked, his movements seemed slower and more methodical.

"Are you a reader?" he asked me out of nowhere.

I blinked. "Um, yeah, I guess."

He nodded slowly without looking at me. "What are you reading?"

I thought. "Nothing really, at the moment. Except for textbooks."

He didn't reply to this. Perhaps I'd given him the wrong answer.

"What are you reading?" I asked when the silence seemed to need filling.

His response was delayed. "Similar material," he said, the smoke dancing as the words left his mouth. "That, and the stars. I am a firm believer in reading what has been written in the stars."

"The stars?"

He looked at me. "I do not believe in coincidences. And because of this, I do not believe it is a coincidence that soon after you moved here you became a Phoenix Keeper, and soon after that I discovered you were one. And I know that the fact that my cellar is the safest place for your Phoenix is not something that happened by chance. There is a reason I felt so strongly about helping you. There is a reason I read that I should help you in my stars multiple times. I am not sure what that reason is. But there is a reason, and I knew that if I did not abide by what the stars told me, I would likely regret it later on."

I stared at him. I didn't really know what to say.

"Why are you telling me this?" I finally blurted. It seemed like an appropriate question.

His eyes were still fixed on me, his lavender irises magnetizing. I could feel his gaze flitting over my face, like a hummingbird flies from flower to flower, searching for nectar. Something about his expression told me that the heaviness in the air I felt was mutual.

Finally, he tore his eyes away from mine, bringing his whirling stare to the garden around us. "I don't really know," he answered.

Again, I wasn't left with much to say, nor was I left with much of an answer to my question. The silence seemed to need filling, but I was grateful to see that the cigarette was just a small stub and he was taking his last whiff. There was a small ceramic bowl filled with sand on a nearby table, where he then put it out. He stared at it for a few seconds for reasons I didn't understand, then approached me.

"Let's go," he told me. The breeze carried the words with their mixed smell of nicotine and alcohol, even from a distance, towards me. I nodded, and we stood.

After the same rather long trek we had made yesterday, we arrived at the little wooden entrance again. Felix unlocked the door, and we headed inside.

The first thing I noticed when I made it to the bottom of the stairs was how much larger Aurora was. She had grown almost twice her size again. I placed the pastries and tea on the coffee table, then walked back over and picked her up. She was noticeably heavier, but still light enough for me to carry. She chirped at me quietly, and her eyes showed signs of recognition. I smiled and gave her a little kiss on the head, snuggling her close.

I turned to look at Felix, who was running his fingers through Fuego's feathers but whose eyes were watching me. I noticed the neutral expression I had seen yesterday washing over his face. It was interesting to me how his lavender eyes glowed so much more beautifully when he wasn't shadowing them in a glower.

"She's growing as expected," Felix said. "She also responded well to the crushed palms I fed her yesterday, and the water, too."

"Crushed palms?" I inquired.

"Yes." He left Fuego and walked over to the large bags in the corner, pulling a handful of palm leaves out of one of them. "Phoenixes love palm leaves. When they're young, it's best to mush them up into smaller pieces to make it easier for them to eat. And if you mix them with water, it becomes a sort of solution that they enjoy."

He picked up a bowl and a thick, wooden stick off the table and then handed them to me along with a few of the palms. "Here. You can crush them up, and then fill it with some water from the trough."

I nodded and put Aurora back down on the floor before cutting up the palm leaves and using the wooden stick to crush them in the bowl. I then brought it over to the trough and dipped it in slightly, filling it with water. I used the stick again to stir it into a mushy, green solution before bringing it back to Aurora.

I sat down beside her and, using my finger, I offered a little bit of the mushed palms to her. She eyed it curiously before taking an eager peck at it with her beak. She gave off a delighted chirp, and I giggled at how cute she was as I continued to feed her.

I looked up at Felix in a way that asked if I was doing what I was supposed to do. To my surprise, he gave me a nod back as he fed the rest of the palm leaves he had gathered to Fuego. He kept throwing glances at me as we both fed our Phoenixes. He didn't react much with every glance, so I guessed I was doing everything well enough that he could leave me to do it in peace.

Aurora finished the mushed palms and then waddled over into my lap and nestled against my stomach. My heart melted at how adorable she was. She made me so blissful that I forgot all about the hell I had to go through with Felix to keep her here. I didn't think something non-human could make me this happy. I had a feeling the amount of gratitude I carried in my heart for her would increase as our bond grew stronger and our lives went on. I was more than prepared for the joy it would bring me.

I bent down and gave her a huge hug, her feathers radiating heat against my chest, and I kissed her head again. "I love you," I murmured into her plumage.

She gave a little squeak in response. I took it as an "I love you, too."

"Ahem…shall we get started?"

I had almost completely forgotten Felix was there, and I looked up instantly, meeting his intrigued gaze as he watched Aurora and me.

I nodded and stood up.

"All right. Sit over there," he instructed, and he motioned over to the couch in the corner. I obeyed, cradling Aurora in my arms while she perched herself cozily in my lap and I settled myself on top of the sofa.

He walked over to the bookshelf and looked at it for a few minutes before pulling out a large, dusty one. He blew the dust off, flicked some stray flecks off the cover and then brought it over to the couch, setting it down on the coffee table. It seemed old, and its thick cover had an intricate, purple gothic design. He then pulled up a chair from the table and sat down across from me in one swift motion.

"I'm going to start with the very basics –the beginning," Felix said. He opened the book to the first page and shoved it towards me. I looked down at it, and realized it was a cover page that had *The Origin of Phoenixes and Phoenix Keepers* sprawled across it in bold.

"I want you to forget everything you've ever learned in your Greek Mythology class, or anything you've ever learned about Phoenixes, and I want you just to focus on everything I'm about to tell you. This right here – "

He tapped the page. " – this is the *truth*. These very books were written – *handwritten*, might I add – by Phoenix Keepers and have been passed down through generations more of them. Everything factual we know about our kind, we have learned from those like us in the past. You understand?"

I nodded, eating a date and taking a sip of my tea, which were both delicious.

"Good. If I repeat something I've already touched on with you, just take it as a reinforcement of your learning – repetition is how we memorize things, after all." He glanced up at me and frowned. "You have something to take notes in, correct?"

I paused mid-chew. "Uh…"

"Oh, for crying out loud." He huffed as he leant forward, opening one of the drawers on his side of the coffee table. He pulled out a couple pieces of paper and a pen, forcefully handing them over to me. "You'll need these."

I cleared my throat. "Thanks," I mumbled, gently moving Aurora over so I had my lap free.

"Now, then, let's begin." He turned the page again. "As you're most likely aware, most humans trace the origins of Phoenixes as a mythical creature to the Ancient Greeks. However, several other civilizations, such as the Ancient Egyptians, had also floated the idea about this bird of regeneration around. In lots of documentation, we see that descriptions of Phoenixes, however, don't align with what you and I know as our Phoenixes today. In Ancient Egypt, there were large birds they called Bennu that could have been mistaken for Phoenixes, for instance.

That being said, the first Phoenix Keeper was a Greek man named Herodotus who lived in Athens, around the 8th century B.C. It was said by those who knew him that he had a bit of a wild imagination, shall we say, and he claims that he had many recurring dreams of a Phoenix – as we know them today – prior to an egg being presented to him. He hatched the Phoenix, and he was certain that he had been blessed by the heavens because he was a dreamer. However, he was also nervous that if anyone found out about the bird, that they would take it from him. So he only ever wrote about it, proclaiming in his writings that the gods had sent him a magic bird, and that if others wanted one, they needed only to dream of it. These writings were only found after he passed away, and of course, not all those who read his writings believed it - but some did, becoming the next few budding Phoenix Keepers at the time. And thus began the cycle of belief, and the cycle of Phoenix Keepers, and the legacy we continue today.

As you can imagine, the writings and the exposure to more and more stories about Phoenixes led to the birth of many Phoenix Keepers. There used to be lots of us in centuries past, but through the generations, those numbers have fluctuated greatly. I believe the decrease of Phoenix Keepers is due to a decrease in the number of people fit to be Phoenix Keepers – ancient civilizations had an easier time believing in something like a Phoenix, and as the world changed, so did the human mind. We focused on other things, and we failed to listen to our own history, and along the way, the stories and the Phoenixes became myths to the masses. When things like wars and turmoil overtake humanity, it's hard for anyone to find faith in anything, after all."

"I can see how that would make sense," I said. Aurora watched curiously as I feverishly jotted it all down.

"Yes. Now, like I said yesterday, it is in your best interest to keep the fact that you're a Phoenix Keeper a secret from mortals, all right?"

"That makes sense as well, but you said that Phoenix Keepers like to pass on stories to their children so that they will become Phoenix Keepers," I said. "Wouldn't doing that sort of defy the keep-mortals-uninformed-about-Phoenixes rule?"

Felix ran a hand through his hair. "Well, if you look at it *that* way, then technically, yes. I think it's a little different when you speak about children, though. Children don't feel the same sense of threat that adults do. It's just common sense to assume that it'd be much easier to have mortals unaware of Phoenixes and their existence than to try and have them coexist," he replied, looking at Fuego. "I mean, say an unsuspecting individual walked down here right now and saw Fuego. How would they react?"

I considered this. "It depends on the person, I suppose. They'd probably be frightened, or surprised, or curious. And based on how people respond to those emotions, I'd say somewhere in there we'd most likely have them going public with a story of their encounter. Maybe we'd even have a picture or video going viral online."

"Exactly, yes. There's our problem. It goes viral, draws enough attention, and pretty soon we have authorities on our hands – the police, the law, animal rights activists, scientists, perhaps the government. And if they find out Phoenixes exist, and that by existing they give us power, I am dead sure that they wouldn't be okay with it. It would be unfamiliar to them; a threat."

"I see. So we're assuming the worst and keeping them a secret because of that."

"Better safe than sorry, in my view. But, that being said, Phoenix Keepers' children are not the police. And when Phoenix Keepers are telling stories or teaching their children about Phoenixes, they're not shoving a Phoenix in their face, so to speak. They're simply introducing the idea to the child. If the child believes it and follows it in the way required, then great – another Phoenix Keeper is born. If they don't, they'll likely forget about the stories, and go on with their lives as a mortal. It's much like parents who tell their children religious stories. A child can choose to believe religious stories or not, and to follow a religion or not, but at the end of the day, no harm was done based on whatever decision they chose. There are many children who are told religious stories quite frequently, but cannot fathom the existence of a God. Same thing with Phoenix stories and Phoenixes themselves."

"Right, that makes sense."

"Good. I already kind of explained to you how the whole Phoenix Keeper selection works, correct?"

I nodded. "Something about the strength of belief in a person?"

"Right, but there's a little more to it than that. Phoenixes look for a very specific character trait in a possible Keeper. Basically, the foundation of a legitimate bond must form for a Phoenix to trust itself to a potential Phoenix Keeper. A legitimate bond is dependent on the type and strength of that person's belief. The belief cannot be forced or thrust upon the person. In other words, the belief in Phoenixes has to develop *before* a person sees a Phoenix, either from stories, lessons from another Phoenix Keeper, wild imaginations, or what have you."

I paused in my writing and frowned. "But wouldn't seeing a Phoenix make someone believe it exists?"

"Yes, but it would be the *wrong* type of belief. It wouldn't be based on the mutual trust a Phoenix looks for in a Phoenix Keeper. Mutual trust comes from the ability to believe without it being forced, you see? Again, it's very similar to religion."

"Is it?"

"Mhm-hmm. Are you religious?"

"I was raised Christian."

"So was I. Now think about it this way – neither of us have seen Jesus, I can assure you, but we still believe He exists, correct?"

I nodded slowly, processing this in my mind.

"That's the kind of belief Phoenixes look for in a Phoenix Keeper. The kind that forms when you let your faith take you wherever it chooses. It's…childlike, but true."

I suddenly felt very flattered that Aurora had chosen me. "I see. Continue."

"Excellent. It also has something to do with the life cycle of the Phoenix."

Another page turn. There was a diagram shown of a

Phoenix egg hatching, a full-grown Phoenix standing with its Keeper, and then a double-headed arrow connecting the two. I copied it very roughly in my notes and scrambled to keep up with the speed of Felix's words as he began talking again.

"Here's the thing – Phoenixes don't technically ever die. When a Phoenix 'dies,' their bond with their Keeper is broken, and the Phoenix bursts into ash. The ash evaporates and vanishes from sight, but it still exists in our world as a lifeform in an invisible state. As soon as the next possible Phoenix Keeper is detected by that Phoenix's ashes, the ashes re-enter a visible state and reformulate themselves using magic into an egg, which is then presented to the next Phoenix Keeper and hatched through a physical awakening."

"Oh, I see. So what happens when a Phoenix Keeper dies?"

"Again, the bond between the Phoenix and the Phoenix Keeper will be severed, and the Phoenix lives on as an orphan. They can still perform magic, but they cannot bond to another Phoenix Keeper."

"All right. So if Phoenixes are reborn to the next Phoenix Keeper, does that mean that Fuego was reborn to you from your father's Phoenix?"

"No. Phoenixes always keep the same name and same type, no matter who they are reborn to. That pendant that they hand you when they are born – they keep that through each of their lives and pass it on to each new Phoenix Keeper. It never changes, and therefore neither does their name. Besides that, Oheň was alive when Fuego hatched to me."

"Oh, I see." I frowned slightly. "If you don't mind my asking, how did your father's Phoenix die?"

Felix didn't respond right away. He held my gaze, cleared his throat, then shook his head and looked away.

"It's my father's story to tell," he eventually replied.

I detected I'd hit some kind of sore spot, so I decided to

just change the topic. "Fair enough. So how do the Phoenixes identify new Phoenix Keepers?"

"That's done through sensing. Sensing is huge in the Phoenix world. Nearly everything depends on their incredible and extremely adaptable senses – especially what we call their *sixth sense,* which is the power of their minds. This is what makes Phoenixes, and their Keepers, so powerful. As soon as you can harness the power of your Phoenix's mind through bonding, you can harness your own sixth sense, and you can use them together to do incredible things. A Phoenix uses their sixth sense to detect belief in their existence in a human, which they then determine to be their next Phoenix Keeper."

I summarized that in my own writing. "Got it. Go on."

Felix nodded, turning to the next page. Now there were multiple illustrations of Phoenixes, ranging in every colour thinkable from yellow and red to blue and green and even all the way to purple and raven-black.

"There are five types of Phoenixes. You've already been introduced to two – Fuego is a Fire Phoenix, and Aurora is a Light Phoenix. There are also Water Phoenixes, Earth Phoenixes and Dark Phoenixes. As you can probably tell, they are based on the elements of the Earth, and so is their magic. Another reason Phoenixes are so powerful – they harness the greatest forces on our planet to use to their advantage. Each type of Phoenix has its own unique ability that it shares with its Keeper. Light Phoenixes, like yours, can illuminate any dark space with no light source. Dark Phoenixes can become invisible. Water Phoenixes can breathe underwater. Fire Phoenixes, like mine, can withstand heat and fire of any temperature without getting a burn, and Earth Phoenixes have healing powers – they can heal wounds of all sorts. In addition to this, each Phoenix gives their Keeper the ability to produce magic related to their element – for example, I can create fire. The Phoenixes hatch with this magic, and can utilize their powers and special gift immediately. But a Keeper can only begin using them once their Phoenix is fully grown."

I jotted this all down. It was incredulous to me, the magic they harnessed and shared with us. I reached out to pull the book closer, but Felix blocked my hand with his.

I frowned at him, to which he explained, "It's old and irreplaceable, and your fingers are sticky from the fruit."

I squinted at him, annoyed.

He opened his mouth to say something else, but was interrupted by the sound of his phone ringing. Frowning, he pulled it out of his pocket, looked at the number for a second, and then put it to his ear.

"Hello? …Yes? I'm fine, Father, just a little busy now…no, I'm with Miss Pierre. Yes…mhm…I'm teaching her right now…mhm-hmm…no. Mhm-hmm…yes, yes, I know…whatever, Father. Why are you calling? …What's that? He's back? How unfortunate…no, I don't think so. Hm? There's absolutely no requirement for their introduction, Father…You're not going to let this go, are you? Mhm…well, then, fine. Let's get this over with. All right, we'll be there soon. Mhm-hmm. Okay. Goodbye."

He pulled the phone away from his ear and looked at me sternly. "My brother has returned from his business trip, and my father is insisting you meet him and join us again for supper at his mansion."

"All right."

"Very well, then. Let's go. We'll pick up where we left off later. Oh, and one more thing – Julius knows nothing about Phoenixes, so don't mention any of that around him."

I widened my eyes. "What? Really? How?"

Felix shook his head. "After trying to make him believe in them and failing, my father thought it would be much simpler to just stop trying. Therefore, he's completely uninformed on the topic other than the little stories my father would have told him when he was a child. He has no idea that I am a Phoenix

Keeper, or that my father once was one. We always kept our Phoenixes in this very cellar, as it's been here even before my villa was built, and we kept everything about Phoenixes a secret growing up. My father and I used to train unbeknownst to him or the staff late at night until I could do everything on my own. He's been told that you and I are just physics partners – which, I suppose, isn't really a lie, so it should suffice."

I nodded without further question, amazed that such a secret could be held from a family member, and we then both promptly left the cellar with Felix leading the way.

CHAPTER 11

As FELIX and I entered Luther's mansion, the two butlers from the previous day ran over to greet us.

"Ah, Felix, sir, welcome!" Benjamin said, promptly taking his jacket. "Your father and brother are in the sitting room."

"Wonderful," Felix muttered unenthusiastically.

George approached me with his hand held out. "Welcome back, Miss Seraphine Pierre. We are delighted to be in your company once again."

I gave him my hand with a polite smile, and he gently kissed the top of it. "Thank you very much, George."

He smiled back and nodded at me before turning to Felix. "Shall I escort you and your lovely guest?"

To my surprise, Felix made a face at him. "I grew up in this home," he replied bluntly. "I would really hope that I needn't any escorting."

I rolled my eyes. "Sheesh, dude. He's just trying to be nice."

The glare that was immediately shot in my direction was perhaps the most animated I'd ever seen those lavender eyes. "You're rather talkative today," he noted with bitterness.

I ignored him and turned to George. "I'll take you up on that escorting offer."

George bowed quickly. "As you wish. Follow me." As I trailed after him, I could hear Felix let out a huff of breath behind me.

The first room George led us through was new to me – I hadn't seen much of Luther's mansion on my previous visit. It was meticulously detailed, and the furnishings were adorned with patterns and colours of vintage splendour. The space, which boasted a grand piano, also had a fireplace, and above it hung a large, framed painting. It depicted a striking young man who seemed deeply infatuated with a painting of himself.

I studied it as we walked past. "Dorian Gray?" I questioned.

To my surprise, Felix stopped walking. Naturally, I did, too. He looked at the painting, and then he looked at me. He had creases in his forehead and a magnifying glass in his eyes.

"You know your narcissists," he said slowly.

I shrugged, holding his gaze. "I told you I read."

"About narcissists?"

I ran my eyes over his features. "They seem to be a pretty common occurrence," I noted simply.

His eyes narrowed. "Hm. And have you learned anything from reading about narcissists?"

I didn't reply right away. "*Oui*," I then said. "I've learned that narcissists are insufferable to those around them." I paused. "But they are ten times more insufferable to themselves."

His eyes widened ever so slightly.

"And I have also learned," I added, "that narcissism is not a synonym for pride, but rather a symptom of self-loathing."

I could feel his gaze as it flickered over my face, my skin, my demeanour. He seemed to absorb something from me.

It was a while before he murmured, "Insightful."

Then he turned quickly, as if he needed to hurry. My brows shook a bit as I followed him and George.

We quickly came to the polished and extravagant sitting room. Luther was sitting with another man on a beautiful, red velvet sofa. The two stood up when they saw us.

"Ah, there they are!" Luther exclaimed. "Seraphine, dear, welcome back!"

"Thank you," I said as I approached him.

Luther motioned to the other young man, whose beaming smile was incredibly charming. "This is my oldest son, Julius. He's been away on business for a few weeks and just returned this morning. Julius, this is Miss Seraphine Pierre. She's partners with Felix this semester, so you'll be seeing a lot of her around here."

Julius held out his hand to me, and I shook it, feeling the materialization of his charm through his handshake. I had seen pictures of him in tabloids and such, but they didn't really do his handsomeness justice. His hair and short beard were a little darker than Felix's and styled well. His eyes were a bright and inviting brown, and his jaw shape and facial structure, though strong, was much less harsh than Felix's. Peeking through the top of his shirt, I could make out a tattoo of what appeared to be a lion plastered on his left pec, and it seemed more body art awaited underneath his shirt sleeve as it lifted slightly with the movement of his arm. He wore a small, gold chain around his neck, a cross earring on one ear, and a feather earring on the other. His skin was warmer than Felix's was; in fact, other than the shape of their nose, which was strikingly like Luther's, the two didn't look or seem alike at all. Julius was slightly shorter and a little stockier than Felix, and he stood with much more receptiveness to people than Felix did. It was obvious while watching the two of them together that Julius oozed charisma while Felix remained frigid and iced. It made me question, then, how on Earth they were even related.

I gave Julius a small smile. "It's a pleasure to meet you, Julius," I said.

"*Mucho gusto!* The pleasure's all mine, Seraphine," he replied, and to my surprise, he leant forward and kissed me on the cheek. The English accent I'd come to expect from the Clarksons was not present, but a Latin American one was, and it danced around his Spanish.

"Oh," I said reflexively as I laughed a bit.

"Not used to being doted on?" Julius inquired with a wink. "That's quite surprising."

Felix made a face and muttered something inaudible under his breath.

Luther rolled his eyes at this and nodded at the three of us. "Supper is ready if you all are."

"Ready as we'll ever be," I responded, and with that, we all headed towards the dining room.

I sat down across from Julius, with Luther sitting at the head of the table and Felix taking a hesitant seat beside me. We were served a delicious carbonara shortly after alongside some asparagus with melted cheese and buttered bread by the butlers. Benjamin poured us each a glass of red wine before disappearing back through a door with George.

There were a few moments of silence before Julius broke it.

"So, Seraphine, tell me a little more about yourself. I know that you're Felix's class partner, but tell me the things I don't know," he said nonchalantly.

"Well, there isn't much to know."

"Nonsense – you've certainly got the looks of a good life story," he said with a grin. I returned the smile. "Start with where you're from. I can tell you're not from here."

"You're right. I came here for school, and I'm originally from Montreal."

"And I understand you're a science student?"

"*Oui,* I'm majoring in marine biology."

"Marine biology, hm? And why marine biology, exactly?"

"Well, I've been obsessed with the ocean for as long as I could remember. Orcas are my favourite animals, so I'm especially interested in orcas and their vocalization. I'm hoping I can do some research work once I get my degree."

"Ah, now that's cute," he said with a wink. "And I suppose you'll find more orcas here than in Montreal, hm?"

I laughed. "You've got it."

"Do you like it better here or back home?"

I shrugged, smiling. "Not sure yet. It's certainly warmer here."

He chuckled. "Yes, that does make things a fair bit nicer."

"Agreed," I said. "So where were you on your business trip?"

"Oh, here and there, really. But mainly between New York and Los Angeles."

"I see. Are you working with Luther?"

"He is a little, actually," Luther answered for him, and I could tell he was so proud to be able to say this about his son. "Sometimes he helps out at my offices – he wants to take over as CEO when I step down one day, so he's preparing for that when he helps out, essentially. I think he'd do great in my shoes. But until then, Julius is actually interested in starting his own business."

"Really? What kind of business?" I turned back to Julius.

"I'm working on a restaurant project right now," Julius explained. "I've got three opening – one here, one in L.A., and one in the Big Apple."

"That's quite impressive," I said. "Especially for someone so young."

Julius grinned. "Well, I had a great mentor, so really, there were no excuses," he replied, patting Luther on the shoulder.

Luther laughed. "A teacher can only really give you theory. You're responsible for putting it into practice."

"This is true," I said. "It's wrong to discredit your hard work."

"Oh, *please!*"

Felix's words rattled the air with the same disruptive energy that shook the dishware as he slammed his fist on the table. "He had it handed to him," he continued sharply through gritted teeth. "That's the only reason he'll succeed. It has nothing to do with his work ethic."

Everyone turned to look disapprovingly at Felix. His eyes darted between us all, before he huffed. "What? I haven't lied!"

"You had every opportunity to get into business yourself, Felix," Luther told him firmly. "Your decision to pursue other interests was one we supported as your family, just as we expect you to support Julius in his wish to try his hand at business."

Julius nodded. "I never denied that Papa had a lot to do with starting me off," he added. "But I haven't just sat down and watched it happen, either."

"Not at all," Luther confirmed. "Your brother is a very hard worker, Felix. Just like you."

Felix made a face. He stuffed his mouth with another bite of food as he mumbled something under his breath, and drowned the grumbling with more red wine as he turned away. It occurred to me that he resembled a toddler who had physically grown up, but had mentally stayed put.

I looked at Julius. "What are the restaurants called?"

"*Clarkson's,*" Julius answered with a grin.

I laughed again. "That's fitting!"

"I thought so, too," Julius said. Luther laughed along with him.

"Well, I'd love to try it out when it opens," I told him earnestly.

"I can most definitely have that arranged," Julius said. "We could use some taste testers for sure."

"My favourite kind of volunteer work!" I exclaimed.

Luther and Julius laughed heartily. "There are certainly

perks to having a restaurant owner in the family, that's for sure," Luther said.

"You two could do some physics homework over a five-star meal, really," Julius suggested.

I nodded enthusiastically, throwing a glance in Felix's direction. He had finished his food and was watching me with a stare so cold that I thought his blood had turned blue. His arms were crossed against his chest, his back slumped against his chair. His lavender eyes flickered down to my plate.

"Are you done?" he asked briskly.

I didn't know whether he was referring to the conversation or my food, but I squinted at him nonetheless. "Am I not allowed to have a good time?"

"We have work to do," was his snappy reply.

I huffed, rolling my eyes. "Party pooper," I muttered. "Fine. Let's go." I shrugged at Julius. "Have to prepare for our next lab," I explained as I stood.

"Sounds like fun," he said sarcastically.

"Oh, plenty of fun," I said with a laugh. "It was nice to meet you, Julius."

He grinned at me. "Likewise. I'm glad you'll be around. Always nice to have beautiful company," he said before tipping his glass towards me in acknowledgement.

I gave him a humoured smile, bid farewell to an equally amused Luther, and then turned to follow Felix back to his place.

CHAPTER 12

WHEN WE GOT to the cellar, we sat as we had before dinner, and Felix turned a few pages forward in the book he had left open. I grabbed the pen and a blank page, preparing my already sore wrist to launch back into note-taking action.

"I'm going to explain to you the basis of how everything you'll ever do with your Phoenix works now," he said. "This is possibly the most important part of being a Phoenix Keeper, so pay attention."

"Got it," I said.

"All right. As I mentioned before, the way we are connected to our Phoenixes differs from anything a mortal human can do, and that is through bonding. As soon as your Phoenix selected you, an invisible, mental bond between both of your brains was formed. This bond strengthens continually for the duration of both of your lives – well, the duration of your life and the duration of this particular life of your Phoenix. The interesting thing about this bond is that the Phoenix's side of it is always slightly stronger than your side, which means that Phoenixes can only bond to their Keeper, but a Phoenix Keeper could bond to a Phoenix as well as another Phoenix Keeper."

"Right, I remember you mentioning that Phoenix Keepers can bond to each other. So how does that work?"

Felix paused, and his nose kind of crinkled a bit. Then he said, "We can circle back to that later. It's not important."

I blinked. "But, I want to – "

"We'll discuss it some other time," he hurriedly reiterated, shaking his head. "I want to cover the more crucial stuff first."

The fact that he was being so suspicious about it made me want to know how it all worked even more. But seeing as he wasn't budging, I simply nodded for him to continue.

He ran a hand through his hair, lifting it and then letting it fall back in front of his face. "You can really summarize the bonding into three levels – minimal bond, partial bond, and fully bonded. Right now, you and Aurora are minimally bonded. I am fully bonded with Fuego. The bond strengthens over time. As the bonds increase and the Phoenix grows, it develops abilities beyond the magic it is born with, such as flight and telepathic communication, which you can then learn from and use through your bond. As well, there's another key component. Remember that pendant you received from Aurora?"

I reached underneath the collar of my shirt and pulled out the pendant, which I had not taken off since it had been given to me. "*Oui.*"

"That pendant acts as an activator for the magic. Without wearing the pendant, the magic can't go through, and it essentially renders you powerless. That's why I told you to never take it off – if you lose it, you lose your power."

I nodded.

"As soon as Aurora is fully grown, the things you'll be able to do are simple, minute tasks – create light, as that's the type of magic she contains, and utilize her ability to illuminate any dark space. Once you've partially bonded, you can begin to learn how to fly her. She will also be able to detect other Phoenixes, and you'll gain the ability to detect other Phoenix

Keepers, so long as they have a sensible amount of the Phoenix Keeper in them."

"So...what defines a sensible amount?"

"Well, when I first sensed you, it was after your belief had started to form – or, in other words, your *bond* had started to form, and that was the moment Aurora's egg was laid."

"Right. Okay." I paused. "But Felix, I thought you said you hadn't encountered another Phoenix Keeper in a long time."

Felix blinked. "Well, yes, I haven't."

"But you just said you can detect any other Phoenix Keepers. Shouldn't you have been able to detect someone before me a long time ago if there are other Phoenix Keepers in the world?"

Felix snickered – I was a little offended by this, actually, but I tried not to care too much about it.

"Miss Pierre, the magic we use from our Phoenixes is strong, but not strong enough to sense other Phoenix Keepers across the globe. Hell, we can't even sense them across the country, or even across town. If you're in the surrounding area, then you can sense any Phoenix Keeper in that surrounding area. But you must be in another Phoenix Keeper's near vicinity to sense them. That goes for your magic, too. You can't be in, say, Africa, and have your Phoenix in North America, and still expect the magic to work. No, the further away you are from your Phoenix, the weaker your magic will be, and after a certain distance, it won't work at all. Being a Phoenix Keeper doesn't make us invincible – it just makes us much more powerful than the average human being, Miss Pierre."

"Oh," I said sheepishly. "Okay, then. That's going to get annoying."

"*What's* going to get annoying?"

"Well, if I'll be able to detect the Phoenix Keeper in you once I'm fully bonded to Aurora, won't my senses be constantly reminding me that you're a Phoenix Keeper?"

He shook his head. "No, Miss Pierre. Your senses will become accustomed to a Phoenix Keeper it recognizes. Think of it like somebody's name – as soon as you learn somebody's name, you don't really forget it, and you recognize them by their name, right? It's the same with the presence of each Phoenix Keeper – we each have an individual presence of our powers inside of us."

"Oh. So…what if I want to find a Phoenix Keeper that my senses have grown accustomed to? Is there a way to tune them back in, for lack of better words?"

"Yes, there is. Simply focusing on the presence of the Phoenix Keeper you're looking for – if they're in a near enough area, of course – will bring your senses' attention back to them if you've tuned them out, and it'll grow stronger as you grow closer to them. Here, look – "

He held up his right palm. There was a brief pause before suddenly, it began to glow red in the center. The glow kept pulsing rapidly, and Felix stood, walking away from me slowly. As he moved further and further away, the frequency of the pulsation slowed.

"Oh, I get it now," I said.

He sat back down on the sofa. "Once you've fully bonded with Aurora, you can telepathically communicate with her. As you probably have already realized, the Phoenixes understand us when we speak aloud, but you can't actually have a conversation with them unless it is telepathic, the reason for that being that they can't respond aloud in coherent words."

Oh, good. So I wasn't completely crazy in thinking that the two Phoenixes understood me when I spoke to them, and that they were responding in their own bird-like ways. One more thing to knock off the "could-possibly-make-me-insane" list.

"As soon as you can telepathically communicate with her, you gain the necessary skills to telepathically communicate with other Phoenix Keepers, too. So, basically, after you've fully bonded with Aurora, you would be able to communicate with her as well as me."

"I see. Understood."

He closed the book and shoved it to the side of the table before looking up at me. "Well, I think that's enough for today, don't you?"

"Yeah," I agreed, standing up as well. "It's getting kind of late."

"Mhm-hmm," he said. "I'll take you home, now. Let's go."

———

He drove me back to the university in his Porsche this time. He pulled up to the curve with finesse and parked the car, turning to look at me as I reached down for my purse, which I had tossed at my feet.

"Miss Pierre?" he said.

I looked up at him. "*Oui?*"

He met my gaze and furrowed his brows ever so slightly. "You never answered my question," he told me.

I frowned in response. "What question?"

"About who was responsible – for the way you act."

I straightened. "Why do you care?"

He measured my face. "A good sailor carries a compass and checks the wind before he sets sail."

I narrowed my gaze. "Are you suggesting I'm an ocean?"

"I've concurred you're a force to be reckoned with. Whether or not you consider the ocean a metaphor for such is up to you."

"Do you consider it one?"

"Most certainly."

I broke eye contact with him, my tongue swirling around my cheek. "Nobody made me who I am but myself," I answered firmly.

"That's a lie."

I shot him a glare, but he returned it with vigor. "Someone made me the way I am, too," he went on. "I can recognize a creation in others from a mile away."

"Are you saying that you're also a force to be reckoned with?"

He seemed caught off guard. "I'm more a candle in the wind, if I'm being truthful," he replied. "Much unlike yourself. You reacted differently to the ones who crafted you."

"You don't know who I am," I retorted with bitterness. "And I don't like your assertion that you do. Your story is not mine."

We stared at each other. Eventually, he cleared his throat.

"It must be nice," he then mumbled with indignation. "To be liked by you."

My brows shook a bit, but I didn't let my gaze falter. My lack of reaction was my response.

He sucked in his lips after the silence became overbearing. "I, erm…"

He trailed off and turned away.

I raised my eyebrows at him. "You…?"

He kissed his teeth, then shook his head. "Never mind. It's not important."

I shifted my gaze between him and the front windshield. "Felix, just tell me."

"No. I already told you. It's not important."

"Well, clearly, it's important to you."

"Yes, but it's not important to *you*," Felix snapped with a sourness I could taste.

I frowned at him. "How would you know?"

"I just do," he said. "You wouldn't understand."

I stared at him. "Felix, just – "

"Have a good night, Miss Pierre," he interrupted sternly.

I raised an eyebrow, surprised he would have the nerve. "Whatever. I'll text you tomorrow when I'm ready," I replied flatly, to which he nodded, and I then promptly exited the car.

I headed for the entrance to the university and stepped inside, shutting the door behind me. It was at this moment, however, that I realized I hadn't heard the rumble of the car's engine. Slightly curious, I threw a hesitant glance out the window beside the door.

The Porsche was still there and hadn't moved an inch. In fact, it wasn't even on. Felix had folded his arms over top of the steering wheel and had laid his head down on top of it, his face buried in them. I cocked my head to the side, curious as to what invitation he was waiting for to start making his way home.

He remained like this for a few minutes before lifting his head up. I couldn't really see the details of his face, but I knew there was an expression of some sort embedded in his features and that it was not his usual scowl. He turned the key in the ignition, and the car lit up. Then he looked at himself in the rear-view mirror.

I thought about the rear-view mirror, how it didn't compare to the splendour of the mirrors in his home. I considered, again, how many mirrors he had in his home and how strange it was. Then I thought about the room with no mirrors, the room with the painting of Echo and Narcissus – the room with the man who'd been cursed to stare at his reflection until he starved to death, and the mountain nymph who had been cursed to only repeat the last word she heard.

I watched Felix look away from the mirror hastily, as if his reflection were becoming harder and harder to look at. It looked as Dorian Gray must have felt – the boy who had cursed his painting to retain immortal youth, only to watch it grow uglier and uglier with each sin he committed until it drove him mad. Eventually, Felix took his sleeve and wiped his nose and eyes. Then, he hurriedly revved out of the parking lot.

As the sound of the engine faded in the distance, I could almost hear it morph into Echo's voice, into the distorted last word of Narcissus – vain.

- F -

The sight of Julius upon entering my home immediately drained whatever energy I had left.

"There you are," Julius chimed as I walked in, giving me that stupid, childish grin of his. "Where's the pretty little thing?"

I was unsurprised that she had quickly become a family affair, but I had no intention of entertaining it. "Why are you in my house?" I grumbled.

"Well, I wanted to borrow a tie, and was also hoping to see some more of that stunning physics partner you've got," he replied. "*Ay, mi Dios,* had I known the girls were that hot in physics, I would have – "

"You have plenty of ties," I cut him off, pushing past him as I kicked off my shoes and made for the staircase. Like a gnat I just couldn't swat away, Julius followed.

"Yes, *hermano,* but I wanted to borrow that one you wore at that gala we were at a few weeks ago."

I frowned at him as we reached the top of the stairs. "The Hermes one?"

"Yeah, with the small horses on it."

"It's still for sale. Go buy one," I told him, heading for my room.

"Well, I only want to wear it once. And I figured if you already have it, why would I buy it?"

"Since when have you made a rational decision instead of

143

one driven by your penis?" I muttered at him, opening the door to my room and slipping my jacket off.

I heard the nuisance chuckle. "Ah, that's where you're wrong, my dear brother. Nina mentioned she thought the tie would look nice on me. I wanted to prove her right and see where that might get me."

I rolled my eyes. I should have known his latest fling had something to do with his incessant pestering.

"Whatever," I said, marching into my closet and yanking the tie from one of my dresser drawers. "Here. Now piss off."

"How very gracious of you," Julius noted sarcastically, taking the tie from me. "Why are you in such a bad mood, anyways?"

"According to you, I'm always in a bad mood," I retorted.

"Well, yes, to a certain degree. But you seem a little extra peeved right now."

"You have yourself to thank for that. Go home."

"Your charm is just infectiously delightful, *hermano.*"

"I need to go to bed. I have class in the morning."

Julius sighed loudly, but finally began meandering towards my bedroom door. "Try not to scare the lovely young woman away with all that suave charisma," he teased before he disappeared.

I let out a breath, walking over to the door and shutting it behind him. My hand rested on the handle for a moment, my forehead gently coming to rest on my door. My eyes shut as his words echoed in my ears.

"It's a little too late," I found myself murmuring into the wooden door, my irritation with him only strengthening my frustration with myself.

CHAPTER 13

- S -

I BEGAN GOING over to Felix's estate daily. Every time I saw Aurora, she had grown more than the previous visit. She was slightly smaller than Fuego, and I was no longer able to lift her off the ground. The feathers on her body were colouring themselves the yellow shades of marigolds and sunflowers, while the ones on the crown of her head mimicked the petals of petunias and buttercups, making her entire body seem like one light-filled gradient. Her citrine eyes were always bright and glowing when she saw me, which always put a smile on my face.

Aurora's presence was a welcome distraction to the endurance of Felix's lecturing. He had spent the three visits following my first lesson teaching me more about Phoenix history, what to do and what not to do around them, and certain rules to follow. Somehow, with each passing day, he seemed to grow more frigid and irritable. It was as if he were sleeping in a freezer and thawing less and less between visits, leaving me to deal with the icy aftermath. Perhaps the problem was that being around him felt like I'd been put on a burning stove; I often found it hard to stop myself from being snarky with him, something he was quite obviously not accustomed to dealing with himself. I would say we mixed as well as oil and water.

On my fourth day of lessons, Felix said it would be only a day or two more before we could start magic training. As prophesized, I woke up Saturday morning with an undefinable feeling in me. It had me paralyzed for a few moments as I tried to decipher what it was. The strength of it was overcoming, and it had filled me practically overnight, surging through me, running through my veins as if they were the path of some unending marathon.

As I laid in my bed with a puzzled frown on my face, my phone rang. I answered it.

"Glad you're awake, Miss Pierre," Felix's voice came over the phone. "How do you feel?"

"Weird," I replied. "I've got this…strong feeling inside me. I don't know how to describe it."

"Just as you should," he replied. "As of this morning, Aurora is fully grown. You're feeling the increase of the strength in your bond. We can start magic training."

"All right. When should we start?"

"As soon as possible," Felix replied quickly. "Preferably today."

"Well, it's Saturday, so no classes."

"Okay. I'll be there in half an hour. Meet me at my car in the front parking lot. It'll be the Lamborghini today."

The Aurora that greeted me was as big as Fuego, her sunshine-coloured feathers a fantastic, bright yellow that gave off rays of light and enhanced just how majestic she had become.

She approached me excitedly, flailing her long wings and flapping them with joy, nuzzling my head and neck with her own soft one and singing a beautiful songbird's melody that filled my heart with glee. She made eye contact with me as I softly stroked her head and brought it down to eye level, and I felt a deep connection as I looked back into her glowing, citrine gaze. The feeling inside of me, the one that symbolized the sudden and imminent strength of our bond, overwhelmed my body like an electric current. It flew through my veins from the tips of my fingers all the way down to the ends of my toes, but the part of me that was most empowered was my head. It exploded with an incredible sensation of willpower and strength, and I smiled at her, kissing her head.

"All right, then, let's start with the bare basics," Felix said, interrupting our moment like sunflowers being shaded by a dark cloud. He was standing beside Fuego, whose wings were lazily dragged at his sides, making him seem larger than he normally was, and whose fiery eyes seemed even more red than usual. It almost looked as if he were aware of the tension between the two of us. Well, to be honest, it was obvious there was some – didn't take a genius to know by now that we weren't exactly the best of friends.

"First off, I need you to get a grasp on your sixth sense, or the energy from the bond you have with your Phoenix, if you will," he instructed.

I blinked. It wasn't like I could reach into my throat and pull the powerful feeling out from the back of my head. "How am I supposed to do that?" I asked.

Felix sighed, letting his patience seep out with his breath. "What I want you to do is focus on it very hard. I want you to shut your eyes and feel how it courses through your bloodstream and up into your mind. And then I want you to think as hard as you can about the strength of the power, and the new sensation of it. Introducing your mind to the idea of it will open your ability to access it."

"So basically, you just want me to focus on the power's existence?"

"Essentially, yes. Making your brain aware of its presence

inside of you will allow the neurons to make connections to it and with it. That's how you'll access it. Give it a try," he said.

I hesitated for a minute. I mean, the idea seemed kind of ridiculous. But then again, here I was standing beside my very own Phoenix, so my own inner questionings soon faded.

I shut my eyes, as he had instructed, and began focusing my energy on sensing that power. I made a mental acknowledgement of it, feeling how it seeped into my bones, up into my spine, spreading through the synapses in my brain and sparking networks in my mind. It became apparent to me that the sensation of the power suddenly became controllable – I could choose whether I wanted to feel it at the front of my head or at the back, and I could even move the power down from my mind into my arms, down through my fingers...

I opened my eyes suddenly in amazement and gazed down at my right hand. It looked no different from the outside, but on the inside, it grew heavy with the power I had sent to it. I understood what Felix had meant now – I had made my mind so aware of the bond's strength that it had become governable inside me, and I was able to manipulate it.

"I have it," I breathed incredulously.

"Good. Where is it inside you?"

"I sent it to my right hand," I told him.

"Excellent."

He walked over to the center of the room, his back tall, straight, and tense. He then spun around on his heel and turned back to face me as he outstretched his hand.

"I'm going to teach you how to do this now," he announced. And then, within seconds of him speaking, a ball of fire burst into view in the palm of his hands.

I gasped as I watched how the fire danced in his hands, never scalding his palms, never causing a single burn. Instead, the reddish-orange glowing orb seemed to flicker powerfully without any sign of failure. It was beautiful magic – almost breathtaking in a sense, especially at the extraordinary fact that he had created it not from matches or a lighter, but from his hand and the power from his Phoenix resting within him.

"Your magic, of course, will be light, but the method to create it is the same," he continued, and he whipped his hand down after that, causing the fire to wane just as quickly as it had appeared. "I want you to try now."

"But...wait, how do I do that?" I stuttered, awestruck.

Felix seemed unamused by my clear lack of understanding. "I want you to focus your entire energy on creating the element," Felix commanded.

I stared at him. "Felix, you must understand that I have no idea what that means. You're going to have to be a little more explicit."

Felix huffed. I think I'd taken up all the tolerance he had.

"Sense the light in you, grab it within, and then express it."

"Express it?"

"Focus on pushing it out of your skin. Don't worry, it won't hurt – it just tingles a bit," he said matter-of-factly.

I took a deep breath, absorbing the information he had just given me. I looked down at my right hand as I outstretched it, located where the power was, and focused on it intently, feeling it bouncing off the walls of my hand and shooting through the bones in my fingers. I pictured the light beaming rays of glorious yellow from the middle of my palm. But try as I might, no matter how hard I focused, nothing was showing up.

"Nothing's happening!" I cried in frustration.

"It takes a few tries," Felix said, but the way he said it was in no way comforting. He grabbed one of the chairs that was by the table and effortlessly swung it over and around so that the back of the chair was opposite him. He then sat backwards on it, folding both hands over top of the back and resting his head atop them while nodding in my direction.

"Go on, now. Try again. Push hard on it, Miss Pierre," he instructed sharply.

I took another deep breath and obeyed, trying my hardest

to achieve the goal in mind. But still, after a long while, nothing was appearing.

I sighed, frustrated, and glared at my hand, willing it so hard to do what I wanted. Still nothing.

Fed up, I grabbed my right hand with my left hand and shook it. Sure, it was worth a try, but it didn't help at all. There was still no light in my palm.

"No, no, no," Felix said irritably, shaking his head as he stood up off the chair. "None of that, Miss Pierre. You're doing it all wrong. Here."

He walked behind me and stood right up against my back, tracing my right arm with his large hands and finally resting my comparably small one in his right palm. He forced it upwards in this jerky motion – one that hinted to me that this wasn't something he did regularly – and then bent my elbow.

"You're too tense," he noted. "Relax your arm."

Try as I might, the harshness of his hand outdid any attempt I made to release the tautness in my body. There was something about his touch that stressed me even more.

"Relax it," he repeated.

I wiggled my arm around a bit, trying to ignore his sensation. But it was as if his stiffness were contagious – my whole body felt as though it had turned to stone.

"I said relax, Miss Pierre!" he exclaimed frustratedly, almost tossing my arm out of his grasp. "What part of 'relax' don't you understand?"

I had no idea how quickly the anger and frustration had bottled in him. Frankly, I didn't understand why such a small thing made him so angry in the first place.

"Well, I can't relax when you're yelling like that!" I shot back.

He scoffed, rolling his eyes and turning on his heel. "You can be so dramatic sometimes," he grumbled.

I watched his back as he walked away from me, pacing. My irritation erupted within me. He hadn't even tried to be patient the entire time we'd been working together. Why should I maintain my composure?

"You really enjoy pissing people off, don't you?" I challenged him. "You get a rise out of being an ass or something, huh?"

He stopped. An eerie silence fell over the room, washing over us all like a silent, thundering rain. I could feel the Phoenixes looking at us with apprehension, a clear understanding of the atmosphere written in their eyes. Everything around us seemed to slow to a halt.

It was a long time before he turned to glare at me. "I beg you, Miss Pierre," he snarled through clenched teeth, "to go and find a hawk. Ask him if he truly enjoys swooping down to the earth below and snatching the humble field mouse from the blades of grass. Ask him if he enjoys being known as nothing but its murderer. Ask him if he enjoys being the last thing that mouse ever experiences before its lights are dimmed."

He began to approach me. "Go and find a lion, and ask him if he truly enjoys sinking his teeth into the heart of a gazelle. Ask him if he fancies the taste of blood on his tongue, the sound of death ringing in his ears. Ask the boa if he enjoys suffocating his prey beyond breath, and the rattlesnake if he enjoys the look in the terrified eyes of those he poisons. I beg of you, Miss Pierre, to ask them, and to come back to me, and to tell me what they say. Because I know it will be no different than what I tell you now."

He left a small gap between us, his lavender eyes alight with tenacity. "They will say they do not know anything different. That it is not a matter of likes or dislikes, of preference or of distaste. It is simply a matter of survival, and that is all they know of it."

He lifted his chin. "There is no desire or lack thereof in a means to an end. Don't attach feelings or emotions to instincts. It is innate for oneself to survive – unless, of course, you are prey. So you can call me names all you want, seeing as you've become quite accustomed to judging me and the things I do. But do not pretend you understand anything about me or my actions, because the fact of the matter is that you haven't got a clue."

I stared at him. I suppose that if Felix Clarkson were a book, he would be the most cryptic, incoherent book the world had ever seen, written in a non-existent language that only someone with incredible patience, enough time, and undrain-able energy could decipher – and even if they did decipher what they could, most of it would still be incomprehensible and open to many different interpretations. That made responding to him even more difficult than translating him.

The response that escaped me was innate. "And I'm the dramatic one?" I sniped at him.

The air around us became edgy very quickly. I could see the way his eyes had hardened, the way the lavender became stone-cold.

"Perhaps we should be finished for today," he then spoke with words of ice. He turned on his heel and began making for the staircase as the words fell like glass, shattering around me in a state of disrepair.

Forfeit – whatever else he'd planned for my lesson, he'd now chosen to forfeit it. The irritation bubbled within me. I was not ready to be done just yet.

I ignored his suggestion and whipped back around to look at my hand. I shut my eyes, trying my hardest to forget about Felix's peculiarity and everything else that was swirling around my brain. I could hear his footsteps growing further and further away, towards the staircase, and I had my determina-tion drown them out. To my astonishment, my mind obeyed me, and I was left with the sense of the light.

I focused on it like a child on their candy, mentally pushing as hard as I could near the palm of my hand and around the tips of my fingers. I could feel the internal light bursting with brightness and sudden flashes, begging for the willpower to be extracted. I fed it more and more and more, trying my hardest, willing the light to be expressed in my hand.

Suddenly, an unfamiliar sensation formed on the surface of my palm, a slight tingle that was not annoying, but rather strange.

My eyes popped open, and there I saw it – a beautiful, shining ball of light, gracefully building in my hand.

I gasped, taking in its beauty. The mix of white and yellow light faded hesitantly for a moment, but became stronger as I steadied my wavering powers. It was as big as Felix's ball of fire, but much brighter and breathtaking, and little sparks danced at its edges, like mini strikes of lightning. I blinked at it, surprised that this had come out of my body. I had – with the help of my Phoenix – *created* this light.

- F -

She glowed with her magic, blossoming like a flower made from the golden rays of an endless, undying star. She was not the one to start a fire, nor was she the one to play in it. She was the glorious, unrelenting light that could set fires through glass, that could spark an entire forest into everlasting flames with a single jolt of lightning. She was kindling, indeed, in her own magnificent and incomparable way.

I crawled out of the shadows of the room as I stared at her in awe, at the magic in her hand. The way she carried it was both intimidating and enthralling. Some may think it's embarrassing to admit how bewitching this woman could be, but I would challenge any man in the presence of her power to try and keep their heartbeat steady.

Miss Pierre was different. She drove me mad in the most addicting, inescapable way. As much as she was frustratingly curt, there was no denying that I rested within the mercy of her hands, just as her magic did.

But they say that things are always clearer in hindsight. I lived in a river of denial, and I would deny the power she had over me until it swept me away like nothing more than the pathetic debris that had washed up on a sandbank.

- S -

The ball of light flickered above my palm for about half a minute before suddenly fading away.

"It is very interesting," I heard Felix say bluntly, "that the moment I tell you something, all you wish is to do the opposite."

I turned and saw he had stopped at the bottom of the stair-well, studying me as he leant against the wall. His lips had curled into this cruel, wicked smirk; it was the same mischief I'd seen in his eyes when he'd ensnared me into these lessons at supper with his father the other night. If I hadn't known it then, there was no denying it now as I stood before him, defiant and vexed.

To him, this was a game. His game. And that made me ever the more determined to break the rules.

I ignored his taunt with a jerky twist of my chin, turning back to look at my palm. I focused on expressing the light again, channeling my infuriation into the power behind the magic. The ball of light erupted in my hands again, brightening the space with an ethereal glow.

"Perhaps a part of you enjoys being an ass, too, Miss Pierre," I heard Felix challenge from behind me.

The light pulsed beneath my hands with the heat of my

fury. Without really thinking, I hurled the ball of light towards him.

He ducked just in time for the light to splatter against the wall, shattering into magic shards of glowing dust that faded into the air. "Bloody hell," he murmured as he straightened, turning to meet my burning eyes.

"Do not *ever* even *think* about calling me that again," I snapped at him.

I was met with lavender eyes that carried a glower of the most guileful variety. The corners of his lips lifted slightly with his jaw as he approached me, looking like a fox with a hen between its teeth.

"I must have done something remarkably wonderful to earn this attitude of yours," he teased. "In a past life, or the present one."

"Shut up," I told him.

"You're the most charming young woman to everyone else, including my sleaze of a brother. But with me – "

He came to a stop about a foot from me, looking me up and down like I was a meal. " – there must be something about me, hm? Something that makes you want to treat me different-ly." His eyebrow rose. "You know, people often behave contrarily with those they admire."

I clenched my teeth, the next few seconds whirling by as I heaved another ball of light at him. He managed to block it with a ball of fire just in time, but stumbled backwards a bit with what I could only assume was an underestimation of the force I could muster.

"Don't flatter yourself," I snarled at him. "I'm here to learn my magic, not waste my time with your petty compensation for insecurity."

To this, he seemed to grow amused. By some miracle, though, he took a few more steps to my right. "All right. Fine. A few more things."

Felix began waving his hand deliberately in front of

himself. Slowly, an entire sheet of fire, almost like a shield, began to form in front of him, burning feverishly in the center of the room. He made it almost twice his size before whipping his hand down, and the fire disappeared with the motion.

"This one's harder, and it will take some time. It's mainly about spreading the magic around instead of focusing it in one place. Give it a go," he commanded.

I took a deep breath and then began waving my hand in front of me. Bits and pieces of a light shield began to form, but they were incredibly weak and faded within seconds.

Felix shook his head and began pacing slowly, almost impatiently. "Once more, Miss Pierre."

I did it again. Little improvement, not much. That seemed to be a common pattern with learning this magic.

"Again, Miss Pierre. Keep going until I say you're done," he stated.

I listened and repeated the magic until I had completely lost track of time and was not making any more improvements. When Felix finally nodded and said it had been enough, I brought my hand down with relief, and the light sheet that was still nowhere near as prominent to Felix's fire sheet faded with my motion.

"It's a start," Felix said. He turned to face me, the expression on his face neither satisfied nor displeased. "The last thing you can do with the power of your bond is your Phoenix's elemental ability – for you, the power to create light even in the darkest of places. Now, because our Phoenixes' elements differ, and my ability is to withstand heat, I can't really demonstrate yours for you...but I suppose I don't need to, anyways. It's simply a matter of grasping the entirety of the power created by your bond and expressing it all outwardly. Give it a try."

I did as he told me, and the room instantly became brighter than it was, illuminated by a soft, yellow glow.

"Not bad," Felix said. "Now, your magic will get stronger over time, but you need practice for that to happen. Lots and lots of practice. As soon as we can get that bond level to half-way, I can teach you how to fly."

I looked at Aurora, and then back at him. "I guess I'll be spending even more time here, then."

"I suppose you will be," he said, his expression unchanging, his lavender eyes dim.

CHAPTER 14

THE FOLLOWING DAY WAS SUNDAY. I practiced my magic for most of it with Felix. I could reliably form balls of light and was beginning to get a handle on sparks as well by the end of our session. It was satisfying to see a lightning strike originate from my hand. They weren't perfect, but they made me feel powerful – and whatever feeling of power I could retain helped me bear with Felix's presence.

By some cruel twist of fate, our usual Wednesday Physics lab had to be rescheduled to Monday due to some upcoming maintenance on the equipment, and I headed to it with heavy feet. I'd spent a lot more time with Felix than I would have liked since our previous lab, and none of those interactions had an overwhelmingly positive effect on our relationship. I was now out of my element in more ways than one, and this was a course I paid good money for and needed to pass in order to proceed, making me even more nerved than anything to do with being a Phoenix Keeper.

Felix was already in the laboratory when I arrived. He looked at me for a brief second as I was setting up my things.

"Hello," he said briskly.

"Hello," I said back. It was an enlightening conversation.

Thankfully, it wasn't long before Lucah entered the lab with a stack of papers. "Good day, everyone," he began. "Let me start this session by handing out your previous marked labs, and then I'll give instructions for your next one. If you have any questions or concerns about it, you may come see me during my office hours."

As Lucah began wandering around the class, I tried my best to look at anything but Felix. The minutes felt like some sort of slow, twisted prank as they passed, the tension seeping into me like poison.

Finally, Lucah approached us. "There you two are," he said, handing us each our own reports. "Felix, well done."

He turned to me, and added quietly with a trying smile, "Don't be discouraged, Seraphine. It's only the first lab – usually not a student's best."

My stomach turned. That was always good to hear.

I gave him a quick nod and a smile that wasn't really a smile, prompting him to move on to the next group. I then opened up my lab report. At the top, glaring at me in red ink, was a big 46%.

I stared at it blankly, not quite processing how I couldn't have even passed. I'd tried my hardest on it, redid calculations, made sure my written answers were clear and concise.

Disgruntled and upset, I peered over at Felix, who had his lab report in his hands. In the same red ink, a 100% was written and circled ostentatiously on his first page. When he glanced over at me, I lost it. I couldn't handle the emotions that billowed up like impenetrable clouds inside of me. I had no words for what I felt; there was nothing left to say.

All my bottled fury and vexation led to nothing but me grabbing my things in one swift motion and rushing hurriedly out of the lab in a fit of rage. It didn't even matter to me that these actions would result in me having nothing to turn in the following day for that lab experiment. That was the last of my concerns. I ran as fast as I could to my dorm, my atrocious lab report in hand, not once checking to see if Felix or Lucah or anyone in the lab had followed in my footsteps. Once inside, I locked the door, threw the lab report furiously at the wall, and collapsed in a heap of anger on to my bed. I channelled every ounce of resentment I had into the inhuman scream I unleashed into one of my pillows.

Was this productive? Probably not. Did it need to happen? Absolutely. I shouted for several minutes into my pillow, letting it all pour out of me like a volcano that had just erupted. When I felt I had exhausted my wrath, I picked myself up to see Emmanuella had appeared in the doorway.

"Who the hell pissed you off?" she asked with a blank look on her face. "And more importantly, are they still living?"

I sighed. "Yeah, he's alive. Unfortunately."

She blinked. "Damn. Who is this guy and what did he do?"

"You remember Felix? My lab partner? You met him the other day."

"Uh, yeah, about – " she reached high above her head " – yay tall and talks like he's straight out of an Emily Brontë novel?"

I snorted as I walked back over and grabbed my failed lab, handing it to her. She looked it over.

"So, you failed your lab because of Heathcliff?" she asked slowly.

"Don't do Heathcliff such an injustice, Em."

She cackled. "Is Felix really dumb or something?"

I shook my head. "No. He's really smart – he got a hundred percent. He just insists on doing all the work himself so he gets it done quickly, and I lose the opportunity to apply what I've learned in class." I huffed. "Not that I really understand much in the first place."

She thought for a moment. "Isn't Elijah majoring in physics?"

I looked at her. "Yeah. I think so."

She raised her eyebrows at me expectantly. I put two and two together, reaching for my phone.

Me

Hey Elijah! I have a bit of a predicament and I was wondering if you could help me.

His response was very quick.

Elijah King

Of course! What seems to be the problem?

Me

Well, I'm having a lot of trouble with PHYS 1A. My partner is really uncooperative, and I don't really understand the concepts too well. I failed my first lab report, and I was wondering if maybe we could go over it to see where I went wrong? I'll need to understand that if I want to make any progress, especially if I hope to do well on the midterm and final lab exams.

Elijah King

I'm sorry to hear all that, but it's good you haven't given up yet! I'd love to help you. I can come to your dorm in an hour or so?

Me

That works great for me. Thank you!

I looked up at Emmanuella. "He's coming over to help me in an hour."

She gave me a smirk. "Do you want me gone, then?"

I rolled my eyes. "He's helping me with my physics, Em. Nothing else."

"Sure, sure."

I shook my head with a laugh, putting the lab report and some supplies to work with on my desk in preparation. Emmanuella let me borrow her desk chair so that we'd both be able to sit at my desk.

An hour later, there was a knock on the door. I opened it to Elijah's smiling face.

"Hey. Heard you needed a physics hero," he said.

I sighed, letting him in. "*Oui*, I'm a damsel in very much distress."

"Let me see what I can do about that."

He sat with me at my desk, and I handed him the lab report. "I really need to pass this course," I told him. "I can't go on in marine biology without it."

"Well, then, let's make sure you pass. Just let me see where we're starting, here…"

He went through it for a few minutes before setting it on the table and grabbing a pen and a piece of paper. "Okay, I think it would be best if we go through these one by one together," he said. "You've got a good start here. I'm honest, you do."

"According to my teaching assistant, I've only got forty-six percent of a start," I said glumly.

"Well, the way I look at it, that's forty-six percent more than zero."

I considered this. "I suppose you're right," I said.

He gave me a smile and rubbed my shoulder softly. "Don't be so hard on yourself. We'll work on this until you feel comfortable with it, okay?"

I blushed, hiding my face a bit. "Okay."

"Let's start with the first calculation."

He began by reading out the question, then going over my answer. He pointed out what I had done right and where I had gone wrong. Then he showed me how he would approach the question, step-by-step, and we solved it together. We repeated this process for the entire lab report, which took us a good few hours. I was shocked at how patient and understanding he remained with me; considering he wasn't really gaining much from the experience, I felt extremely humbled that he would spend the hours helping me instead of working on his own studies or spending time doing something fun.

When we'd finished going through the lab report, I felt a lot better about the concepts. "Thank you so much for helping me," I told Elijah. "I appreciate this a lot."

"No problem! Glad I could help," he said.

There was a bit of a pause as we both smiled at each other. Elijah then glanced at the clock by my bed. It read five o'clock in the evening.

"Do you have any dinner plans?" Elijah then asked, looking back at me.

I tucked a strand of hair behind my ear. "Not currently, no."

He shrugged. "You want to grab a bite to eat somewhere off campus? Maybe do that tour of the city we talked about?"

I smiled. "I'd like that."

He thought for a second. "I know a good place not too far away – about fifteen minutes by bus."

"Sounds good to me. Let me just grab my purse."

With my purse over my shoulder, Elijah led the way out of my dorm. We hopped on a bus and arrived at the restaurant shortly after. It was a family-owned Greek restaurant, which excited me as I enjoyed all the Greek food I could get my hands on. A young waitress led us to a table for two in the corner of the small building. We thanked her and sat down, ordering ourselves a feast to share. It was a lovely evening; he made me laugh a lot, and it was nice not having to cook. He paid before we headed out on a walk through downtown San Diego. He showed me some of the city's landmarks and hotspots, all illuminated by the lights of the drawing night.

When we had made it back to campus, we both stopped outside my door. "Thank you for your help, and for suggesting we have dinner," I told him. "I had a good time."

"So did I," he said with a grin. "We should do it again soon. And if you need any more help with your physics, let me know."

I smiled. "Thank you, Elijah."

His eyes drifted down to my lips, and he kissed me softly. "Have a good night, Seraphine. Talk tomorrow," he then said, and disappeared down the hallway.

Blushing, I headed back in my dorm and shut the door. I could hear Emmanuella singing from her room, but she must have heard me come in, for she soon stopped and appeared through the entrance to the bathroom, her arms crossed across her chest expectantly.

"I see your afternoon consisted of more than just physics," she said with a smirk.

I cleared my throat. "I see you've got quite the voice," I noted. "You sing really well. Have you taken lessons?"

"Now, don't you try and change the subject. I need a full report."

I giggled. "He took me to dinner and for a walk around the city."

"Where'd you guys go?"

"This Greek restaurant about fifteen minutes away."

"Did he pay?"

"*Oui.*"

"Did you guys kiss?"

I bit my lip, grinning.

She rolled her eyes. "I'll take that as a yes," she then said, laughing. And we spent the rest of the evening studying together before we were off to bed – all in all, it was the perfect way to distract myself from how upset I had been. I had forgotten all about my frustration with Felix by the time I fell asleep.

- F -

I stared at the calculations on the page. My hand trembled as I gripped the pencil so tightly that my fingers were going white. It seemed I couldn't connect my limbs to my brain. I couldn't properly think the calculation through, either. Frustrated, I huffed as I scribbled out whatever I'd written, tearing the page out of the notebook and crumpling it. Then I threw it against the wall, expecting a bit of catharsis. There wasn't much of one.

"Felix," I heard Fuego say slowly in my mind. *"Why don't you just call her and –"*

"Stop talking," I snarled at him. "I'm trying to focus."

He snorted. *"Clearly doing a stellar job at that,"* he muttered.

I crumpled another sheet of paper and threw it at him. He jumped, grumbling a bit as the paper bounced off his scarlet feathers. Then he shimmied away from me, tucking himself in a corner to preen. I didn't hear another word from him as I carried on with my fruitless attempts at my calculus assignment.

I swallowed as I cupped my face in my hands, forcing myself to reread the question again. Movement distracted me before I could decipher it any further, and I lifted my eyes to see Aurora nudging one of the crumpled papers away with her beak. She met my gaze, her bright yellow eyes wide with inquisition.

She knew I couldn't get her Keeper out of my head, that

much I could tell. She knew I had something to do with her absence. Try as I might, I wouldn't be able to convey a convincing enough argument against that – most likely because she was not wrong on either account.

That look she had given me just before she'd stormed out – it was etched in my mind, replaying over and over. It made me feel sick, the amount of frustration I'd seen in the way she viewed me, the very frustration I had caused. She loathed me. She was in good company; I didn't particularly care for myself either. Perhaps that was the worst part – that she wasn't completely unfounded.

The sound of footsteps brought my attention to the stairway, where my father was just entering the cellar. He looked tired from the day, as he usually did if I saw him late at night. I questioned why he was even still awake.

"Hello, son," he greeted me, approaching Aurora. He rubbed her neck soothingly, and the Phoenix nuzzled his hand in response.

I looked back down at my calculus. "Hello," I grumbled. "What are you doing here?"

"I came to see how everything was going with Seraphine," he explained, glancing around. "Has she gone home for the evening?"

I didn't reply right away. "She didn't come tonight."

"Oh?" Father questioned. "Is she all right?"

I shifted, tapping my pencil against my book. "Don't know. Don't care."

"Don't care?" he questioned in surprise.

The tapping intensified. "It isn't my job to worry about her wellbeing."

"Well, sometimes, we as humans volunteer to care for one another."

"I'm not feeling charitable," I spat back.

I could feel my father's frown bearing down on me. "What's going on?"

I huffed, halting my tapping of the pencil and motioning to the question in front of me. "I've been stuck on this calculus problem for two hours."

There was a pause. I didn't make eye contact with my father as he came and sat down beside me on the couch. I felt his hand on my shoulder.

"Is that truly what's gotten you so up in knots?" he asked me slowly.

I scrunched my nose up, avoiding his gaze. "It shouldn't be this difficult to figure out."

I knew he didn't believe me. He waited for a moment — what for, I don't know.

Eventually, he said, "Well, I'm no calculus expert. But when I'm faced with a problem that's really grinding my gears, the first thing I try to do is step back and look at the bigger picture. Perhaps I haven't given to it as much as I've taken from it. Perhaps I've gone about it the wrong way. Sometimes all you need to do to solve a problem is consider how to best approach it."

I brought my eyes up slowly to meet his as he stood. He was watching me carefully as he added, "But unless you're willing to admit to yourself that what you're doing isn't working, you'll never be able to take that necessary step forward in adopting a new strategy."

I held his gaze for a moment, then turned back to look at my assignment. Father began making his way for the staircase.

"Maybe you need some rest. I certainly do," he said. "Have a good night, son."

I swallowed. "Good night, Father," I mumbled back to him before he began ascending the stairs.

I considered what I'd heard when he'd disappeared from view. I'd never cared enough to change my social strategies. To be frank, nobody who needn't be near me had stuck around long enough to make me care. I had Fuego, my father, a pathetic excuse for a brother, and myself. That was more than enough.

I rubbed my face with my hands. My actions didn't even make sense to myself. I was constantly torn between fear and desire, between pulling her close and pushing her away. It was a wonder she hadn't killed me with that look in her eyes. I wouldn't have blamed her.

But I didn't want her to feel that way. And upon that realization, I knew it was over. Whatever horse I had in this race of bargaining with myself had collapsed and died tragically in the dust and dirt. There was no sense trying to fight my feelings or my fate any longer.

I had lost to the most powerful force in the world, the one anyone could recognize and nobody could deny; there I went, swept away in the mouth of a boundless sea I would likely drown in.

My eyes fell to my other binders and textbooks on the coffee table. I easily found my physics lab reports amongst the array of materials.

Decidedly, I tossed my calculus assignment to the side and plucked them out from my pile of supplies. I picked up the pencil with a reasonable grip, and then I got to work.

CHAPTER 15

THE NEXT MORNING, I met up with all my friends in the lounge for breakfast. After my classes, I decided to go over physics once again – the more I revised and practiced, the better I would understand.

I was about an hour into going over what Elijah and I had worked on the previous day when I felt a tingling sensation in my hand. I frowned and glanced down at my palm. It was glowing slightly, a faint yellow light emitting from it in irregular waves. I could feel the magic within me pounding on the underside of my skin. It grew quicker and quicker, then more even, until suddenly, there was a knock at my door. I blinked, got up, and opened it.

I was met with Felix, and as soon as I saw him, the pounding and the glow in my hand vanished. He had a solemn look on his face, and his dress was nothing short of the usual fancy attire.

"Oh. It's you," I said, blinking at him.

He studied me. "Oh. It's you, too," he said quietly.

I looked him up and down – he held a slim binder in his hands. "What are you doing here?" I asked him bluntly.

He looked down at the binder, and then handed it to me. "I came to give you this," he said.

I took it from him slowly, a little baffled that Felix was giving me anything at all. With crinkled brows, I pried open the binder. My eyes widened. It contained pages upon pages of notes – physics notes. There were the things that had been discussed in the first lab; he had written the concepts, the formulas, the problems I could be asked, and how to solve them. Then there was the lab report he'd solved with explanations on how he completed the experiment and answered all the questions. He'd done the same thing for the lab I'd run out of.

I looked up at him in shock. "...What?" was all I could make out.

He looked down at the binder. "It's to make up for the fact that you didn't get to be a part of the lab work on our first two experiments. But that won't happen again. I want you to be involved from now on."

I blinked. *Who was this man and what had he done with Felix Clarkson?*

His eyes drifted to the floor. "I was wrong. It's my fault you failed the first report, but I want to make sure you don't fail any others," he continued. "I've provided all the values and information you need to complete the lab you missed, and you still have plenty of time to write it up and turn it in before it's due."

Baffled, I fumbled for words. "Felix...I-I really appreciate this. Thank you."

He nodded, and then seemed to remember something. "Oh, right. And then there's this."

He reached into his pocket and pulled out a small box, one that looked like it could contain jewelry. "I know this doesn't exactly make up for the fail," he said. "But I thought you could use a new one. I'm not sure if it's the best apology. Truthfully, I'm not very good at them."

I took the box carefully from him, beyond astonished. I

opened it to reveal a gold keychain, around which dangled a small charm of an orca.

"I couldn't find a Phoenix charm," he chimed in. "So I tried to get you the next best thing."

I ran my finger over the delicate charm; the entire keychain felt heavy and sturdy, like it carried expense. I had no doubt it was made from real gold, knowing Felix. But its value had nothing to do with what it was made of. Its value was attributed to what it meant.

A peace offering. A truce.

Eventually, I looked back up at him, my face soft. "Thank you, Felix," I said. "I appreciate your apology, and I forgive you."

He nodded once at me. His eyes still seemed fervent.

I took the keychain with me to my purse and pulled out my keys. I unclasped them from my current Eiffel Tower keychain and carefully attached them to my new one.

I was about to throw out the old keychain when Felix blurted, "Don't throw it away."

I stopped and stared at him. "What?"

"The old one. Don't get rid of it," he said again.

I blinked. "But…it's old…"

He cleared his throat. "Well…maybe you can get it polished up someday."

I frowned, then shook my head. It was a strange suggestion, but it wasn't the first from him, and it certainly wouldn't be the last.

"All right, then," I said, replacing it back in my purse.

There was a pause as we both stood facing across each other in the doorway. I felt a strange air about us. Not necessarily bad or good. Just strange.

"Tell me, did you sense my presence before I arrived?" he then asked me.

"*Oui*, my palm was glowing and pounding," I said,

suddenly remembering what he had taught me. "And that means that – "

"You and Aurora are fully bonded," he finished for me, nodding once. "Then we can begin learning to fly."

I gleamed. "Perfect. When do we start?"

"The sooner the better." He cleared his throat again. "Well, especially because Aurora seemed sad yesterday. I think she missed you. It would be good to see her," he added in a hurry.

I held his gaze for a moment. He'd dimmed the light that had come and gone, but not quickly enough for me to oversee it.

"I missed her, too. Let's go," I eventually said.

As soon as we had stepped into the cellar, Felix pulled a little electronic device out from one of the coffee table drawers and pressed one of two large buttons on it.

Almost instantaneously, the skylight in the center of the room began to shift. The glass split like two double doors and opened outwards, revealing an entrance accessible and large enough for the Phoenixes.

"This is how we get the Phoenixes in and out of the cellar," Felix explained to me. "It can close right behind us, too. And in the summer, I like to let in a little air, as it can get quite hot down here."

"I bet," I agreed.

"There's a large clearing above us, so there's very little chance of crashing into trees and such," he went on. "I mean, unless you do something incredibly stupid."

I shrugged. "I'll try not to."

"That's the spirit, Miss Pierre," he said, approaching Fuego. He greeted his Phoenix with a hug, bringing his face down to his own and nuzzling him softly. It was touching to see in a weird sort of way – such a hard man made softer by a lovable creature. I hadn't quite gotten used to it.

I turned to Aurora, who had approached me quietly, and kissed her head. She cooed softly and nuzzled her head against my neck. I closed my eyes and hugged her tight.

"Hey, girl," I whispered to her. "I missed you, too, baby. Oh, I love you so much."

Aurora chirped in response. I giggled and hugged her tight again, stroking her beautiful, yellow feathers.

It was a long while before I pulled away and turned back to face Felix, and I was surprised to find him watching me curiously. I saw warmth shining from the lavender in his eyes and falling like rays of sunshine on my face. It seemed like the unique, melting colour in his irises was causing the rest of his face to glow faintly, like a star in the night sky.

"Are you ready?" he asked.

I nodded.

"All right. Mounting a Phoenix is sort of like mounting a horse. Have you done that before?"

"*Oui.*"

"Excellent. Why don't you give it a try?"

I turned back to Aurora, walking around her until I was facing her right side. I then grabbed her back gently, to which she responded by lowering herself closer to me. I pushed off the ground, hoisting myself in the air, and I had myself balanced in the air for a few seconds before my grip suddenly loosened and I fell back towards the ground.

I hit the floor with a loud thud, and a few moments later I heard Felix burst out laughing.

I rolled my eyes and stood up before reaching over Aurora's neck again. I pulled myself up with such strength that Aurora jumped in shock and shook me so hard that I fell on the other side of her, flat on my face.

Felix laughed again, and the sound of it was somewhere

between light-hearted and teasing. "Bloody hell, how did you even manage that one?"

"I don't know," I grumbled into the floor. "Physics was never really my forte."

"Don't be discouraged, Miss Pierre! Come now, get up and try again. You can't give up that easily," Felix said.

I sighed and got up, walking around to Aurora's other side. Taking another deep breath, I reached for her neck and began to pull myself upwards slowly, making little progress.

"Oh, for heaven's sake, here!"

I felt his hands suddenly grab both sides of my waist, and I gasped at the unexpected touch.

"It's okay, it's okay, I've got you!" he exclaimed from behind me. "Grab hold of her feathers and try again! I'll push you up!"

I obeyed and grabbed her feathers once more, this time getting a better grip on her back. I began to pull forward just as I felt Felix's strong grasp push me upwards, and somehow, I found myself plopped dead center on Aurora's back.

"There you go!" Felix said, and he didn't even seem strained from lifting me in the slightest. "Wait there."

He then walked over to Fuego, who lowered himself towards the ground. Felix grabbed hold of Fuego's back and hoisted himself up effortlessly, almost as if it were something that came completely natural to him.

"All right, first things first – you don't have to worry about being seen while flying," Felix began. "The Phoenixes have the ability to conceal themselves and their riders once they are in flight. The magic to do so can be triggered once they reach a certain speed, which they do quite quickly – you'll see soon enough."

"Really?" I questioned. "So we're untraceable in flight?"

He nodded once. "If you were close enough to a person, they may feel a gust of wind as you soared past, but so long as we're in motion, we can remain unseen. Now, that being said, we do have to pick our landing spots carefully. As soon as the movement stops, so does the concealing magic, so it's best to avoid people when landing. Unless, of course, you have a Dark Phoenix, as they have invisibility powers regardless of if they're in flight or not. Make sense?"

"Sure, but – what about each other? How will I know where you are?"

"Ah – I was unclear," he replied. "The magic doesn't conceal us from the view of other Phoenixes or Keepers. We'll still be able to see each other. It hides us from everyone else, though."

"Got it," I said, relieved. The thought of having to navigate the skies completely on my own was a bit daunting.

"Good. We're going to start off nice and simple. No sudden movements, no hesitation. You understand?"

"*Oui!*"

"Okay, I want you to lift on Aurora's neck slowly and gently, you hear? That'll get her to stand tall."

I did as he told me and found myself even higher off the ground atop Aurora's back as she stood to her full height.

"Good! Now, when you're ready, I need you to pull up on her feathers again, and that should get her – "

I didn't hear the rest of his sentence because I had done as he had asked much too eagerly and was too busy screaming as Aurora bolted up and out through the skylight.

As I wrapped my hands around her neck and clung on tightly, I realized just how fast the two of us were slicing through the air. In a few moments, we had already flown high off the ground and were soaring faster by the minute, making the trees and garden below us smaller and smaller with each passing second. Her wings beat with such strength and power that every flap propelled us further and faster than the last. After the shock of the sudden movements had sunk in and instead changed to the appreciation, I felt my heart lift with my spirits. We were flying, Aurora and I, together through the crisp, empty, late afternoon air. The wind rushed through my hair and brushed swiftly on either side of my body, cooling off the warmth in the surrounding atmosphere and filling my lungs with freshness and lightness. I laughed happily and lifted my arms in the air, feeling the wind gust against them, as I pressed tightly against Aurora's sides. For the first time ever in my life, I realized what it truly meant to be free.

I felt a strong whoosh pass my left side, and turned to see Felix and Fuego had suddenly appeared beside us, matching our speed.

"You were supposed to wait for me, Miss Pierre!" Felix yelled over the sound of the wind, but it wasn't in a tone of accusation. It was a happy tone, a light tone, a tone that completely contradicted the cold Felix I had gotten to know and instead better convinced me that a warm Felix did exist somewhere inside that icy body.

"Sorry! I didn't realize she would take off on me like this!" I yelled back with a large smile.

Felix laughed, loud and bright. "It's all right! They tend to take full advantage of every opportunity to fly free!"

"As all birds do!" I shouted back.

His smile was wide, further indicating that this moment right here was where Felix was the most blissful. "All right, do you want to try some basic directing?"

"*Oui!*" I said.

"Okay, I want you to grab hold of the base of her neck – they respond best to commands from there, I find!"

I did as I was told.

"Good! Now, it's quite simple really – if you tug right, she'll go right. Tug left, and she'll go left. Up for up and down for down. Pretty straightforward. There are certain manoeuvres you can learn to do, but those usually come after you get used to the basic handling of the Phoenix's speed and direction. The speed, especially. Phoenixes are the fastest fliers the world has ever seen – we could make it to London by late this evening if we really wanted to!"

If I hadn't been on the back of a Phoenix soaring so quickly through the air, I would not have believed that we could make it so far in such little time. But, as I was in the midst of flight, I could definitely see how we could. Aurora and Fuego flew at such an incredible speed that it would be weird if we didn't make it so far should we decide to continue flying through the afternoon.

"Go ahead and give some of those a try!" Felix continued. "We'll follow your lead!"

"All right!" I said, and for no particular reason, I tugged right.

Aurora responded to my movement almost instantly, and suddenly we were cutting right through the clouds and soaring on over towards the Pacific Ocean. My inner daredevil had me tugging downwards, and then plummeting straight down towards the water.

Just as we were about to crash through the waves, I lifted upwards on the back of her neck ever so slightly, and I found ourselves cruising just above the dark blue water, flying faster and faster away from land and into the horizon. The vista was splattered with pinks and purples and oranges, as if a child had waved paintbrushes drenched in the colours all over the sky; the water sparkled down below.

I saw a shadow in front of me and looked up to see Fuego and Felix soaring boundlessly above us. In what seemed like split seconds, Felix had directed Fuego to fall back and swiftly fly in line with Aurora and me, over to our left side.

He looked over at me and gave me an encouraging nod. This was the longest I had ever seen him seem so fulfilled and at peace with his surroundings, his Phoenix, and possibly even himself.

"You're doing good!" he shouted.

Being one of the only compliments I had ever received from him, I beamed in response.

We flew for a long while over the water, so long that the sun was setting just as I began to pull up. At first, I was simply just going to make a wide circle and turn back towards the estate, but as we flew almost straight up, I had a clever idea. Giving her back a tight tug inwards, I had Aurora flip backwards in a large, vertical circle, doing half a loop before I turned myself right-side up. We were then positioned exactly the opposite direction we had come and were flying straight back towards land.

"Very good!" Felix shouted from behind me, and I looked back at him to see that he had done the exact same thing. "You've got the hang of it!"

"Thank you!" I yelled back.

Within the next hour, we were flying over land again. Felix took the lead, motioning for me to follow him. Aurora and I took our place behind him and trailed as he descended towards the trees. It wasn't long before I could spot the clearing with the skylight that led to the cellar.

"All right, we're going to head back in there now!" Felix told me. "Aurora will understand that we're landing as soon as we make it through the skylight, and she should respond to that, so don't worry too much about technique! Just head straight down!"

"Got it!" I said. And with that, we both found ourselves slicing downwards through the air and into the cellar.

Almost as quickly as the movement of flight had started, the movement ended as Aurora positioned herself to land feet first. The momentum of the wind caused her to rush forwards, but she counteracted it by pushing backwards with her powerful wings, and within seconds, we had stopped.

The wind gushing, the fast rushing, all of it came to a quiet, peaceful halt, and for a moment I had to stop and take it all in as the change in motion had me plastered against Aurora's back and neck, breathless.

"Not bad at all!" Felix exclaimed, and I looked over at him to see him hopping off Fuego's back and walking over to me. "A great first ride!"

I smiled and pulled myself upwards, lifting my right leg over Aurora's back to push myself down from her. I hesitated as I realized I was a lot further off the ground than I thought.

"Here," Felix said, offering me his hand. I took it, and he helped me down, having me land on my own two feet with a soft thud.

"Thanks," I said, and he nodded before releasing my hand. "That was amazing."

"It's one of my favourite things to do," Felix said. He was still being warm and friendly – the nicest version of himself I'd ever seen.

"I can see why," I breathed. "So, what next?"

He nodded once. "Practice, practice, and more practice," he said.

That night, after I had finished the second lab and handed it in an hour before it was due, I eagerly fell asleep with anticipation for the next day. I didn't really feel the time go by in between that moment and the following Wednesday afternoon, when I successfully managed to mount Aurora without falling, and we were airborne atop our Phoenixes once again.

We were flying over the palm forests of his estate, close enough so that I could watch the details of the beautiful grounds below and appreciate them as they whizzed past me. Aurora and I had gotten very familiar with each other's movements quite quickly, and the amount of difference it made in our technique was astounding. Reading each other's sense of directions, we were able to turn tighter, make decisions faster and fly more gracefully than our first try, and Felix had taught me that this would improve even more with practice.

"We're going to fly past the property pretty soon!"

I turned to look at Felix, who's bright, warm gaze was staring back at me with what looked like an excited twinkle in those stunning lavender eyes. My senses hadn't alerted me to his presence when he had come to pick me up that morning – they were already accustomed to him.

"Are you comfortable going beyond there?" he continued.

I nodded enthusiastically.

"Good, good! Go ahead, take the lead!"

I followed his instruction and pulled Aurora ahead, cutting through the wind like a knife through butter. We soared past the fence that separated the Clarkson estate from the rest of the world and flew above a large, barely vegetated mountain.

"All right, Miss Pierre – let's try something new!"

I looked over at him. "I'm in!"

"Perfect. Mirror my actions!"

"Got it," I said, not quite sure what I had gotten myself into but a little too curious to back out.

He nodded, and then slowly, he brought one leg over Fuego's body so that both were on the same side. He looked at me, gave me a grin, and then launched himself from Fuego's back.

I gasped. "Felix!"

I watched Felix fall frighteningly fast. Seconds after he'd sent himself plunging, Fuego dove downwards and scooped him back up. In a matter of moments, they were both flying beside us again. Felix's hair was a mess, but his smile – a real, genuine smile – was the brightest thing I could see for miles.

"That rush is like no other, I tell you!" he exclaimed, looking expectantly at me. "Come on, now! I said to mirror my actions!"

I blinked at him. "Are you insane?"

He scrunched his nose, holding up two fingers slightly apart, a hand motion that translated to, "Just a little." I had different opinions on the matter.

"You want me to fall off Aurora's back?" I asked.

"Yes," he replied as if it wasn't crazy.

My eyes were about to pop out of their sockets. "On purpose?"

"On purpose," he insisted. "Trust me, Miss Pierre. It'll be worth it."

"Worth more than my life?" I questioned.

He shook his head. "You're not going to die, Miss Pierre. You have to trust me."

I gave him a skeptical expression.

He raised his eyebrows at me. "Do you trust me?"

"I did a few minutes ago, but now I'm not too sure," I replied.

He rolled his eyes. "Miss Pierre, you're going to be all right," he assured me. "You saw me just now. And I'm back here again, very much alive."

I took in a deep breath, studying him again for a very long time. This time, I think my brain knew it was being fooled and decided to go along with the lavender bullshit anyway.

"All right. Fine. I'll do it," I finally said. "But you have to do it with me."

He shrugged and swung his leg over again. I sighed, shakily moving one leg over Aurora's back, trembling a bit as I sat with them both to one side.

He raised his eyebrows. "All right. On the count of three."

I nodded. "One…"

"Two…" he continued as I inhaled sharply.

"Three!" I exclaimed, and at precisely the same time, we both slid off our Phoenixes and on to…well, air.

Gravity took immediate effect, and so did my lungs as I began to scream. The wind rushed all around us, flapping our clothes and hair crazily in the wind. The air beat against my body quickly, but not as quickly as my heartbeat, which was racing with the sudden dose of adrenaline that seemed to have been injected into my veins. The sight of the ground looming beneath us and growing closer and closer by the second did not subdue the effect of the adrenaline injection.

My screaming eventually subsided when my lungs ran out of its supply of yelling, and when my noise stopped, I became aware of Felix's. I brought my head up to look at him instead of the impending doom below me, and I found that he was grinning and laughing as we fell.

It took my body a few seconds to respond to this information, but when it did, it responded with a grin and explosive laughter. The adrenaline had suddenly turned from fear to excitement. Instead of scared, I began to feel invigorated. My panic morphed into rejuvenation. I was revived in the most primal sense of the word. There are not enough ways to describe the feeling of contentment that comes with complete airiness after coming to accept its sensation. There was pure delight in the absence of footing.

I felt a swoosh of wind from behind, and I was suddenly thrust against Aurora's back as she appeared underneath me without warning. I gasped as I hit her body, but managed to get a quick grasp around her neck to prevent myself from falling. She chirped loudly, and I grinned, readjusting myself so that I was riding her as I had been before Felix and I jumped.

It took very little time after that for Aurora to coast down towards the ground and land abruptly atop a grassy field. The sudden landing took me by surprise, and the momentum of it had me flung off her back. It was barely a fall compared to what had just ensued in the air, though, and it didn't hurt that much. In fact, as soon as I had stilled after collapsing off my Phoenix, I faced the sky and I laughed once again.

I heard a thud come from beside me, and I turned to see that Felix, too, had fallen from Fuego on to the ground beside me. He looked over, met my gaze, and beamed. I returned his Cheshire cat smile and sat up ecstatically.

"Oh, my God! That was *incredible!*" I squealed.

"I told you it would be!" he responded.

"I can't wait to do that again tomorrow!" I exclaimed, standing up. "We *are* flying again tomorrow, right?"

His grin thinned, and his smile suddenly became sincere as the stars in his lavender eyes brightened. He seemed pleasantly surprised, his shimmering irises bursting with an interminable and contagious light as the muscles in his face relaxed all at once.

"We sure are," he replied.

When we had landed in the cellar, the sun was just beginning to set over San Diego. I took a moment to readjust myself – especially my hair – after dismounting Aurora, and then Felix and I climbed out of the cellar.

He led the way to his garage. We hopped in the Koenigsegg, and when we were both buckled in, he backed out on to the road and took off towards the entrance of the estate.

"I'm really enjoying learning how to fly," I told him soon after we'd started driving.

He nodded. "Mhm-hmm. You're doing well, Miss Pierre."

"Thank you."

There was a pause after this as we came to a stop at a red light. I glanced out the window, looking at our surroundings, and seconds after I did so, my phone buzzed with a text from what appeared to be a group chat.

Everly Jones
Hey girls! What's everyone up to tonight?

Chenoa Bernhard

Not much, really. Was just planning on finishing up some readings.

Myra Nakaoka

Same. Have a paper due in two days that I was planning on working on, but it can wait.

I added my response.

Me

Don't really have anything planned!

Emmanuella Rosa

Me neither.

Everly Jones

Sweet! One of Roscoe's friends booted for him — he's got a lot of booze and he wanted us all to get together in his and Sajan's dorm and drink it up. Are you girls down?

Me

Sure, I could go for a couple of drinks!

Emmanuella Rosa

Me too!

Chenoa Bernhard

Free drinks? Are you joking? Count me in.

· · ·

Myra Nakaoka

Oh, Chenoa…

Everly Jones

Myra, are you coming?

Myra Nakaoka

Yeah, sure, what the heck?

Everly Jones

Okay, sick! I'll see you girls at Sajan and Roscoe's!

I put my phone away and noticed that Felix was looking at me.

"Something up?" he asked quietly.

I nodded quickly. "Oh, yeah, no, everything's fine. That was just my friends asking if I wanted to hang out with them tonight."

"Oh. I see," he replied. "You and your friends going to some crazy party or something?"

I grew amused. "Not a crazy party, per say. We're just getting together and having a few drinks."

He considered this. "That sounds like fun."

"Mhm-hmm," I said. "How about you? Do you have any plans?"

He seemed surprised. "Me? Oh, no. I'll probably just study a bit and then go to bed. Maybe I'll get a couple photos in." I could tell these had been every one of his evening's 'plans' for a very long time.

"A couple photos in?" I asked.

"Yes. I just got my new camera. I'd like to try it out," he answered.

"Do you do that often?"

He nodded. "Photography is therapeutic for me."

"That's kind of like writing for me," I said with a smile. "I do it to escape reality for a bit. And dance, too. I love to dance."

He considered this. "Writing is difficult, and writing something that people enjoy even more so," he replied. "If I do write, it's mainly for me, though. And as for dance...I can appreciate how others find it to be rewarding. I'm not much of a dancer, though. I'm more of a capturer of things rather than a creator of them. I think it's because I'm better at it."

"Well, that would make sense," I said with a laugh. "We like doing things we're good at."

"Of course," he agreed. "That's how I ended up in pre-med."

"Yeah?"

He nodded. "I started out in business and did a few years of it. I never really liked it. I mainly went into it because of my father, but I remember always taking a liking to science, especially in my later years of high school. And I think it was after taking a chemistry class as my science elective last semester that I realized I liked science better than business, and the possibility of medical school from there intrigued me. So I switched to science to prepare for it."

"Oh, I see," I said. "So you've actually been in school for a while now, then?"

"Yes. Well, I took a year off after high school. Then I did three years before I decided on switching, so I formally began as a science major this semester. After I finish my bachelor's, I'll apply to medical school. I've got a long way to go, but that's okay with me. I do enjoy school. Keeps me occupied."

"I enjoy school too, *oui*. I can understand that, for sure. I'm glad you've found your niche," I said. "You seem to be really good at physics, too."

"I think physics is the most interesting science," he said.

"I'm fascinated by it. I spend a lot of time reading about it. Even when I was in business, I'd find myself gravitating towards physics books – " he grew amused with himself " – no pun intended."

I chuckled. "Good one."

The rest of the drive back to the university was relatively quiet. After he pulled the Koenigsegg up to the curb and parked it without turning the engine off, Felix turned to me.

His lips turned ever so slightly at the corners. "I had fun today, Miss Pierre. I look forward to tomorrow."

"As do I. Thanks for the ride," I said as I stepped out of the car, my hand on the top of the car door.

"You're welcome," I heard him say from behind me, and I shut the door softly.

When I entered my dorm, Emmanuella was ready to go. We headed over to Roscoe and Sajan's dorm to find that all our friends had already gathered there. A little portable stereo was playing some songs by popular artists on shuffle, and three bowls of different kinds of chips sat in the center of their desk, surrounded by an ungodly number of alcoholic beverages.

"There they are!" Keiffer exclaimed.

"Yeah," Emmanuella said with a grin. "Were you waiting for us to bring the party or what?"

"Obviously!" Sajan laughed.

We all began drinking, and Roscoe brought out the game Cards Against Humanity. The offensively hilarious game became more and more hysterical as the night went on and the drinks were poured.

A couple hours in, as I was pouring myself another drink, Elijah came up from behind me and slid his hands around my waist. "Hey, you should've told me you wanted a drink – I would've made a special one for you."

I grinned, handing him the cup with very little liquid in it. "You still can," I said.

He grinned and took the cup from me, mixing in a concoctive array and handing it back to me after stirring it all together. "There you are."

"I didn't realize you were a mixologist," I noted.

"Secret talent," he replied.

I took a sip, and then another. He watched me curiously. "So, what do you think?" he asked.

A sly smile took over my face, and I brought myself very close to him. "I think...we should go to my room," I whispered, nibbling his lips a bit before I kissed him.

He raised his eyebrows, and I took his hand in mine, slipping us both out of the room quietly and back to mine.

I'd come to realize that sex, when I craved it, was one of the things that reminded me I was alive. Every new man I permitted to my bed was a different artifact to discover, a new world to travel. I relished the way human bodies were designed to collide when they desired one another, and I took delight in being ravished – when Elijah touched my breasts, I lingered in the tingling sensation. I felt satiated when my touch, my body, and my movements brought men to places high above the Earth. For me, it was empowering.

Elijah was clumsy, but light-hearted and fun. And when he lost it unexpectedly in my mouth, I swallowed before pulling my lips away to look up at him. "Thought you said you would do everything in your power not to disappoint me," I teased.

He wiped his forehead. "You're just too good," he gasped breathlessly. He had this apologetic look on his flushed face that made me snicker.

He tried to make up for it with his fingers, but the technique he used convinced me to reach for the vibrator in my bedside table instead. I straddled him as I showed him what my pleasure should look and feel like, collapsing beside him afterwards in a heap of tranquil liberation.

And as I reeled from the sensations of the day, the flying and fooling around, I found myself impatient for the next rush I'd feel.

CHAPTER 16

Elijah and I both woke up late the next morning, and we scrambled our naked bodies out of bed to get to classes. When I'd finished my last, I told Felix I was ready to fly whenever he was. About half an hour later, there was a knock on my door.

I opened it to see Felix standing in the doorway, wearing a typical Felix getup consisting of his staple black Armani jeans – *seriously, how many pairs of Armani jeans did a guy need?* – an olive-green Versace shirt and sneakers that had red bottoms; they must have been Christian Louboutin. He gave me one of those smiles that weren't really smiles and that people used when they felt embarrassed, awkward, or shy – it was more just him bringing the corners of his lips up as he sucked them in.

"Hello," he said quietly.

I blinked. "Oh. Hey. You could have just texted me to come down to the car."

"Thought I would switch things up," he said with a shrug.

My expression relaxed as I turned to grab my purse. "Well, all right, then."

"Does that bother you?"

I frowned. "Well, no. Why would it bother me?"

"I'm not too sure. I just know there are a lot of things I do that bother you. I'm learning as I go here."

My lips twitched into a humoured smile as I turned back to face him, my purse slung over my shoulder. "Well, this isn't one of them," I said. "Let's go."

We began walking side-by-side through the hallway and down the stairs quietly.

"How was your not-crazy-party?" he inquired, breaking the silence as he held the door to the courtyard open for me.

"Good, thank you," I replied, stepping outside as he followed suit. "How was your quiet night?"

"Good, thanks."

"Good. That's…uh…that's good."

He sucked in his lips and nodded. "Lot of good in this conversation."

"Well, good is better than bad, right?"

"Right. And right is better than wrong. So we can have a lot of right in this conversation, too, and it wouldn't be such a bad thing."

I cracked a small smile. "What about left?"

His lips curled. "Oh. Right," he said, humoured. "I forgot about left."

I giggled softly. Quiet began to slowly creep back into the atmosphere as we strolled through the campus gardens on our way to the parking lot. We clambered into Felix's Aston Martin, and he started the car quickly. Although there wasn't much said, the silence was not uncomfortable. We both seemed eager to get back in the air, because minutes after we had arrived in the cellar, we departed it atop our excited Phoenixes.

We flew in a different direction this time, soaring over the rolling hills of San Diego speedily and freely. The mountains of San Diego were stunning to me. Even though they weren't heavily populated with plants, the mere shape of the twists and turns that ran between them were so intricately beautiful that I found myself gaping at their art-like form.

"It looks so beautiful from up here!" I yelled to Felix.

"I agree!" he yelled back. "The California mountains are some of the most intriguing forms of landscape I've seen! Not the best view, but up there on the list!"

I glanced over at him. "What are some of the better views, then?"

He thought for a moment, his hair flapping crazily in the wind, revealing both of his eyes for only seconds at a time. "Well, I especially love the aerial view of the coastlines!" he finally stated.

"Really? Which ones?" I shouted.

"The ones off San Diego are lovely!" he said. "Australian coastlines, as well – watching the Great Barrier Reef from above is amazing! Hmm…Hawaiian ones too! The Caribbean waters are also quite beautiful…come to think of it, anything tropical is breathtaking to see from the eyes of a bird!"

"Oh, I bet!" I said.

"That's not to say they're the only beautiful views in the world, though!" Felix went on. "Seeing the Rockies from above is just as remarkable! The Himalayas, the Great Lakes, the Alps, the Sahara Desert, the Andes, the Red and Mediter-ranean Seas…and landmarks, too! I saw the Great Wall of China and the Eiffel Tower from above for the first time before I ever visited them on the ground!"

"Wow!" I exclaimed. "You've travelled a lot!"

"Well, why wouldn't I if I was given this beautiful gift?" he shouted, motioning towards Fuego. "No hassles for visas, no holdups at the airport – I fly where I want, and I leave before it causes any trouble!"

I smiled widely. "Do you have a favourite travel destina-tion?" I shouted back as I turned and motioned towards the horizon before us.

"A favourite? Hmm…I think perhaps my favourite could be…"

He drifted off.

"*Oui?* What is it?" I prompted.

He shook his head and shut his eyes, frowning. But no sound came from him.

I raised my eyebrows at him. "Hello?"

He reopened his eyes, but his gaze did not meet mine. It seemed blank and distant as he stared out into the sky.

I snapped my fingers in front of him, yelling, "Is anybody home?"

He shook his head rapidly and suddenly met my gaze, seemingly focused on me once again. "There's another one."

I frowned. "What?"

"There's another one."

"Another one?"

"Yes."

"Another *what?*"

"Another Phoenix. And another Phoenix Keeper."

"What?" I exclaimed, my eyes suddenly scanning the Earth below. "Where?"

"Nearby. Fuego just notified me about the Phoenix. If you listen carefully, your senses may have tuned into the Keeper."

I straightened, taken aback, and then shut my eyes. Sure enough, I could feel a slight sensation in my hand; I glanced down and saw that it had faintly started to glow.

"Oh!" I said, looking back at him. "You're right!"

Felix nodded once at me before looking down towards the ground. "What should we do?" he asked.

I stared at him. "What should we do? What do you mean, what should we do? We should go find them, that's what we should do!"

Felix sucked in his lips. "I'm not sure that's a good idea."

"Not a good idea? In what universe?" I blurted. "Up until now, the only Phoenix Keeper besides your family that you've met is me! And when another one pops up, you're too afraid to go find them?"

He scowled. "I'm not afraid. I'm just…vigilant."

"Vigilant? About what, exactly?"

"Perhaps this Keeper isn't welcome to receiving strangers as company," Felix offered. "You certainly weren't convivial with me in the beginning. Isn't that something to be mindful of?"

I gave him a look of disbelief. "You're trying to be courteous to a complete stranger?"

"Why is that so surprising? I am a considerate man."

"You're a chicken, that's what you are."

"I am not!" he snapped, turning away. "I'm a guy – I'd have to be a rooster," I heard him add.

I rolled my eyes and grabbed hold of the feathers around Aurora's neck. "You made me do the freefall yesterday. Now it's my turn to decide what potentially dangerous activity we do, and I say we go find the Phoenix and its Keeper."

Felix huffed, but grabbed Fuego's feathers, too. "Miss Pierre, I swear you will be the death of me," he muttered.

I rolled my eyes. "Well, give Satan my best when you get to the underworld, you cock," I told him.

He gave me a shocked expression. "What?"

I raised my eyebrows along with the corners of my mouth. "You said you were a cock," I explained. "You know…cock? As in a male chicken? A rooster?"

Felix narrowed his eyes before turning away. "I'll see you in hell," he scoffed before yanking downwards on Fuego's feathers. The movement had the bird plummeting towards the ground, and I had Aurora do the same shortly after.

As we drew closer to the ground, the volume of my senses increased. Felix and I used our senses to direct us towards the Phoenix and its Keeper, changing course only if our senses grew more frantic in frequency and sound. We soared just above the mountains we had found ourselves over, following what seemed to be a single winding road that would occasionally branch off into the driveway of a small, remote home. Eventually, the two of us had our senses going wildest overtop of one small house, which had us landing a little ways away from it in a cluster of bushes.

Felix and I dismounted the Phoenixes and took in the scene before us. The house seemed to be single-storey and rather shabby, and a wire fence enclosed a rather large amount of land around it. The yard looked unkempt, and the paint on the house needed a touch-up. Perhaps the most striking part of the property was the ominously large shed out behind the house, towards which Felix immediately pointed.

"I bet their Phoenix is in there," he mentioned.

"Agreed," I said, my eyes scanning the property once again. "I wonder what kind of person lives in a place like this…"

"Someone who's main priority is neither hygiene nor property value," Felix replied.

I turned to the front of the house, where a gravel driveway led to the tarnished front door on one side and the road that continued through the hills on the other. "Let's find out who it is," I said.

Felix hesitated, but then turned and instructed the Phoenixes to stay put before following me out of the bushes towards the front door. Upon reaching it, the two of us looked at each other before I raised my hand to knock.

My hand did not make contact with the door before it opened suddenly, startling both Felix and I. Sheltered somewhat behind it was a middle-aged man with beady, black eyes and raven-coloured hair. The pounding of my senses practically exploded in my palm upon seeing him before quickly coming to a halt along with the glow of yellow light. He looked at me, then at Felix, and then parted his lips into a smile, revealing yellow-stained teeth.

"Keepers?" he asked in a bit of a hush, his voice brusque.

Felix and I nodded slowly.

"Oh, how exciting!" the man exclaimed, his pale skin seeming to glisten. "It's been a very long time since I've met another Phoenix Keeper! You sensed me, didn't you?"

"*Oui*," I replied. "We were flying over the hills and were alerted to your presence."

"Ah, yes, yes…indeed, I am glad you two decided to stop by and say hello!" the man said. "Tell me, what are your names?"

"I'm Seraphine, and this is Felix," I replied.

"Seraphine and Felix…wonderful! Come…come, follow me! I'll take you to my little Phoenix hideaway, if you will," the man said before bustling out of the door and shutting it behind him. We let him pass us so that we were walking behind him over to a gate in the wire fence, which he opened to provide us access into the yard.

"We didn't catch your name," Felix noted flatly as we followed him.

"Oh, forgive me! My name is Alchnost," the man replied.

"Alchnost," I repeated.

"Pleasure," Felix added, but the way he said it lacked any trace of pleasurable emotion. I threw him a glare, but he avoided it.

"It is an odd name, indeed," Alchnost remarked. "Not to worry – I'm familiar with the reaction."

"It's unique," I piped up. "There's nothing wrong with that."

Felix threw me a look, which I blatantly ignored.

"Ah, dear, you sound like my mother. Always optimistic," Alchnost said with a laugh as we reached the door of the shed. He opened it and motioned for us to step inside.

I followed behind Alchnost and looked at the inside of the weathered building. It was dimly lit by a single, hanging bulb in the center of the room, and it had no windows but was also quite large for a shed. There was a cheap bookshelf in the corner filled with old books and a narrow wooden table beside it, atop which were a few more books and miscellaneous items. Hung above the table was a giant corkboard, the contents of which I didn't pay much attention to. The wooden floor of the shed was covered in multiple different rugs that didn't seem to have a rhyme or reason to their placement. There was a tattered couch and armchair in the corner to my left, and in the corner furthest from where I stood was a sack full of palm leaves and a pile of large, randomly strewn pillows. Atop them sat a fully-grown, black-feathered Phoenix.

The Phoenix, of course, immediately drew my attention. It would have been missed due to the dimness of the room had it not been staring at me as I entered with glistening, cinnabar eyes. They were strikingly similar to Fuego's, but against the stark contrast of its sable feathers and the murkiness of the shed, they stood out much more than Fuego's did. It looked at me intently; I found its mystery intriguing.

"This is Oscuro," Alchnost said as he motioned towards the Phoenix. "He's a lot friendlier than he looks, I assure you."

I smiled slightly, approaching the Phoenix. He stood up as I neared, and I reached my hand out slowly to his neck. The feathers I made contact with were a bit coarser than Fuego and Aurora's feathers, but Oscuro responded well to my touch, studying me with his scarlet eyes as I soothingly stroked his neck back and forth.

"A Dark Phoenix?" I heard Felix inquire from behind me.

"Indeed, Felix," Alchnost responded. "Please, have a seat."

"I'm all right standing, thank you."

"Suit yourself. Say, your Phoenixes are around here, are they not?"

"They're out in the bushes near your property."

"Well, you're most certainly welcome to bring them in."

"It would get much too crowded," was Felix's blunt refusal. Why was he being so stiff?

"As you wish. Care for some coffee or tea, either of you?"

I was going to turn and accept the offer, but Felix beat me to it. "No, thank you. We won't be staying long."

"Ah. Places to go, people to see, my boy?"

"You could say."

"Mhm. You and Oscuro seem to be getting along, eh, Seraphine?"

I turned and smiled at Alchnost, who was now sitting in the armchair. "I'd like to think so," I said.

"Tell me, what kind of Phoenix do you have?"

"A Light Phoenix."

"Ah, I see. Suits you, sweetheart," Alchnost noted, looking over at Felix. "And yourself, Felix?"

Felix didn't look at Alchnost – he was busy studying the giant corkboard. "Fire," he answered quietly.

"Hm," Alchnost said, turning back to me. "Your friend here is a man of few words, isn't he?"

"I suppose so," I replied, my eyes still on Felix. He seemed mesmerized by whatever was on that corkboard, his gaze flitting over the multiple papers pinned to its surface like a cat follows a laser pointer. He brought his fingers up and grazed them over one paper in particular, his eyes narrowing at what was before him. I wondered what was so fascinating about it.

"Do you two know any other Phoenix Keepers?" Alchnost asked me, bringing my attention back to him.

"No. Well, other than you and each other, no," I replied. "And you?"

He shook his head. "Never met any others."

"Really?" I asked with wide eyes.

He shrugged. "I wanted to teach my daughter when she was young, so we could connect that way. Who better to share such magic with than your own family, hm? But…well, let's just say she developed more of an allegiance to my ex-wife and her ways of being." He chuckled a bit sadly. "As far as I know, she's become her mirror image. But I haven't seen much of her since they left."

I gave him a sympathetic gaze. "That must be hard."

"Well, she always got on much better with her mother than she did with me," Alchnost mentioned. "It wasn't much of a surprise that they gave her sole custody after the divorce. I'm sure she would have chosen to go with her mother regardless."

I could see Felix tense.

"I'm sorry to hear that," I offered.

"No apology necessary, dear," Alchnost responded. "I'm sure they – "

"What is all this?" Felix suddenly queried.

Alchnost and I both turned our attention to him. He was still staring at the contents of the corkboard; it was safe to say whatever they were had lured him into some kind of trap.

Alchnost chuckled. "Why, you've been staring at it so much, I thought you'd already known," he replied.

I was curious enough now to part with Oscuro's feathers and approach the corkboard. There were a few maps on it – seven, actually; one for each of the continents. Each map had pins which identified what seemed like sporadic locations and led to further information that was linked to it through connected strings. Many of the places had Xs over them, like they had been crossed off or eliminated. Thrown in alongside the maps were what looked like old pages with messages that seemed to be written in riddle. There were a few depictions of a Phoenix, and the most striking thing about it was that it was golden in every single drawing.

"I don't know anything about this," Felix said slowly. "But it looks…interesting."

Alchnost cocked his head to the side. "Tell me, Felix – what do you *think* it is?"

Felix paused for a second, looking over the maps and messages. "It looks like you're trying to find something."

"Find something, you say? What do you think I'm trying to find?"

Felix's eyes immediately fell to a depiction of the golden Phoenix. "This," he said slowly, nodding his head towards it.

"You're absolutely right, my boy."

Felix sucked in his lips as he continued staring at the drawing. "I don't understand," he then said, shaking his head as he turned to look at Alchnost. "How can you be looking for a Phoenix? Phoenixes hatch to their Keeper – we get one, and one only."

Alchnost cocked his head to one side, a sly smile suddenly creeping over his lips. "Is that so?" he asked slowly.

Felix held his gaze. "That's what I've been taught."

"Well, I'm afraid to tell you that you've been taught wrong."

I studied Alchnost as he leaned back in the chair, propping one leg over the other as he pulled a cigar out of his pocket. He lit it, put it in his mouth, and proceeded to puff out a hefty cloud of smoke. Keeping the cigar loosely clutched between his pointer and middle finger, he then returned a pair of raised eyebrows towards both of us.

"You two look rather stumped," he noted. "It's quite amusing."

I glanced at Felix; he looked as if he'd just discovered his entire life had been a lie. "There's a way to acquire more Phoenixes?" he questioned.

"Yes," Alchnost replied.

"How?"

"You find them, of course."

Felix squinted at him. "*Where* do you find them?"

"Why, boy, that's what I'm trying to find out. Hence the corkboard behind you."

Felix turned his attention back to the corkboard. "So…are you telling me this golden Phoenix is just stumbling about the world, waiting for someone to discover it?"

"No, no. That Phoenix is special. That's Sedaurea, the Golden One, the most almighty and powerful Phoenix to ever live," Alchnost explained. "You don't find her – you create her."

"*Create* her?" Felix repeated in disbelief. "How?"

Alchnost grinned, rising from his seat. He approached the

table, on which sat an old, dusty book. He brushed it carefully before opening it, his movements slow and taunting. Felix and I exchanged glances.

"This story may take a little while to go through in its entirety," Alchnost then said, turning to face us. "I hope that doesn't deter your interest."

I reached into my jeans pocket, pulled out my iPhone, and pretended to check the time as I accessed the recording feature. When it was set, I replaced it.

Felix simply stared at him expectantly. "We're listening," he said.

"Well, then, I'll simply start from the beginning," Alchnost declared as he began to pace back and forth. "I'm sure you're familiar with our little friend Herodotus? The first Phoenix Keeper who dreamt Phoenixes into existence?"

We both nodded.

"Right. Now, before Herodotus, and before the five types of Phoenixes originated, there was only one Phoenix that existed in the entire world. Her name was Sedaurea, but she's referenced as the Golden One because she was covered in shimmering, golden feathers from top to bottom. She was a mixture of the five elements of the Earth – fire, earth, water, light, and darkness, therefore rendering her the most powerful Phoenix to ever have lived. Her magical abilities surpassed that of any other Phoenix, and she had the power to perform all five of the kinds of magic and even infuse them with different spells that had bewitching effects on their recipients.

Now, Sedaurea did not have a Keeper. She was a free Phoenix, capable of bonding to a Keeper but not finding anyone suitable enough to take control of her. The ancient civilizations of her time knew also of her, and they knew of the capability to take control of Sedaurea. And so, great battles ensued over the Golden One – people fought and killed to get a chance to approach her and bond to her, but she never chose a Keeper because she never deemed one worthy enough. All they had was a lust for power. This frustrated the people who tried so hard to get to her, and suddenly, Sedaurea became a target of destruction rather than of attainability. And so, she did the only thing she could do to protect herself. She separated herself into the five elements of the Earth, producing multiple of the five types of Phoenixes that exist today.

The people of her time learned of her disappearance and assumed she had been destroyed. Thus, the memory of her and of Phoenixes were lost, and generation after generation, it dissipated further, until they merely became a forgotten myth. That is, until Herodotus, who imagined and dreamt the first Light Phoenix into existence with his open mind, and triggered the belief of Keepers after him. This gave rise to the Phoenix Keepers like you and me, worthy of mastering one element and one element alone. But that was not the end of Sedaurea."

He stopped pacing and turned to face us. "You see, along with living Phoenixes, Sedaurea hid one of each type of Phoenix egg in its own sanctuary somewhere in the world, known as the Sanctuary Phoenixes. Their purpose was to act as a gateway for a Phoenix Keeper to reawaken Sedaurea. The sanctuaries were well hidden in ways that would prevent anyone who had no business being there from getting in and disturbing the eggs; Sedaurea sought out the most protected and most clever hiding places, the places that were the most durable and near impossible to destroy. They were related in some way to the Phoenix they enclosed. Since only one type of Phoenix is hatched to a Phoenix Keeper, these Sanctuary Phoenixes make it possible for a Keeper to attain all five types of the Phoenixes, and if they die, they simply reappear in their egg form back in their appropriate Sanctuary. It's all described in this book here – " he tapped the page he had turned to with his index finger " – and in the instructions she composed, she states that when all five types of Phoenixes are brought together, Sedaurea will once again form and awaken from their combination. This action proves the Keeper worthy, and thus,

Sedaurea will be in control of the one who wakes her. The person who brings them together may not even be the Keeper of all the Phoenixes. They just have to be the one who physically connects the Phoenixes and themselves together. Even given this loophole, no one has successfully brought Sedaurea back to this day. But the potential to bring her back and bond to her is still as valid as ever."

He closed the book and outstretched it towards me. "There's much greater detail in here – but essentially, that's the basic knowledge of her legacy."

I took the book hesitantly from him. *The Legend of Sedaurea* was scrawled on its aged cover. I began flipping through it, my curiosity bursting, my thoughts overwhelmed.

"Well, what does 'City of the Sun' mean?" Felix suddenly blurted. I glanced at him and saw that he was looking intently at a piece of paper on the corkboard with the words 'City of the Sun' scribbled on it and circled many times.

"Oh – Seraphine, dear, turn to the last page, will you?" Alchnost replied.

I looked at him, and then down at the book as I flipped the pages over, stopping at the last one. Nothing was written on it but four lines, which I read aloud:

"Your journey begins in the City of the Sun,
Slumbering there is the light of the Golden One.
Locate the monument older than I
And there you will find the first of five."

"Ah," Felix said. "So it's where to begin looking."

"Indeed, Felix," Alchnost replied.

"And where is the City of the Sun?" I asked, closing the book and handing it back to him.

"Not too sure. But I'll find out eventually," Alchnost said with a chuckle.

I eyed him. "This seems like it'll take you a rather long time."

"Oh, sure it will. But Sedaurea is well worth the hassle."

I narrowed my gaze. "And that would be…because…?"

"Well, she's the most powerful Phoenix a Keeper could have!" Alchnost exclaimed. "A combination of all the elements of the Earth, with the ability to perform magic no other Phoenix can muster! And, of course, she bestows those powers upon her Keeper, too."

I considered this. "So you want the best of the best?"

"Easy way of putting it, yes."

"Why?"

Alchnost shrugged. "I'm an aging man with nothing better to do with my time, dear," he said. "When you get to this age, any adventure is worth pursuing – especially one that could be the most rewarding adventure ever partaken in."

This response seemed to lure Felix back into the conversation. "One might argue that giving such power to a single man could be a dangerous thing," he remarked.

Alchnost winked. "And yet, we have presidents and gods and kings," he countered.

Felix tensed a bit.

"I've nothing against the world, Felix. You must understand that. I'm a moral man. I'm just simply seeking an escapade," Alchnost continued. "Everyone desires a good expedition of some sort at some point in their lives, now don't they?"

I fidgeted again with my phone. I found myself both relating to his passion for the undertaking and still a little hesitant about the nature of his quest.

Felix, on the other hand, seemed impermeable. He cleared his throat as his eyes stayed locked to Alchnost's. Then, after a brief pause, he spoke without ever lifting his gaze.

"Miss Pierre, we best be on our way," he stated.

I did not argue, and simply nodded. The two of us made our way towards the door, and after Felix opened it, I quickly stepped out into the yard. Felix followed suit.

"Your company was lovely, Seraphine and Felix," I heard Alchnost say, and I turned to see he was now standing in the doorway.

I gave him a small smile so as not to be completely off-putting, despite Felix and I's blunt departure. "Thanks for the hospitality," I said.

Alchnost grinned. "My pleasure, sweetheart."

I turned and began walking with Felix promptly to the gate in the wire fence. As we opened it and made our way through, we heard Alchnost's distant voice.

"Happy adventuring!" he called, and neither Felix nor I responded.

CHAPTER 17

As soon as we had landed in the cellar, Felix had dismounted Fuego and was determinedly stomping up the stairs.

"Felix!" I said, trying to get off Aurora's back as fast as I could. "Felix, hold up!"

"I'm going to speak with my father," I heard him growl from the stairwell.

"*Oui, oui,* that's fine! Just…just wait for me!" I cried, but the stomping did not cease. I huffed, deciding that focusing on dismounting Aurora rather than halting Felix would help me off her quicker and therefore allow me to catch up to him sooner. I finally managed to jump off Aurora and booked it up the stairs, falling in pace behind him on the pathway through the garden.

He was walking briskly, angrily. "I can't believe he would keep that from me," he was mumbling when I caught up with him. "I can't believe he wouldn't tell me."

"Okay, Felix, just relax – "

"Relax? You're telling me to relax?" he snapped, turning to face me; his eyes were wide and his nostrils were flared. "Do you even understand how betrayed I feel?"

"I'm, uh, beginning to get an idea, but – "

"My own father not informing me, his own son, about something so near and dear to my heart? Something so crucial and significant in the world of Phoenixes – the world I live to be a part of? Do you know the extent to which I'm hurt, Miss Pierre?"

"I'm going to go out on a limb and say you're pretty hurt, but I, uh – "

"You think this is a joke, do you?" he snarled. "You think this is some kind of fun little game?"

"No, no!" I assured him. "I don't! I understand how you feel! I just…I….maybe your father has some kind of explanation for all of this?"

"Oh, he better have some kind of explanation, all right!" Felix declared as he began marching his way down the path again. "And it better be a fucking good one!"

Poor Luther, I thought. *He has no idea what's coming for him.*

Felix kept simmering to a boil like a kettle on a stove for the duration of the time it took us to get to his garage. He mumbled under his breath incessantly as he drove us to Luther's mansion in his Porsche.

When we had arrived at Luther's front door, Felix vigorously banged on its surface. A startled Benjamin frightfully opened it.

"For Heaven's sake," he muttered. "You'd think someone was dying, the way you're knocking!"

"It may be you who dies if you don't stop wasting my time," Felix snarled at him as he pushed past the poor butler and marched into the mansion.

Benjamin turned to me with a sigh. "Greetings, Miss Seraphine. You're looking lovely as – "

"Yeah, yeah, she's lovely. We all know. Where's Father?" Felix snapped at him, cutting him off.

Benjamin seemed unaffected by Felix's brute demands. "He was in the study, last I checked," he answered him.

"Great. Come on, Miss Pierre," Felix said, bounding up the magnificent staircase two at a time. I followed without hesitation.

We travelled down a long, elegant corridor and finally turned left into a small, extravagant study covered in oak wood. There was an oak table that carried a printer and a lamp in one corner and a bookshelf in the other that mainly contained little décors and photos – I picked out one of a ten- or eleven-year-old Felix and a much younger Luther sitting together on a fancy yacht. On the left wall was a massive, timely-looking world map. A large, oak desk was placed beautifully in the center of the room, atop which sat a large computer screen, a mug filled with writing utensils, and multiple papers. Luther himself sat at the desk, and he was squinting at the computer screen, a pair of reading glasses low on his nose.

He looked up and seemed surprised to see us so frazzled. "Felix! Seraphine! Why, what a pleasant – "

Felix was evidently not listening to what his father had to say as he slammed the door to the study shut. The sound from the banging door echoed throughout the entire room, and Felix locked it before approaching his father and smacking his hands down on the desk. "You never told me we could have more than one Phoenix!" he bellowed.

Luther frowned, his eyes wide. "What?"

"You never once informed me! Not *once!*" Felix went on, using one fist to hit the desk so hard that I could feel the ground around it shake. "How could you not think to mention such a thing?"

Luther's eyes were darting between his son and I rapidly. "Felix, my boy, what in the world – "

"Oh, don't 'my boy' me!" Felix roared, pointing a finger in his father's face. "I want more information on this! *Now!* And don't pretend like you don't know! I know that you know and I don't know why you wouldn't tell me that you know! All I know is that I don't know and now I want to know! So tell me what you know, damn it!"

Luther seemed dumbfounded. "Son, I have no idea what you're talking about!"

"Oh, don't feed me that bullshit. Miss Pierre and I just heard of this from some lone, reclusive Phoenix Keeper out in the hills! If he knows, then you ought to know!" Felix replied irately.

Luther turned to look at me. "A reclusive Phoenix Keeper?"

"*Oui*," I said, and in contrast to Felix's rumbling, my voice seemed a lot calmer and more collected. "We sensed him while flying. His name was Alchnost, and he had a corkboard full of information he was trying to decode. He told us he was trying to find some Phoenixes in some sanctuaries and create a golden Phoenix."

Luther raised his eyebrows. "A golden Phoenix, you say?"

"Yes, that's what she said – I don't see why you feel the need to repeat her! You're just wasting our time!" Felix snapped, shaking his finger horrifyingly close to Luther's face. "A golden Phoenix, yes! He called it something else too – oh, what was it? S…Sedaurea! That was it!"

I had never seen someone look so stunned in my life. Luther's eyes were growing almost too big for his face, which was now frozen in a look of complete and utter astonishment. His eyes fluttered in surprise at his son's sudden motion, and he stared back at him with the eyes of a frightened deer.

Felix was growing impatient. "Father, why are you looking at me like I killed a man? I want to know all about this! Now!"

Luther cleared his throat, slowly using one hand to gently

bring Felix's finger away from his face. "Felix, I already told you," he responded. "I don't know what you're talking about."

Felix straightened and took a step back as Luther stood. He looked at me, then at Felix, and then let out a bit of a huff, seemingly relieved Felix hadn't started ranting again.

"I'm sorry, son, but this is news to me," Luther went on. "It most certainly sounds interesting, but I'm afraid this is also the first I'm ever hearing about this. I don't really know what to make of what you're telling me."

This finally seemed to register with Felix, who instantaneously returned to a calmer, yet colder, state. "Oh," he said in what was the most anti-climactic resolution to an argument I'd ever witnessed. "Hmph. Too bad you weren't with us. You could have heard it straight from the source."

"He still can," I chimed in.

Both the men looked at me with a deep frown as I produced my iPhone from my jeans pocket. "I recorded him speaking after he picked up the book," I explained to Felix.

Felix's eyes widened in surprise. "Bloody hell, I can't believe I didn't think of doing that myself," he exclaimed.

I turned to Luther. "Care to listen?"

"Yes, please, let me hear it."

I pressed play and let the recording of Alchnost's storytelling take up the room. We all listened intently, Luther especially.

When the recording ended, Luther took in a deep breath. "My," he mumbled. "That is ever the more intriguing. I've never heard of such a thing."

I looked at his desk. "Luther, may I borrow pen and paper?"

"Yes, of course," Luther said, stepping away from the desk. "Help yourself."

I approached the desk, grabbing a pen and a piece of paper before I replayed the part where Alchnost began speaking about the City of the Sun. I wrote down the four lines from The Legend of Sedaurea:

> *"Your journey begins in the City of the Sun,*
> *Slumbering there is the light of the Golden One.*
> *Locate the obelisk older than I*
> *And there you will find the first of five."*

When I was done, I held up the paper, rereading the lines over and over. Then, I turned back to Luther and Felix.

"I want to find them," I said simply.

Luther and Felix exchanged glances. "It seems like quite the undertaking," Luther then replied.

"If it all even exists," Felix added.

I frowned at him. "What do you mean? We just learned about it from Alchnost."

Felix motioned to his father. "And, yet, he knows nothing about it. What if this isn't what we think it is? What if we waste our lives searching for something we think is real, or die in the process?"

"We could die in a car accident on our way home to the university," I said with a shrug.

"Transportation is a necessary risk – that's different than a treasure hunt, Miss Pierre," Felix said. "I don't know. I'm not convinced."

"The stuff on Alchnost's corkboard seemed convincing enough to you," I countered. "And convincing enough for you to march in here demanding answers from your father."

"And those answers I did not receive," Felix responded. "So I'm having doubts."

I looked at Luther, who nodded once at me. "It seems outlandish, Seraphine," he cautioned. "I can understand the excitement, especially given how many nearly unbelievable things you've experienced recently. But I don't think it's wise to pursue this any further."

I couldn't believe how easily I had been overruled. It had all the inner workings of something completely plausible. Alchnost had spent nearly an hour explaining it all to us, and Luther had convinced Felix to shut it down in less than a minute. As much as I respected Luther's age and wisdom, I questioned whether we should truly leave the final decision-making to him. But seeing as Felix's personality indicated he wasn't going to budge, I knew that any pursuit of the idea would have to be undertaken alone. Truthfully, I didn't know where I would even start. I felt stuck.

I looked down at the ground and nodded in response to Luther. I could feel them both watching me.

"I'm sorry, Seraphine," Luther added.

I shook my head. "All good," I replied, bringing my eyes back up to him. "You're probably right."

"It was an interesting story, that's for certain. But unfortunately, I believe a story is all it is," Luther sighed, rubbing his eyes tiredly. "Now, I must give my regrets to the both of you. I must have the Autumn Ball completely organized and prepared by tomorrow, in addition to what seems like a million other things at this point."

Felix suddenly threw his head back with a groan. "Ugh, that's tomorrow? I'd forgotten about that."

"Well, it's a good thing I reminded you, then," Luther stated.

I frowned. "The Autumn Ball?"

"Yes, m'dear. I often host events with business partners and their affiliates – builds rapport, you see," he explained, nodding to Felix. "My sons often are a part of them."

"Sadly," Felix murmured.

Luther rolled his eyes, but continued. "I like to do different themes – seasonal gatherings, costume parties, that sort of thing. It keeps it fun. So tomorrow's our little

Autumn-themed ball. Autumn colours, autumn treats, the works."

I smiled. "That's neat."

"Indeed. Despite the amount of work they are, I do quite enjoy them myself," Luther said as he eyed me. "Say, if you've nothing planned tomorrow night, it would be lovely to have you attend as well. I'm sure Felix could bring you to and from."

I cleared my throat, suddenly a bit nervous. A room full of rich socialites didn't seem like the kind of place I should be spending my Friday night. "Oh, sir, I don't think I'd consider myself a business partner."

"Oh, nonsense. That's no requirement," Luther insisted. "You're company of the host."

I looked at Felix. Where I expected some form of objection, I merely got a shrug that read, "It's up to you."

I nodded at Luther. "All right."

"Excellent," Luther replied with a grin. "It'll be wonderful to have you there. Dress is formal, and make sure it's a colour of fall. You know, reds, browns, yellows, oranges."

I racked my brain, trying to picture my closet and whether it included a formal dress in any of those colours. "Sounds good. I appreciate the invite," I said.

The drive back was relatively quiet. As he pulled up beside the university's entrance, Felix turned to me.

"I'll pick you up at six tomorrow," he said.

I nodded before heading back to my dorm.

That night, I lay awake and blinked at the ceiling for a while. I couldn't shake the curiosity that had exploded within me. I both envied and questioned how Felix could have done so if he'd even been half as curious as I was.

I sighed and turned to stare at the wall. I trusted Luther's judgment – at least, I thought I did. I couldn't decide whether I was upset with his judgment call, or if I just didn't believe it altogether. Either way, he'd persuaded Felix. And that was a feat to be considered.

A thought entered my mind. I shut my eyes, and a small smile formed on my lips.

Considered, sure, but perhaps without consequence.

PART III: THE RESOLVE

CHAPTER 18

IT TURNS out my closet did not contain what I would consider a formal enough dress for a Clarkson event – neither in fall colours, nor in any other colour. I scrambled to try and find a nearby thrift shop on my phone's GPS, and after determining the closest and a plausible bus route, I grabbed some spare cash and made my way towards the bus stop.

As luck would have it, I spotted Felix smoking by a few picnic tables on the way. He waved when he saw me, and I waved back as I approached him.

"Off to class?" he asked me.

"No, off to the thrift shop," I replied as I kept walking. "I realized I don't have a dress for tonight."

I caught a glimpse of his brows furrowing. "Oh, I see."

"Hopefully I'll find something nice," I said as I began hurrying past him. "I'll see you later!"

I hadn't walked very far before I heard Felix call, "Miss Pierre, wait!"

I stopped and turned. He was just throwing the cigarette in a sanded bowl and had begun rushing over towards me, fumbling in his pant pockets for what seemed to be his wallet.

"Here," he said when he'd caught up to me, and he handed me a credit card.

I stared at it, then at him, my brain short-circuiting. "Wait, what?"

"Go to a bridal store or something," he said. "Get yourself something fine." He extended the card closer towards me, almost awkwardly. "I insist. You can tap up to a grand on it, so you won't need my PIN."

I felt as though my mind had been boggled. "Felix, I can't accept this – "

"Sure you can. You wouldn't need to buy a dress if it wasn't for my father's event. And if you're going to go out of your way to buy one, it might as well be something you really like." He gave me a trying, anxious smile. "Go on, take it. You can give it back to me tonight."

I swallowed, my brows shaking a bit as I hesitantly took the card from his hands. "I-I don't know what to say."

"Then don't say anything at all," he told me. His eyes were alight with some kind of charming nervousness, as if he weren't accustomed to the action he'd just made. "But get something burgundy."

"Burgundy?"

"Burgundy. That's the deal, kindling. You get something burgundy on me."

"Is there a reason for that?"

"Yes."

I raised my eyebrows expectantly. "And that is…?"

He shrugged. "It's a surprise."

I let out a bit of an amused breath. "All right. Burgundy it is."

I ended up finding a one-shouldered dress in burgundy that was well under a grand at a nearby bridal boutique. I hummed and hawed about it for a while, questioning if it was good enough or if I should keep looking for something fancier. It was hard to know how far to go with the Clarksons sometimes. But when I received a text from Felix saying he would be ready to go in an hour, I concluded my pondering and bought the dress before rushing back to campus.

After I'd finished throwing my hair in an updo and putting on some similarly coloured makeup, I gave the completed outfit one last glance over in the mirror and grabbed a small purse before heading out the door. Felix was waiting in the parking lot, and I made my way over to his Porsche and opened the door.

He had changed, and I would say he was dressed well, but he always was to some degree. Perhaps it was just a cut above the norm. The most notable thing about the Givenchy suit he wore was that it was burgundy. So was the tie that hung around his neck, contrasting nicely against the white dress shirt.

I stared at him, the corners of my mouth twitching. "You wanted to match?"

He scanned my dress. "Happy accident," he said unconvincingly. I could see the hint of a small smile on his lips.

I smiled myself as I shut the door, and I tossed his credit card in the cup holder as he began driving. "Thank you for letting me borrow your card," I said. "I hope I put it to good use."

He nodded once. "I would say you did." His brows shuddered a bit. "Why? Do you not think so?"

"Well, *oui,* I do. Or at least, I think I do. I just don't go to many formal events. I didn't know if this met the requirement."

He looked at the dress again. "It looks just fine to me."

"Oh, good," I said, relieved. "Thank you."

"You know how to dress, Miss Pierre. You shouldn't worry."

I was surprised. "I don't know. I just don't have...like...you know..."

"Money doesn't buy class. Nor style. Common misconception, though." He shook his head. "I've met enough rich people to know that most of them couldn't pair a blazer with trousers to save their lives. If they didn't have stylists, they'd be a walking Picasso – " he paused " – well, Picasso after his art was a mess."

I didn't answer right away. "I kind of like messy Picasso. It's...different."

He threw me some side-eye. "Would you be daring enough to wear a dress if it bore the design of a messy Picasso?"

I sucked in my lips.

He chuckled. "That's what I thought." I grew amused, too.

When we arrived at Luther's mansion, Felix pulled over close to the entrance. There were many other luxurious cars parked on the cobblestone driveway. After he shut the car off, Felix and I both exited the Porsche and headed for the front entrance.

Benjamin smiled at us from the open doorway as we approached him. "Greetings, Felix and Seraphine," he said.

Felix nodded at him. "Nice to see you, Benjamin," I said.

"And you as well, Seraphine. You look beautiful, as usual," he said. "Everyone has gathered in the ballroom."

Felix turned to me. "Come, this way."

He led the way to the ballroom. As we neared, I could hear music growing louder and louder, until we turned into a doorway which opened into a staircase that led down to the massive space. A gorgeous chandelier overflowing with shimmering crystals hung in the centre of the room. Dark hardwood covered the floors while the walls remained a light cream colour, accented with intricate, ornate detailing in the crown moulding and window frames. The huge, arched windows showcased a scenic view of the ocean in the distance, seemingly the focal point of the room. There were many round tables that were topped with delicate, white tablecloths and completed with harvest bounty centerpieces – brown branches and maple leaves in those beautiful tones of red, yellow, and orange. Hanging from the ceiling were string lights that gave off a faint, yellow glow. At the front of the room, by the windows, there was a little raised wooden stage, where a pianist played on a grand piano. Around the room, people stood, all dressed well and nearly all holding fine glasses filled with champagne. Chatter competed with the piano for volume.

"Wow," I said, taking in the sight before me. "It's beautiful in here."

Felix shrugged. "I suppose."

"You don't think so?"

"Perhaps I've just seen it too many times. There's only so much that a change in décor can do to the same room when you frequent it as much as I have."

I thought about this. "Well, maybe it isn't supposed to be about the décor," I said, looking back out over the room. "Maybe it's about the reason for gathering. Or maybe it's about the company you're in."

I saw him turn to look at me out of my peripheral vision. "Money. That's the reason. And it's also the company." Another pause. "I've failed to see a genuine splendour in these gatherings for quite some time. It's all very staged and overdone."

I turned to face him again. "So you're no longer charmed by your wealth?"

He held my gaze. "It's like this room. It loses its charm when you spend too much time in it."

Before I could really digest this and respond, I heard Luther's voice coming from below. "Seraphine! Felix!"

We both turned to see him waving at us from the foot of

the staircase. I returned the wave and began making my way down. Felix followed.

"I'm glad to see you," Luther told me with a grin. "You look wonderful."

"Thank you, sir," I said, returning a smile. "I was just telling Felix how beautiful the room was."

"Oh, why, thank you, m'dear," Luther replied, looking around. "It's one of my favourite rooms in my home – when it's full of life, it's very cheery. Now then, have you two had some champagne?"

"Not quite yet," I said, and in response, he promptly waved down a waiter who carried a tray of champagne glasses.

"Here. Take your pick," Luther insisted. "It's a Krug, hm?"

I widened my eyes. "Whoa," I said as Felix and I each picked up a glass. I was hesitant to drink it as I knew how expensive the champagnes ran, but after one taste, there was no going back. My eyes instinctively fluttered closed as the glorious, bubbly mixture swam down my tongue and throat. It was like drinking liquid magic.

I heard Luther chuckle and quickly opened my eyes. "One of the finest champagnes ever created," he noted. "I fancy Krug quite a bit myself. I never tire of that feeling it brings."

"I can see why," I said, taking another sip. As I did so, Felix returned his now empty glass to the tray and picked up another, to which I blinked in surprise. He'd drunk the first one as if it were water, and he proceeded to take a large gulp of the second.

"Well, if it isn't my favourite Canadian!"

I turned around and met Julius' cheery grin. He was dressed very well – his dress shirt was a pale yellow and his dress pants a dark brown.

"Hello, Julius," I said with a smile.

"Hello yourself! You look gorgeous, *hermosa!*" he exclaimed, his hand winding its way around my waist as he pulled me in for a hug. "What a lovely dress – or, should I say that you make it lovely?"

"Or you could say nothing at all," Felix mumbled grumpily, placing the second empty glass on the tray and picking up glass number three. "Excuse me, all of you."

He then turned and disappeared amongst the other guests. I didn't have much time to wonder where he was going before Julius offered me his arm.

"Come, I'll show you to the hors d'oeuvres," he said with a wink.

I linked my arm in his. "Enjoy!" I heard Luther call out behind us as Julius led me to the spread of delicacies.

There was a long table in a corner of the room, filled with an appetizer for all. Mini pot pies, cranberry brie bites, pumpkin hummus, apple crumble cups – my mouth was watering as I filled my plate with some of the delectable teasers. When we were done selecting, Julius and I sat down at one of the tables, and he waved over a waiter to bring us some more champagne.

"So, first impressions of a Clarkson event?" Julius asked me with a grin. His eyes were so much warmer than Felix's, and that smile was irresistible. It was hard not to fall completely head over heels in love with his charm.

"This is awesome," I replied, my mouth full of apple crumble. I had given up on trying to eat politely in front of the Clarksons. Their food was much too delicious not to scarf down.

His grin widened even more, if that was at all possible. "I'm glad to hear," he said. "Maybe you'd like to be a regular on the guest list."

The thought of more tasty food and ridiculously cheerful champagne made my stomach do a happy dance. "I'm in," I said without hesitation, shoving another one of the apple crumble cups in my mouth.

Julius laughed – such a vivacious sound. "Do they starve you at the university or what?"

"If I say they do, can I take some of this food home?"

He laughed again. "I'll see if I can't find you a takeaway container somewhere."

"You're a gem."

He winked. "As advertised," he crooned.

The sound of a guitar meandered its way to my ears, and I turned my attention to the stage. Sitting at the foot of the wooden structure, the guitarist cradled his instrument in his arms, plucking and strumming the strings in smooth motions. The music rose beautifully from the guitar, dancing with the chords the pianist sent with it, in a beautiful salsa.

The music seemed to enchant the guests as much as it had enchanted me. I watched as slowly, all around us, people began to dance between the tables, in the corners, beneath the stair-case – in any space they could find. I beamed at the sight. It was one thing to dance with your friends at a club. But to be at an event like this...

"You like to dance?"

The sound of Julius' voice reminded me he was there. I turned back to look at him, nodding with a smile.

He flashed those pearly whites. "Do you want to?"

I blinked. "Like...with you?"

He stood, offering me his hands. "*Si, señorita, conmigo,*" he replied. "*Vamanos!*"

I giggled a bit as I took his hands and he led me away from the table. Before I knew it, I was being bustled through foot-work I could barely keep up with, shimmying to and fro, spinning left and right. But I didn't care if I was bad at it, didn't care if anyone saw me stumble a couple of times. The music was good, the steps were fun, the man was striking, and I was laughing the entire time.

The salsa ended, and I clapped along with the others in the

room. "*Bueno, bebesita!*" Julius exclaimed. "You move your hips like a Colombian, you know?"

I snorted. "I doubt it."

"Hey, the hips don't lie, and I don't lie about the hips either." He waved a single finger at me. "No, no, *guapa*. Those are some fine hips, I tell you."

I rolled my eyes, but I had to bite my lip to keep my grin from exploding across my face.

I heard someone call for Julius then, and I turned to see two other young men who he appeared to know approach him excitedly. He politely excused himself to talk to them. I smiled and nodded, turning back to watch the stage.

The guitarist and the pianist began a waltz. Everyone in the room began pairing up, bringing each other in close and swaying in circles. My heart thumped with joy. Now *this* was a ball, straight out of a fairy-tale.

"It seems your dance partner has disappeared."

It took me a moment to truly recognize Felix's voice as it came from behind me, coated with a caramel silkiness I could have sworn I felt as his words breezed through the air. I turned and met his gaze, which was accompanied by a lazy grip on his champagne glass and a slouched lean against the wall. The grumpy mood I'd last seen him in had morphed into something less salty and more…honeyed.

"I think he went off with some friends," I replied.

Felix made a face, glancing away as he took a sip of his champagne – a large sip of his champagne. "I see," he said flatly.

I turned back to watch the dancers flitting across the ballroom. The swishing of fabric and the combined rhythm of everyone in the surrounding space was hypnotizing.

But then, Felix spoke again. "Well, now."

I threw a sidelong glance at him, but I could have accepted something had certainly shifted within him even if I was blind. He had set the glass of champagne down and was in the process of removing his suit jacket with quick, unhesitant motions.

"It's very unchivalrous to leave a lady without a partner in the middle of a waltz," he went on. "But given this is him we're talking about, I can't say I'm surprised."

He looked straight at me, locking my gaze with an inexplicable sort of key. "I am the better brother, after all."

I raised my eyebrows. The man before me, though he looked and sounded very much like Felix Clarkson, was not, in fact, the Felix I'd become accustomed to. The sudden and unexplained suave glaze that layered his deep, English accent, combined with the velvet in those lavender eyes, harboring famished pupils that were larger than life…

It was like the flick of a switch, and I was looking at the same face on a different man. Where he'd come from or gone so drastically, I couldn't be sure. It was as if he'd eaten – or drunk – an entirely new personality.

Though flirtatious and hungry, he didn't intimidate me. Instead, I found the shift rather…intriguing.

"The better brother?" I questioned slyly.

He didn't seem phased. "As well as the taller brother," he added. "And the bigger brother."

I let out an amused breath. "You two weigh yourselves together or what?"

"I wasn't talking about muscles," was his swift response.

I rolled my tongue around my mouth, biting back a smirk. "That's sweet. You measured each other instead."

He scoffed, dusting a speck of something off his shirt. "There was never a need for a ruler."

I threw my gaze upwards with attitude. "That's subject to opinion, don't you think?"

"There's no room for subjection to an objective fact."

"How bold of you."

The way he was staring at me felt as though I'd been

hooked on a line. "My brother doesn't play with the same toy twice, and I don't share mine."

I crossed my arms, sucking my lips. "It's a good thing women aren't toys, then."

Those lavender eyes were whirring. "Nevertheless, I think we should play a little game."

"Is this a different game than the one we've been playing since we met?"

A twisted, humoured smile. "And what would that game be?"

I shrugged my shoulders. "Cat and mouse?"

He chuckled. "Cute, indeed. But I prefer a more dignified game," he replied as he outstretched his hand towards me. "Please allow me to compensate for my brother's lack of manners."

Dance. With Felix Clarkson. At a Clarkson event. What exactly had *happened* in the last month? Didn't I move out to San Diego to study marine biology? Now I was a Phoenix Keeper, trained by the son of a wealthy CEO, propositioned to dance with him at a business event. I didn't have that one on my bingo card of life, that's for sure.

But for some reason, something about the action made the corners of my mouth twitch. "Since when do you care about rectifying your brother's mistakes?" I asked.

Felix shook his head. "Oh, I don't care to rectify any of his mistakes. But I do care to prevent me from making my own." His eyes traced every one of my features, from the top of my scalp down to my shoes on the floor, before they returned to my gaze. "Some may say it would be a mistake to let an open door close."

My lips pulled at the corners.

He glanced at his hand, then back at me. "Dance with me, kindling," he said.

It was not a question, nor a plea. It was a demand.

I let out an amused breath, and then slowly slid my hand

over top of his. As soon as I felt his skin, I felt the warmth within his touch, the burning fire beneath that coursed through his veins like rapid rivers of flames. He grasped my hand tightly, burying me in the flares as his back straightened and his eyes hardened.

He led me away from the table, far from any other dancers. Slowly and gently, as if I were glass, he then raised our joined hands up in front of us and placed his other hand on my lower back. He began waltzing us around, and I followed his lead. The movements he led me into were smooth and swift, perfectly in time with the music and always natural for me to follow. Considering he never once glanced at our feet on the floor, I found this impressive. His eyes, though fervent and active, never left mine.

After we'd been dancing for a few minutes, I became curious. "I thought you weren't much of a dancer," I noted.

He gave me a half-smile. "Much in the same way I keep telling myself I'm not a smoker. Yet the nicotine makes me do it anyways."

I returned a small smile. "How did you learn to dance?"

"My father had us taught privately," Felix replied. "So that we would be able to participate in his events." He studied me. "And you?"

"I took lessons, too. It's good exercise. And it's fun."

He nodded slowly, considering.

"Is there always dancing?" I asked.

Felix thought for a moment. "Most of the time. Somehow, music just ends up moving people."

I glanced around at the other dancers around us. "Julius offered for me to be a regular on the guest list because I liked the food so much. But I think the dancing is even better than the food."

He dipped me. "You want to come to another event?"

I shrugged when he brought me back up. "I wouldn't mind."

Felix's eyes were measuring my expression. "And you'd want to dance again?" he asked as he twirled me.

"Oh, most definitely."

He brought me back to face him. Those lavender irises were suddenly alight with a curious spark.

"With me?" he inquired in a bit of a hush.

I didn't respond right away, the music carrying our bodies as the air carried the feeling of uncharted waters. "Would you want me to dance with you again?" I queried.

Almost immediately, his gaze was up in flames. I thought I saw a tug at the corner of his lips. "I wouldn't mind," he replied.

And suddenly, I was spun so quickly I nearly lost my footing. I felt his hands grip both my shoulders as he pushed me firmly against a wall. I gasped with surprise as I felt him press up against me, one of his hands coming to rest beside me as the other supported him from above.

He leaned in so close that his lips were by my ear, his breath warm and steady as it fell on my skin. "You know, there's usually a lot of fucking at these parties, too."

The small hairs on the side of my face tingled as the scent of alcohol and cigarettes wandered to my nose like strangers in the night – an intoxication all on their own.

"Mhm," I responded. "So you were just after sex all along, weren't you?"

"I didn't say that," he retorted evenly, his lips brushing my ear lobe. "But I could devour you, if you allowed it," he whispered.

"Devour, hm?" I snickered as I slithered out from under his strong body. "That's some big talk."

He grabbed my wrist and pulled me closer to him. "I never commit to something I can't deliver."

I lowered my gaze as I studied his - if I could have painted the lavender eyes I saw, I would have coated them with insatiable, lustful hues of red. "Where's this all coming from?" I asked him slowly.

His face was vivid, unstoppable, as he brought us so close again that our foreheads were touching. "I think you and I were always destined to be complicated," he replied in what was nearly a whisper.

I exhaled with amusement. "I think complicated doesn't do it justice."

"So you admit it," he pounced immediately, his eyes flitting from my eyes to my lips and back again. "The tension that's been between us —"

I took one hand and pushed on his collarbone. "I haven't admitted anything."

He lifted his chin as he put a bit of space between us, a sneer pulling on his features. "I should have known you'd play hard to get."

I snorted. "And you'll have to try a lot harder than that," I purred.

"Harder than the attitude I've already suffered through?" he challenged.

I laughed, letting my hands and body drift from his. "Sweetheart, that was just the appetizer," I hummed as I gracefully sauntered away.

CHAPTER 19

I DANCED with several other men and ate many more delicious things before I took the opportunity to make my way up the grand staircase, gazing down at the room below. It was a perfect people-watching spot; the room was alive, and bustling, and glowing.

"Everything all right, dear?" came Luther's voice from behind me.

I turned and nodded at him with a small smile. "Absolutely. Just admiring the event."

"Ah, I see. Very good," he said, leaning against the railing beside me. "It came together well, no?"

"Very well. Everything is lovely."

"I'm glad to hear."

There was a pause.

I then looked at him. "Luther?"

He met my gaze. "Yes, m'dear?"

"I've been meaning to ask you something, but I haven't found the right place or time. It came up during my training, and Felix directed me to you."

He frowned slightly, but straightened. "I see. In that case, come. Let's go somewhere a bit quieter."

He led me out of the ballroom and back out into the corridor. At the very end, he opened a pair of double doors, and we walked into a massive library fit for a king. Dark wood wall-to-ceiling bookshelves lined three out of the four walls, leaving just the doorway we entered through. The fourth was a series of wall-to-ceiling windows that showcased Luther's fabulous garden. Books of every size and every colour filled the tremendous amount of shelves, and ladders that were attached to the shelving units but could be moved from side to side were made available to allow access to the books on the highest shelves. There must have been hundreds of thousands of books in the room. Four sofas sat forming a square in the centre of the room.

"Oh, wow," I breathed, drifting into the room and circling around myself to get a panoramic view of all the books. The thought of all the different kinds of stories resting here within the grasps of my fingers filled me with bliss. I felt like a child in a candy store, my heart racing at the sight of so many literary wonders.

My feet were drawn to the shelving on the left side of the room. On the shelf at my eye-level, I read the spines of the books aloud, filling the space created by the high ceilings with the echoes of titles.

"*To Kill a Mockingbird. Othello. Northanger Abbey. For Whom The Bell Tolls. The Picture of Dorian Grey. Jane Eyre. Lolita. The Great Gatsby. Pride and Prejudice. The Tenant of Wildfell Hall. Ulysses. The Sun Also Rises. Sense and Sensibility. As You Like It. The Importance of Being Earnest. Great Expectations. Wuthering Heights*...oh – " I involuntarily reached for Emily Brontë's masterpiece, one of my personal favourites, and ran the pages softly between my fingers – "Luther, I could spend all my years locked in here and not be bored a day of my life!"

I heard him chuckle as he closed the door behind us. "I can relate. I quite enjoy books myself, Seraphine. Now then, what were you meaning to ask me?"

I turned to face him, leaving the books on the shelves. "I apologize as this may be a bit personal."

"Nonsense, dear. You're practically family now. Go on."

I nodded. "While Felix was teaching me about Phoenixes, I asked him how Ohên had passed. He told me it was your story to tell, and it seemed to upset him. I was wondering what happened."

Luther took a deep breath in, pausing for a moment. "Ah, yes. I assumed it would come up in conversation sooner or later. Let me begin answering that by asking you this – have you noticed anything unusual in your visits here?"

I blinked. "I'm not sure I should answer that question."

He chuckled. "I won't be offended."

I considered his inquiry for a moment. "I have noticed some things that have struck me," I then responded. "For one, Julius and Felix are suspiciously unalike, in personality and appearance."

"Mhm-hmm. And anything else?"

I thought again. "*Oui.* There also seems to be an absence of women in the immediate family. I never paid much attention to the personal lives of celebrities growing up, but I will say this confuses me, as I do remember hearing about your wife from the media a few times."

"Ex-wives," he corrected.

My brows shook. "Hm?"

"I had two. Therein lies the beginning of the answer to your question," he explained, sitting down on one of the sofas as I sat across from him. "Felix and Julius are technically half-brothers. My first wife, Marlli, was Julius' mother. I met her on a business trip to Colombia, and we married. Six years after Julius was born, however, she had an affair with one of my business partners. Shortly after the divorce, I met Iliza, who I later married. She was Felix's mother, and unlike Marlli, she was also a Phoenix Keeper. The strange thing, though, is that she didn't want Felix to be one."

I frowned. "Why?"

He sighed. "She believed being a Phoenix Keeper was more detrimental than beneficial, that the responsibilities it carries outweighs and negates the advantages it provides. She was worried it would put her baby in some kind of danger, I suppose. I disagreed wholeheartedly. We fought endlessly about it, until one day, I decided I would just go about the process of making him one without her. I just thought to myself that she'd come around eventually. And so, I started telling him stories, as I had done unsuccessfully with Julius. It wasn't that I was planning to keep the entire thing a secret from her forever – I couldn't have even if I tried, as she would have sensed him. I just didn't think she would react the way she did."

I widened my eyes. "What happened?"

"Well, in stark contrast to Julius' aloofness, Felix caught on very quickly. A few months after he'd turned five, Iliza began to sense the beginnings of his bond with Fuego. When she asked me if I could feel it, though, I would lie. I told her I couldn't sense anything and didn't know what she was going on about. I made the poor woman think she was crazy for a bit there, but alas, Fuego eventually appeared to Felix, and on the same night, he hatched him. Iliza caught Felix, Fuego, Ohên, and I moments after we'd made it to the cellar. She lost it; she began screaming at me, saying how I'd betrayed her, that Felix wasn't only my son. I fought back. Somehow, someway, it escalated to the point where she attacked Fuego with what would have been fatal magic – I suppose her strategy for solving the problem was to destroy the problem." He took a deep inhalation in. "Ohên leapt in front of him, taking the blow. It was so strong with anger that it killed him."

My mouth fell open.

"I was livid with her. Felix was hysterically crying, clutching Fuego and huddling in the corner, terrified of losing his own Phoenix. I screamed at her to leave, that I never wanted to see her again. I didn't mean it as such – you know how you say things you don't mean when you get upset, hm? But it was too late; she took it to heart, clambering aboard her Phoenix and making her way out right before my eyes. It was the last time any of us saw her; the divorce papers were mailed to me shortly after."

He shook his head. "We both overreacted that night. She killed my best friend, and because of me, Felix lost his mother." He met my gaze. "It's had a horrific effect on Felix himself. I'm relieved he didn't lose Fuego – I don't know how he would have coped without him. But witnessing that drama and then going through the repercussions of his mother's abandonment has had drastic consequences on his life. He is not the same man he would have been had she not left him."

I studied Luther. "Do you wish she would've returned?"

He shrugged. "Some days I do, and some days I still believe what she did was unforgiveable."

"Do you think Felix wanted her to come back, even after seeing all that?"

"Well, he undeniably loved his mother. I don't doubt that at least a part of him misses her, and I don't think he's ever felt truly whole since she left." He paused. "I don't think he can really wrap his head around the fact that his mother never made the effort to see him again, and truthfully, it puzzles me, too."

I took this in. "I'm sorry to hear all of this."

Luther stood, giving me a small smile. "It's how the cookie crumbles, I suppose. But I do hope it answers your question."

"It did. Thank you for sharing. I recognize that must have been difficult."

"Don't worry about it. Any other questions you may have, don't hesitate to ask me. Now then, let's return to the party, shall we?"

I nodded, and we made our way back to the ballroom. When we returned, he waved goodbye to me as he climbed down the staircase towards a group of guests who were beckoning him. I remained at the top, leaning against the railing once more, my eyes drifting back out over the crowd.

"Miss Pierre?"

I turned at the sound of my name. It was Benjamin.

"Sorry to disturb you, miss," he said with a quick bow.

"Not at all," I told him. "What's up?"

"Felix had asked me to give you a message before he left," Benjamin said.

I crinkled my brows a bit. Left?

"He said he was...not feeling very well," Benjamin added a bit hesitantly at the change in my expression. "But he would like for you to enjoy the ball for as long as you wish. When you are ready to leave, you can come and find me. He asked me to give you options for departure."

"Oh, thank you. That's very kind," I replied. "What are my options, if you don't mind my asking?"

Benjamin gave me a curt smile. "Well, it would be my pleasure to drive you home. Or – " he cleared his throat " – Felix suggested that you may experience what he coined as 'a change of heart,' and wish to accompany him at his residence for the evening. I can drive you there as well."

I eyed him, but really, I was seeing straight through him. My mind raced in a frenzy as I became aware of the opportunity that had just fallen into my lap.

"You know what," I said, smiling innocently to conceal my mischief. "I *have* had a change of heart. And I think I'm ready to leave now."

The butler nodded once. "As you wish. To Felix's villa, I presume?"

"Please," I replied.

He motioned for me to follow him, and the smirk was hard to keep off my face as I meandered through the crowd in his footsteps.

CHAPTER 20

As Benjamin pulled up to Felix's villa, I peered through the windows. The lights in the foyer seemed to be off.

"Here you are, miss," the butler said as the car came to a stop. "He mentioned he would leave the door unlocked."

I beamed at him. "Thank you so much for the ride."

"Of course." He nodded once at me as I stepped outside the vehicle. "I hope you have a pleasant rest of your evening."

"Oh, I will," I replied as I shut the door. As he drove away, I turned and headed into Felix's villa.

There was no one in the foyer – in fact, the house seemed incredibly still. I waited a few moments to gauge if I could hear any signs of movement. When silence was all that returned, I hastily took off my heels and hurried towards the door to the garden.

I managed to make it all the way to the room with Echo and Narcissus without running into anyone, throwing a glance behind me before I quietly made my way back outside. I rushed down the all-too familiar path as swiftly and silently as a cat. When I reached the cellar, I softly pried open the door, checking over my shoulder once more to make sure I hadn't been followed. Then, I slowly climbed down the stairs, and upon peering into the room, I was pleased to see Felix wasn't with the Phoenixes.

Excitedly, I greeted Aurora, and after finding the remote for the skylight, I hopped on her back and had us flying out into the night.

It was difficult to find Alchnost's property in the night, but eventually, enough retracing of our previous flight led me to the house and its odd shed.

I attempted to sense Alchnost, but I couldn't seem to tune into his presence. There were no lights on anywhere throughout the property. I assumed he must be out.

I coasted Aurora to a graceful landing outside the shed. After dismounting, I slowly made my way to the door and pushed gently on it. It creaked open. I smiled to myself.

Peeking through the slight crack in the doorway, I couldn't see or feel any movement coming from within. I pushed the doorway open and used my magic to create a small ball of light, which dimly lit the room. Aurora and I entered it slowly.

It looked pretty much identical to the last I'd seen it. I made my way to the corkboard, but it didn't seem like anything on it had changed. I glanced around the room and spotted it – *The Legend of Sedaurea.*

Lifting it as if it might break, I carefully brushed away a small layer of dust and pried the book open, skimming through the pages. It was too much to read here – I had to take it with me. I knew it was wrong. But I couldn't resist. I'd already broken into the shed. Might as well leave with the thing that drove me to break and enter.

I closed the book decidedly, turned, and came face to face with Alchnost.

"Oh!" I gasped in surprise, stumbling backwards. I nearly dropped the book in the process.

Alchnost snickered. "The thief is the one surprised? How cute." Behind him, I could see Oscuro's red eyes lingering amongst the mound of ebony feathers.

I cleared my throat, my heart racing. "I-I was just so curious – "

"You really didn't strike me as a kleptomaniac," Alchnost interrupted, looking down at me with a sneer. "But you did strike me as foolishly naïve. To make your way back here despite your little friend's trepidation – and not only that, but alone!"

He laughed. I grew even more unsettled. Aurora let out a few panicked screeches, to which Oscuro growled.

"Well, you've done most of the hard work, getting yourself here and all," Alchnost went on. "But I can take it from here. Given I won't have to worry about your counterpart getting a little too adventurous, rest assured I'll be free of any meddling in my quest after tonight."

My brain wasn't working properly. I didn't know how to defend myself. Anything Felix had taught me about my light magic seemed to be slipping from my mind. I glanced around frantically – there was nowhere to run.

An eerie orb of dark magic formed in Alchnost's hand, and before I could react, it was hurtling at my face. I instinctively raised my arm to block it, and it collided with such a force that it knocked me off my feet. I yelped as a stinging sensation spread from the area of impact, my head and back hitting the ground hard. Twisted and gnarled shadows burst out in front of me like fireworks as the dark magic exploded against my skin. I screamed as the shadows pierced my body, bringing such horrid sensation as they etched their way into my arm. The Legend of Sedaurea flew from my hands.

I didn't have much time to straighten before another dark-ened orb smashed into my stomach. I shrieked and arched backwards, the pain shooting through my veins. The shadows seeped into the fabric of my dress like snakes, darkening to a charcoal black and sparking in different directions with a sizzling sound. I could hear Aurora screeching as she and Oscuro squabbled. I couldn't believe my actions. I'd killed us both.

I hopelessly glanced upright to see Alchnost forming another dark orb. I tried to muster any strength to form a ball of light. But it faded and flustered until it burnt out, my hands shaking with resounding pain. I had no fight in me.

And just when I'd completely given up, there was a flame.

It appeared in the center of the room, catching Alchnost and I both by surprise. And then it grew, and grew larger, and as it began to overtake the wooden structure, the ceiling came crashing down.

I gasped and shielded my face as the wood came toppling on top of me. There was pandemonium as the fire enveloped the building, and as I turned, I could make out bright red feathers amid all the chaos.

Relief flooded through me. Felix leapt from Fuego's back, grabbing a stunned Alchnost by the neck and slamming him harshly into the wall. I saw a flurry of punches amongst the flames, but the billowing smoke and growing heat made it hard to watch for long. I coughed harshly and turned my eyes away from the scorching fire, spotting The Legend of Sedaurea untouched in the corner.

I tried to stand, but I became aware then that my legs were buried in toppled wood. Determinedly, I twisted my body and pulled myself closer to the book, clenching my teeth as nearly every part of my body rang with pain. I eventually managed to snatch it and held it to my chest, wincing as it made contact with my injured stomach. Seconds later, I felt the heaviness of the wood loosen, and turned to see Felix yanking wood and flinging it backwards. When my legs were free, he grabbed me harshly from underneath both my arms and pulled me upwards.

"Get out now!" he yelled at me.

I frantically searched the burning room. Aurora was heading right over to me, screeching. I stumbled on to her, collapsing and writhing in pain. She made up for my lack of form with readjustment in hers, and within moments, we were soaring out of the hole in the roof, the book clutched tightly between my arms. I glanced backwards just in time to see Felix and Fuego rushing out of the building as the smoke and fire swallowed it whole.

I turned back to stare into darkness as we flew through the night. I had a chance to catch my breath for the first time in what had felt like a long time. As the adrenaline started to wear off, the pain became stronger and more overpowering. I was sore and overheating. I had aches and pains all over. As the wind slapped me, I could feel it hitting bare skin where the fire had burned holes in my clothes.

We landed messily in the cellar. I clambered off Aurora's back, shaking, and I was so weak that I couldn't keep myself up on all fours. I fell to the ground, crying out in pain as my body made contact with the floor. The only thing I could keep a grip on was the book.

I felt Felix suddenly at my side. "What hurts? Where does it hurt?"

"Everything!" I exclaimed, and I could feel tears streaming down my cheeks. "Everything hurts!"

I felt him reach underneath me, and I winced when he lifted me into his arms. I cried as he carried me out from the cellar and into the garden.

"You're so bloody stupid," he muttered. "I can't believe you would do that. You are so incredibly fucking stupid."

The fact that he was being so harsh didn't help my tears. Gone was the man who'd made peace with me, who'd wanted me to wear a burgundy dress, who'd danced with me earlier that evening, who suggested he devour me. Instead, I was being carried by the truculent arse I'd met in my physics lab. It was frightening how intense the disparity was. How many Felix Clarksons could there be?

I kept crying as he rushed me inside the villa and through a few rooms I'd never been in at the back of the house. We ended up in a luxurious bathroom, complete with a soaker tub, which he lowered me into.

"Give me that," he instructed, yanking The Legend of Sedaurea from my hands. "I need to get as much of your skin exposed as possible, to see the injuries."

Before I could process what this meant, he was unzipping my dress and pulling it off. I didn't resist much because any thought of relief from the pain hindered my ability to consider whether I was comfortable with Felix seeing me without clothes. He tossed the small purse I had thrown over my shoulder away and left my bra and underwear on, studying my skin quickly and pausing over my forearm.

I glanced down and was shocked to see it was darkened with a black marking; at the place of impact was an inky, vile orb, from which stemmed fading layers of black rays. It almost appeared to depict a blackened sun. Wisps of shadows lifted from my skin, waning mere inches from my arm as they poisoned the air around my hideous new stain.

"He hit you with magic?" he asked.

I nodded, sniffling. "On my stomach, too."

He quickly looked down at my stomach. I did, too. No marking there – but a hefty bruise.

"Your dress must have prevented a blotch there." He sighed and turned on the bath water without so much as a warning, which I would have appreciated considering the water was freezing cold. The obscene marking sizzled, the shadows hissing with what sounded like repulsion as they vanished back to wherever they came from.

I yelped at the sensation, to which Felix shrugged. "It's

going to suck. Unfortunately, it's how you deal with swelling," he explained. He kept a watchful eye on the marking, though, as the water continued pouring – I had a feeling he didn't quite expect a reaction from it.

When I was shivering in a tub full of what felt like ice, Felix turned off the water. "Stay in there," he said, standing. "I'll be back. I need to get something."

"Okay," I said quietly, and he disappeared through the doorway.

I glanced around uncomfortably. The bathroom was entirely white – tiles, marble, fixtures, everything. It seemed so pristine and untouched that I could believe Felix if he were to tell me I was the first person to ever set foot in the tub. Somehow, I felt very guilty about dirtying the space and energy of the room. I felt the same sort of shame when I looked down at what I'd let happen to my body.

And yet, when I glanced over at the book that Felix had set to the side, the remorse subsided. I had it now. The adventure was mine if I wanted it. And despite the pain, I couldn't deny how intrigued I still was about what could be explored and uncovered.

Felix returned with two bottles – one of an anti-inflammatory cream, and one of Macallan. He sat down beside the tub with both, and opened the bottle of whiskey. I stared at him as he took a long swig.

"I thought you'd left the party because you weren't feeling very well," I said bluntly.

"That is true."

I blinked. "Is alcohol going to help?"

He laughed almost manically – it wasn't a pleasant sound. "Oh, no. Alcohol will most likely make it much, much worse. But I've just killed a man." He shrugged. "The treatment for that takes precedent over my…other issues."

I stared at him. What may have happened to Alchnost hadn't occurred to me.

"You really think…?"

Felix took another long, hard sip as he avoided eye contact. "The building collapsed seconds after we were out. I didn't see him escape, so he must be."

It took me a minute to process this. As much as I was thankful to be alive, it wasn't necessarily in my plans for Alchnost to die, either. "I'm sorry I made you do that."

Felix didn't respond. He simply kept drinking the whiskey in large, slow gulps.

I glanced at The Legend of Sedaurea. "But hey, I did manage to get – "

"Oh, would you give it a bloody rest already?" Felix snapped, turning angrily to glare at me. "Your adventure is over, you hear me?"

I frowned. "But I just got the book! I haven't even started!"

He rolled his eyes, huffing. "Miss Pierre, you're literally sitting with injuries in my tub of freezing water right now. Can you not see that this has gotten a little out of hand?"

I shook my head. "Isn't the whole point of burning to rise from the ashes?"

He laughed mockingly. "Oh, for fuck's sakes," he responded, taking another swig. "You really ought to stop chasing death."

I watched how his face scrunched slightly when he swallowed the whiskey, how his fingers clutched the glass bottle in a way that suggested it may escape him. I eyed his features and how he worked hard to control them, how he fought to hide something underneath them. I was silently pondering him for so long that, eventually, he met my gaze.

I looked down at the bottle, then back up into the lavender. "I don't think I'm the one chasing death here."

He squinted at me, and then turned away. "I'm here to live. Not to survive."

"And why do you think you can stop me from doing the same?"

"You heard what my father said as well as I did."

"I get to make my own choices, same as you. At no point did I say you shouldn't listen to your father, even if I choose not to."

He shook his head. "This is not in your best interest, Miss Pierre. You should know better."

I scoffed. "What the hell is this? You're not my dad!"

He didn't answer. He simply stood and made his way over to the book, picking it up slowly. He ran his hands over the cover, shaking his head. Then he made for the door.

"Where are you going with that?" I demanded.

"Putting it away," he answered without looking at me.

"That's mine!" I exclaimed.

"Forget about it, Miss Pierre."

"It's not for you to decide what I do!" I shouted, stumbling upwards into a pathetic attempt at standing. He ignored my movement, continuing out of the room. There was no way I would catch up with him, let alone fight for it, given my current state.

"I'll trade you!" I suggested desperately.

He stopped in the doorway. I was surprised he did, given I didn't even know what it was I could offer him that he didn't already have, or that he couldn't buy for himself.

Slowly, he turned to frown at me. "Trade me?" he asked.

I nodded frantically. "Anything you want," I added, not really understanding the gravity of what that meant until the words left my mouth.

He looked me up and down. Then he walked back to me. He stopped on the other side of the tub, bringing his face mere inches from mine. His breath bore that whiskey he'd drank like water and a cigarette he must have had recently, for the scents were fresh and inebriating. The only thing I could really see written on his face was a stern, unbreakable displeasure.

He stared at me for a long time. His eyes travelled down my

exposed body, lingering over the injuries, and then slowly meandered their way back to my own.

Then, he scoffed. "All right, then."

To my surprise, he bent down and snatched my purse. I frowned as he reached inside, rummaged around, and eventually pulled out the Eiffel Tower keychain I'd thrown in there a few days ago. He tossed my purse down to the ground and turned back to me. Forcefully, he shoved the book in my hands.

"Your funeral, kindling," he muttered angrily. He then turned on one foot and left the room, burying the keychain in his pocket as he marched away and slammed the door shut behind him.

CHAPTER 21

I DIDN'T QUITE KNOW what to do with myself. I stood dripping over the bathtub for a long time, dreading any sort of movement for fear of the pain it might cause. Eventually, I forced myself out of the cold water and onto the plush mat outside. Leaving a trail of water behind me, I searched the bathroom cabinets to eventually find some luxurious, white towels. I draped myself in them gingerly, feeling a stinging sensation as the material met my burns. When I was somewhat dry, I slowly sat at the edge of the tub and grabbed the cream Felix had left. Gently, I began applying it to my bruises.

"Miss Seraphine Pierre?" I heard from outside the door. "Are you in there?"

"I am," I called back.

"Are you decent?"

"As much as I can be, but do come in."

Francis entered through the doorway. "Miss Pierre, I've been advised you'll be spending the night here. I've had a room prepared for you, and I can show you to it if you're ready."

"Oh," I said, taken aback. "Sure. Thank you."

I grabbed The Legend of Sedaurea and followed Francis slowly out of the doorway, trying not to make it obvious that I was injured or carrying a book that may contain the possible location of Phoenixes. He led me to the second floor of the house and into a beautiful, neutral-coloured guest bedroom with a matching ensuite. There was a robe folded neatly on the bed accompanied with some chocolates. I felt like I had checked in to a luxury hotel.

"Please make yourself at home, and don't hesitate to let me know if you need anything," Francis told me.

"Thank you so much," I replied, and he nodded before scurrying off.

I closed the door behind him and slipped out of the towels, draping myself in the robe instead. I put the precious book by the bedside table before I walked into the bathroom, where a fresh tube of toothpaste and a toothbrush awaited me by one of the two glorious sinks. There were also several different creams, moisturizers, and oils available to me. I brushed my teeth and applied a combination of skincare – mainly driven by how much I liked the scent – to my face. Then I went back into the room, shut off the light, and lay down hesitantly in the bed.

The only position that was comfortable for me was on my back. My legs still ached. My stomach pinged with pain. Sleep eventually came, but it was the kind of sleep where it felt like a nightmare I couldn't escape. The soreness seemed to have infiltrated my thoughts. That being said, it wasn't easy for me to wake up. There was a depth to the uneasy rest. I felt like I was in purgatory.

As my dreadful sleep carried on, I thought I heard voices wafting through the window, but I couldn't be entirely sure that they weren't a part of my dreams.

- F -

"She's gone completely mad!"

I was livid, trying my best to convey the seriousness of the matter while still being quiet enough that an eavesdropper wouldn't hear. My gardens were quiet this early in the morning, and that left opportunities for wandering words. The only ones awake to hear those words, though, were probably my father and me. My father was a bit of an early riser. I, on the other hand…well, I didn't sleep very much on a good day, and this was certainly *not* a good day.

"Some might call it passion," was my father's reply. I couldn't understand why he wasn't more concerned about what I'd just explained to him. Miss Pierre had nearly killed herself in pursuit of that damned book, and she still wouldn't give up on the idea that left her bruised and battered.

"It's stupidity, that's what it is," I hissed, waving off his previous words.

"I wouldn't dismiss it so punitively, son," Father replied, still ridiculously calm. "She sees things differently than you do. That doesn't mean either way is wrong."

"Let me remind you that you also thought it was a bad idea," I said.

"Why, of course. I'm entitled to my own opinions. But my opinions aren't law."

I huffed in frustration, rolling my eyes. "There's got to be a way for me to get that bloody book from her and put an end to this."

"I think that would be wrong of you," my father cautioned.

"Wrong?" I challenged. "Wrong to be the voice of reason?"

"Wrong to try and influence what she does," Father corrected.

I scoffed. "Even if it's for her own benefit?"

"You only think it's for her benefit. You don't know that for sure."

"Father," I snapped. "I do know that for sure. I witnessed the consequences of her actions firsthand."

"Sure, but you don't know what happens next. Nobody does. None of us can see into the future."

"Since when did you become so philosophical?"

He ignored my snarky statement and shook his head slowly. "You cannot control people. Especially not a woman, and even more so a woman like her." He looked at me. "If you try to stop her, she'll only resist more, you know."

I let out a groan and pulled out a cigarette, coming to a stop on my garden path. "You're no help," I muttered as I discreetly lit it with the tip of my finger and inhaled sharply.

The fix only slightly eased my nerves. I puffed the nicotine in and out slowly, watching the leaves on one of the trees move slightly in the soft wind as I tried to supress my irritation. When it was proving to be a fruitless task, I turned back to face my father. To my astonishment, he was watching me with a smile.

I squinted at him. "What's that look for?"

He wasn't phased. "This seems like an awful lot of fuss over a woman who's wellbeing you recently claimed not to care about."

I gave him a baffled, almost insulted stare. No – this was between me, myself, and I. The last thing I wanted was anyone getting involved with my emotions, especially when it came to her.

"Whatever you're trying to suggest is not only absurd, but vastly misguided," I snapped at him. "I couldn't care less what she does. I just don't want to be held responsible for any short-comings or unfortunate accidents, and I certainly don't want to keep finding myself in the middle of her disasters, either."

My father chuckled. "That's a well-worded excuse that any other person may believe," he retorted. "A person besides the man who raised you."

He placed a hand on my shoulder. "Don't forget that you're

my son," he said. "And I've no reason to make suggestions where I've made observations. Perhaps you should reconsider the true reasoning behind your concerns."

I pushed his hand away, narrowing my eyes. "I'm telling you that you're wrong."

He only shrugged once as he turned back to head the way we came. "And I'm telling you that I'm not, in much the same way I wasn't wrong about the smell of tobacco on your clothing when you were seventeen."

I didn't have a chance to reply before he walked away, the smoke from my cigarette billowing all around me like a shroud of fog.

- S -

When my eyes fluttered open next, the pain had morphed into an excruciating soreness. I groaned as I fumbled myself upwards, trying to find a comfortable seated position in bed. When that proved impossible, I muttered frustratedly to myself and slowly swung my legs over to the side of the mattress, forcing myself to stand. Sure, I was sore, but I wasn't dead. I glanced at the bedside table and was pleased to see The Legend of Sedaurea was still there.

I hobbled over to the adjacent ensuite, flicking on the light. My face looked worse for wear in the mirror. Underneath the robe, there were bruises and small nicks I could have done without. I turned my attention to my forearm; the shadows were gone, but the black marking sat like a proud intrusion, prominent as ever. I frowned as I scrubbed at my skin; there was no pain, but no sign of it lifting, either. It almost seemed like a tattoo – a dreary, ugly tattoo.

I sighed as I dug into my bag and found some extra

strength pain medication, swallowing them graciously before I looked around. I quickly concluded that my dress was nowhere to be found. I tied the robe back up and was going to settle for wearing it out of the room when I noticed colour in the closet on the other side of the bathroom. Curious, I made my way into the walk-in to see a few dresses hung in an otherwise empty room – and a large one, at that.

I thought it strange that Felix would have dresses in his home as I approached one sundress that had sunflowers on it. I ran my fingers over the fabric. It seemed like an older style of dress, but it had been very well taken care of. I decidedly plucked it from the hanger and held it up to my person. It seemed like it would fit, so I undid its front buttons and draped it over me. It did fit – a nearly perfect fit, in fact.

I shrugged and made my way out of the bedroom into the hall, The Legend of Sedaurea in my hand. The house was still. I located the winding front staircase and descended slowly, trying not to strain my sore legs. When I reached the bottom, I followed the same route through mirrored rooms that Felix and I had taken many times to get to the garden.

I entered the room with Echo and Narcissus. I couldn't help but stop at the photograph for a moment. The pain in Echo's eyes was one that stemmed from sacrifice. And Narcissus could see pain looking back at himself, a self-induced injury to the soul. It was difficult to say which was worse.

I looked down at my arm, at the marking now etched in my skin. I ran my fingers daintily over it, then over the rest of my bruises, studying how different levels of pressure caused different levels of pain. I sighed and turned for the doorway, and I could see Felix through the glass, standing in the garden.

He was staring at me, his face weary. His brows furrowed ever so slightly as I opened the door and stepped outside. As I moved towards him, he never once let his eyes stray from me. He seemed focused on the sundress, and he watched it flutter with the breeze that came after each step.

When I stopped a little ways from him, he met my gaze. Felix had become a little easier to read since I'd continued getting to know him, and I'd learned the secret to translating him was to be the last to break. I could feel the torrent of emotions in his eyes as they gushed through the space left between us, filling it with a tension so strong it was almost impermeable. But it wasn't enough to convince me that the fire I had inside me wasn't just as strong.

I suppose he cracked first, because eventually, he lowered his face – first back down to the dress, and then further down to the ground beneath us. "I am glad you are feeling well enough to dress, but you shouldn't snoop in other people's things," he mumbled as he fidgeted in his pocket.

"I couldn't find my clothes," I replied bluntly.

He produced a cigarette, lit it with a flame from his finger, and puffed on it slowly. "Your Phoenix is unharmed," he went on simply, glancing at my marked forearm. "As for that…I'm not sure how to remove it."

I swallowed, crossing my arms so that the eerie tattoo was hidden.

He cleared his throat. "Let me know when you want to go home."

For the brief second his eyes flickered to mine, I thought I could see something like…pain.

Before I could respond, he walked away, towards another part of the garden. I watched the trail of smoke waft behind him as he disappeared into greenery and flowers.

I let my thoughts linger with the faint smell of tobacco as I continued towards the cellar. When I made it down, I approached Aurora and gave her a thorough look. Felix was right – she didn't appear to be injured.

I sighed with relief as I sat down beside her. "I'm glad you're okay," I told her as I gave her some loving scratches. "Last night was unreal. I'm sorry – I should have planned that better."

She nuzzled my hand once, throwing a curious gaze at The Legend of Sedaurea in my other hand.

I glanced at it, too. "I'm a little banged up at the moment, but I want to keep at it when I'm better," I went on. "There's something to this...I just feel it."

She cooed, and I felt her nudge one of my bruises.

I smiled at her. "If I promise to be more careful, are you in?"

She chirped and nodded quickly.

My smile morphed into a grin. "Glad you like adventure as much as I do."

Aurora shifted her bright eyes to the other corner of the room. I followed her line of sight to Fuego, who was watching us both carefully.

I gave him a somber look. "I'm sorry to you, too."

Fuego fluffed his feathers, tossing his neck towards the seating area. I frowned a bit in confusion as I stood slowly, making my way over to where he'd motioned.

As I neared, I noticed there were some things strewn about on the coffee table. There was an empty whiskey bottle. There was another whiskey bottle, but this one was only half-empty. And then, there was the keychain Felix had traded me for The Legend of Sedaurea.

I stared at the items for a moment before I turned to look at Fuego again. His eyes were on me, contemplative and soft. He made a movement that resembled a shrug.

I cleared my throat and took a deep breath in as I faced a feeling I didn't want to admit to. Then, I decidedly nodded once at Fuego, grabbed the book, and made for the cellar staircase.

When Felix eventually found me in his kitchen, he appeared to be a mix of puzzled and startled. "What are you – "

I held up the apple crumble I'd made with the recipe my mom had taught me long ago as well as the ingredients and bakeware in his kitchen. "Your repayment, as previously discussed," I announced to him.

He stared at me, and I watched the corners of his mouth twitch. "My repayment, or my apology?"

"Don't play semantics. Just eat."

"So…you used my stuff to make the debt you owe me?"

"Do you want the dessert or not?"

He swirled his tongue around his mouth to keep from smiling. "I was a fool to think you'd be any less mouthy while injured," he replied as he grabbed himself a fork.

"Because I'm trying to be nice here, I will not comment on that statement," I said.

"How very kind." He took the apple crumble from me and sampled a large bite, chewing it slowly. His eyebrows rose a bit when he swallowed.

I watched him expectantly. "Well?"

He nodded slowly as he dug up another forkful. "It's delicious," he said. "Tastes like a mother made it with love for her children. Yours will be very lucky – " he eyed me " – though I must admit I sympathize with their father regarding your attitude."

I kissed my teeth. "I'll let that one slide, too."

He stifled a chuckle. "So it seems I'm not the only one who is terrible at apologizing."

I scoffed. "You got the apple crumble, didn't you?"

"Sure, sure. But I didn't hear anything along the lines of – " he pretended to be deep in thought " – oh, what's that word? Could it be something like…sorry?"

I crossed my arms. "Don't even get me started on the apology I am not demanding from you."

He gave me a bewildered expression. "From *me?*"

"For yelling at me, and for trying to fuck me before that."

Felix's eyes doubled in size as he choked on his mouthful. "I beg your ever-loving pardon?" he spat. "I tried to do *what?*"

"Don't pretend you don't remember."

"I absolutely do not recall such a thing."

I laughed with no hint of delight. "That's convenient, now isn't it?"

He held his hands up defensively. "I would tell you if I did. But truthfully, I'm hungover as all hell and I haven't really slept, so my memory is as good as rubbish at the moment."

I rolled my eyes, exhaling with exhaustion. "Sounds like excuses to me."

Felix cleared his throat and took another bite of the crumble. "Well, I do apologize if I came on to you in my drunken stupor."

"*If?*"

"I told you I don't remember."

I rolled my tongue around my cheeks. "How evasive."

He frowned at me. "You got your apology."

"I'm smart enough to know what a pathetic, half-ass attempt at a conditional apology is, Felix."

He stared at me, then shook his head rapidly as he turned away. I watched as he consciously avoided eye contact with me and the forkfuls of apple crumble became bigger, occupying his mouth longer as he chewed erratically.

I turned to look at my nails as I flexed one hand. "You know what else I'm smart enough to know?"

I could feel his gaze fall back to me.

"That drunk minds speak sober thoughts," I went on, my eyes flickering up to challenge his.

His eyes narrowed as he lifted his chin, placing the fork and half-eaten apple crumble down on the counter. "Is that wishful thinking I hear?"

I cackled. "Get over yourself."

His eyes traced my face as I returned a sneer, his posture

becoming tensed as he stood up taller, broader. And as we stared at each other, I took in the exhaustion that creased the lines of his face, the dullness to his skin. In his eyes, there was defeat, like he'd lost a game he'd wanted desperately to win. Something had been awakened in him at the party last night, but it slumbered now, nowhere to be seen.

I still couldn't comprehend what had summoned such an altered personality and shut it out all within a night.

He eventually let out a breath and tore his gaze away from mine, pushing away the remaining dessert. "I suppose I should save some for the next time you nearly get us both killed?" he said with a pinch of salt.

I shook my head firmly. "Nobody told you to come help me. That was entirely your choice."

He sighed. "I'll take that as a yes, Little Miss Adventure," he muttered as he motioned for me to follow him. "Let's get you to the university."

CHAPTER 22

"WHAT THE HELL HAPPENED TO YOU?"

The harsh question came from Emmanuella, who – along with the rest of my friends – looked at me in shock as I entered the lounge. The dress I'd borrowed from Felix did not do a very good job of hiding my marked forearm or my other injuries, and I assumed my face still bore the wear of my hellish night, so I couldn't really blame them.

"I fell," I lied.

"Off a cliff?" Roscoe added.

"Down a flight of stairs," I replied, rubbing my eyes with my hand. "I was drunk at a party."

"Well, I would hope so," Keiffer snickered. "Otherwise, that's just embarrassing."

"Says the man baby with the cheese fetish."

Chenoa snorted as Sajan coughed into his hand to keep from laughing.

"Hey," Keiffer warned, shaking a finger at me. "Don't judge, stair assaulter."

"I didn't assault – " I took a breath. " – Whatever."

"Come, sit down," Elijah said as he stood and offered me his spot on the sofa. "I'll get you something to eat."

"Thanks, Eli."

As he went into the kitchen, Emmanuella made a mocking kissy face at me. I stuck my tongue out back at her.

"Did you get a new tattoo while you were drunk?" Hakeem asked, nodding at my forearm.

...Sure, I guess that works.

I huffed loudly. "Apparently."

"What is it a tattoo of, exactly?" Myra asked, studying it with a frown.

"Your guess is as good as mine."

"Looks like an eclipse," Roscoe noted, coming in to get a close look. "Like when the moon passes in front of the sun."

"Maybe drunk me is an astronomer," I mumbled.

Suddenly, the door to the lounge opened. Felix appeared in the doorway, holding the dress I'd worn to the ball.

"Miss Pierre, you forgot your – "

He stopped as all my friends turned to stare at him – arguably with more bafflement than when they'd seen me waltz in with my injuries. "Oh," he said. "Hello, everyone."

Nobody returned the greeting. Instead, they all slowly turned to look inquisitively at me.

I cleared my throat. "Hi," I said to him, my brain scrambling to come up with some kind of explanation. "Thank you for, uh, getting that cleaned after I...puked all over it."

He nodded slowly, his eyes flickering to my friends' faces. "It was covered in a lot of vomit," he confirmed.

Emmanuella frowned at him. "You guys went to the same party?"

I eyed Felix, who eyed me back. "No. Well, yes...sort of," Felix answered unconvincingly. "We didn't go together, per se. I just ran into her...by happenstance – "

"He found me at the bottom of the stairs after I fell," I interjected quickly. "And, uh, puked. A lot."

"It was a lot," Felix added.

I laughed nervously. "So embarrassing. Anyways – "

I motioned for him to toss me the dress, and he did so hurriedly. "Thanks again for helping me out," I told him.

"Don't mention it," he said, waving at the group. "Goodbye, everyone."

As soon as he was gone, Emmanuella whipped around to face me. "So you forgave him for making you fail your first lab or what?"

"*That's* the lab partner that made you fail?" Elijah piped up from behind the kitchen counter.

"You didn't know Felix Clarkson was her lab partner?" Emmanuella directed towards him.

"Felix Clarkson?" Sajan exclaimed. "*That's* Felix Clarkson? That businessman's son?"

"Yeah," Roscoe noted. "You didn't recognize him?"

"To be fair, he's kind of elusive if you're not really tuned in to the business world," Myra commented. "Or if he doesn't unexpectedly show up in your chemistry lab," she added, looking over at me.

I sighed, rubbing my face with my hands as I tried to avoid the bombardment of chatter. "Guys, he just happened to be there yesterday and got me straightened out. Would you all chill?"

Keiffer snickered. "Poor guy had to deal with your pukey, drunk ass, huh?"

"That was nice of him to get your dress cleaned, at least," Everly said with a shrug.

Emmanuella eyed the dress. "That's a pretty fancy dress for a college party."

I glanced down at the pile of fabric in my hands. "It was a Gatsby theme," I fibbed.

"That's fun," Chenoa mentioned. "Sounds like you had quite the night."

I threw my head back with a groan. "You wouldn't believe the half of it," I muttered tiredly.

I spent the rest of the weekend resting, and my classes at the beginning of the week enveloped me in assignments that made them fly by quickly. I pawned through parts of The Legend of Sedaurea when I could, but the pieces I read didn't provide any more information than what Alchnost had already revealed to us. I would need to go through the ancient text in its entirety to determine if I was missing anything, and given its thickness, that would take me a lot more perusing.

By Wednesday, I was feeling much better, and my bruises had subsided tremendously. As I walked into my physics lab, Felix nodded at me in acknowledgement – the first I'd seen him since the dress return fiasco.

"Vomited at the bottom of anymore stairs this weekend?" he teased as I set my stuff down.

"Fuck off," I sniped at him. "I was covering my tracks."

"Forgive me for my lack of empathy when it comes to the trouble *you* got yourself into." He glanced at my arm. "You seem better, at least – except for that wonderful new addition to your arm, of course."

"I am better. And you wanted me to face consequences for my actions, so here's the consequences," I told him, tapping the marking. "Anyways, I miss Aurora. Can I come by tonight?"

He shrugged. "Sure. But can we avoid anything chaotic?"

I groaned. "Such a bore."

He eyed me firmly.

I sighed, rolling my eyes. "Fine. No chaos. I promise."

We began going through the motions of our lab, during which Lucah came around with our work from the previous week. "Well done, Seraphine and Felix!" he exclaimed as he handed back our marked reports and hurried off to the next group.

A glance at the top of my page showed I'd scored an 87%. My eyes widened as I gasped. "Felix! Look!"

Felix peeked over my shoulder. "Well, congratulations," he said with a small smile. "Your hard work certainly paid off."

I squealed. "I can't believe it! It must have been all the help I got from you and Elijah!"

"Me and who?"

"The guy I'm seeing – he's a physics major," I exclaimed as I hurriedly shoved the graded report into my bag. "I can't wait to show him – he'll be so proud."

Felix turned back to the lab we were working on, his smile thinning. "Right," he noted plainly as he cleared his throat. "… That he will."

We finished the lab relatively quickly. I stopped by my dorm and grabbed The Legend of Sedaurea before meeting Felix by his Ferrari in the parking lot.

Upon sight of the old book, he shook a finger at me. "I thought we agreed on no chaos."

"Since when is reading chaos?" I retorted.

He gave me an accusatory expression. "May I remind you – "

"No. I'm sick of your reminders," I interrupted. "Stop trying to tell me what to do."

He sighed as he unlocked the car. "I won't be surprised if I find your picture next to the definition of 'stubborn' in the dictionary."

"I prefer persistent," I corrected as we sat down in the vehicle.

"…I think it's more along the lines of inflexible."

I shook my head. "Determined or persevering is more like it."

"I could settle for dogged."

I glared at him. The corners of his lips twitched, but his amused smirk never took full form as he started the car and began driving.

When we made it to the cellar, we greeted our Phoenixes and promptly took them out to fly. Our little excursion took several hours; by the time we made it back to the estate, the sun was beginning to set.

"That was a nice ride," Felix noted as he dismounted Fuego.

"Definitely," I agreed, patting Aurora's neck as I swung my leg over her back and hopped down. She cooed before settling into a sit and starting to preen.

As Felix started preparing some crushed palms, I walked over to the bookshelf full of Phoenix-related material. I studied the spines for a long while, eventually concluding that there wasn't anything blatantly related to Sedaurea or a 'City of the Sun.' I sat on the sofa and thought for a moment, then pulled out my phone.

I did a quick Google Search for 'City of the Sun.' I didn't expect anything about Phoenixes or sanctuaries to come up. But what it did bring up was a book by Tommaso Campanella with the same title.

I raised an eyebrow, clicking on the link. The philosopher had written the book after he'd been imprisoned for ideas opposing orthodox religious doctrine and encouraging rebellion against the monarchy. An interesting guy with an interesting mind – the book essentially detailed his idea of a theocratic society, and a prophecy that the Spanish kings and Pope were destined to be a part of some Divine Plan, where True Faith would rein victorious and seep into the world. The work was published in 1602.

I pondered this for a moment, and then did a search for Tommaso Campanella himself. He was born in 1568 in the Kingdom of Naples. A picture of his house at Stignano even came up – there seemed to be a plaque marking the location at the door.

I stared at the photo. I couldn't tell if I'd found a clue or a coincidence, but I knew there was only one way to find out.

"I'm going to Italy," I announced bluntly, standing up off the couch.

Felix, who was still in the process of making the Phoenix's food, whipped around. "What the bloody hell do you mean, you're going to Italy?"

I showed him my phone. "This philosopher guy published a book called 'The City of the Sun,' and his house is in Stignano. It might have something – "

"Miss Pierre," Felix interjected, shutting his eyes with frustration. "You. Promised. No. Chaos."

"A trip to Italy isn't chaos."

"Right – that is, until you get lost, or you get mugged, or you run into some ungodly predicament related to this…*disastrous* quest you're chasing for reasons I just cannot comprehend."

"None of those are guaranteed to happen. There's an equal chance I could find what I'm looking for."

"For the love of all that is holy, would you please just – "

"*Felix*," I barked, lifting my chin with my voice. "Enough."

He blinked in surprise at my loudness, my firmness.

I stood as tall as I could. "I'm going," I said with vigor. "End of story. I can take care of myself."

The minutes slowed and the air became as still as a cold, winter night. We stared at each other, our breaths so shallow as we held our respective grounds that it looked as though both of us had traded respiration for the strength to be the most persuasive.

Felix's body was still, but his irises were ablaze with a frustration I hadn't quite placed in them before. It was as if the lavender in them begged for water to put out their fire, only to be given gasoline. His lips pressed together unevenly as he bit his own gums; I'd never seen him so…angry.

"I can't be bothered with this shit anymore," he eventually spat with a venom I could nearly taste. He furiously tossed the bowl of palms he'd been mixing, and as it shattered against the wall, he stormed up the stairs of the cellar with steps so harsh I thought it would raise hell itself.

I watched him until he disappeared, my back still straight, my decision unimpacted. I turned to look at Aurora, who was already eyeing me. Behind her, I could see Fuego's eyes darting between the two of us.

"You still with me, or do you want out?" I asked her.

She gave me a single, sturdy nod.

My eyes flickered to Fuego. His gaze did not hold resentment, nor the fury of his Keeper. He just seemed…bored, like he'd already known the scene that had played before him was bound to occur eventually.

I returned my eyes to my own Phoenix – my companion. "Let's go."

- F -

"Fucking nonsense," I grumbled as I kicked the ground along which I stomped. "Such utter ridiculous fucking nonsense."

She was insufferable. Maddening. Infuriating.

How could she be so idiotically headstrong?

I gritted my teeth as I walked, my fingers curling into fists and unfurling with an irrepressible tremble. I couldn't get a handle on myself. I crunched a branch on the path, and a flock of small birds shot out of a nearby bush – terrified little creatures.

Why wasn't she like that?

Why couldn't she see it the way I saw it?

The sound of whooshing air caught my attention. I shot a glance over my shoulder just in time to see her sitting resolutely atop her Phoenix as they rushed out of the cellar skylight and into the evening sky. Within seconds, they'd vanished into the clouds.

I scowled as I halted.

She was really going. She was really doing this.

I let out an angry shout as I began trekking my way back to the cellar.

I heard Fuego's telepathic snicker in my mind as I descended the staircase. *"And there he is. Right on schedule,"* he teased.

"Piss off."

"I warned you. She's a fierce one. You can't change her mind, no matter how much of a temper tantrum you throw."

"I said, piss off," I growled at him as I hopped on his back. *"Follow them."*

"What's the magic word?"

I clenched my teeth. *"...Please."*

"That's more like it," he said, and we were off.

- S -

Aurora and I chased the night as we soared through the clouds to Italy. I kept us flying below the puffs of white so I could keep track of where I was in the United States. When the Atlantic Ocean came barrelling into view, I brought us upwards, over the clouds, beneath the night sky. It was comforting to have the constant night stars on the horizon, even after so many hours.

Eventually, I felt a change in the air, and saw a difference in the pattern of the clouds. I had Aurora dip us down again and saw we were nearly finished crossing the Atlantic; I could see the details of the Western coasts of Europe and Africa down below.

I had searched for aerial views of Italy prior to leaving, so that I could identify the shape of the country and thus where I needed to land. The village of Stignano was located in the Calabria region of the country. Italy was distinct in its shape, and spotting the little nick where Calabria would be, about halfway down the 'boot' figure, was not difficult.

I scanned the ground for a covered area to land in, which was difficult to do in the dark. Eventually, I spotted a cluster of trees, and I directed Aurora down towards it. We coasted smoothly through the leaves to the ground below. I dismounted and turned to pat her softly on her back.

"Stay here. I'll be back," I told her. She cooed, and promptly made herself comfortable under the shade of the trees.

I made my way out of the greenery and onto the old, cobblestone streets. Even in the dark, everywhere I looked seemed like a picturesque postcard. I felt as though I were walking on history as I made my way down the well-worn road.

I had the location of Campanella's home pinned on my phone's maps. Using it, I navigated through the narrow walk-ways, between the ancient architecture that had somehow stood the test of time. It was breathtaking to be a part of the present moment and the past at the same time. I found myself mesmerized with the village and its people as they scurried about, seemingly unphased by where they resided.

My phone buzzed to let me know I was nearing the turn I needed to make. I followed the direction and ended up at a very old and ruined building. The doorway was a bit sunken into the ageing stone. The familiar plaque I'd seen online was fixed beside the entrance.

I studied what was written on the plaque. It had been

etched in Italian, so I grabbed my phone and entered the wording into an online translator.

In this house was born the philosopher
Tommaso Campanella
who came to eradicate the three extreme evils:
tyranny, sophistry, hypocrisy
Stignano 1568 - Paris 1639

I turned to the doorway. I grabbed the handle and pulled – it was locked.

I took a step back and studied the building again as a whole, slowly making my way around it. I couldn't believe it was still standing. It appeared older than I thought possible, but despite its deterioration, there didn't seem to be anything particularly enthralling about it. In fact, if anything, it seemed creepy. I felt uneasy around its aura on the dimly lit road.

I returned to stand in front of the plaque, getting lost in my thoughts. Three extreme evils – oppressive governmental rule, clever but false arguments, and the implication of higher standards than one assigns for themselves. It seemed there hadn't been much progress made since Campanella's death, as I could think of very relevant and pertinent examples in the society I lived in. I wondered how it had been determined that this had been his life's purpose, and I also wondered how he would feel about the state of the world several hundred years after his passing. The apprehension seemed to envelope me when I considered the stagnancy before me.

"So nothing?"

I screamed at the sudden voice, and without thinking, I instinctively threw my elbow backwards with the force of my shock. I ended up elbowing Felix square in the stomach.

"Agh!" he exclaimed, stumbling backwards and grasping his torso as he hunched over.

I gasped. "Felix! What the hell?"

"What the hell, me? More like what the hell, *you!*" he shouted. "Fuck! Why would you do that?"

"You scared me!"

"Oh, I bloody scared you, did I? Well, fancy that!" he taunted. "Little Miss Adventure is frightened of something after all! But is she willing to put her little journey to self-fulfilment aside to acknowledge that fear? Of course not! It couldn't be dangerous, now could it? Oh, no, not at all – no journey like this could be dangerous. What even is danger, anyways? Something someone could have warned her about, hm?"

I ignored his little rant, becoming more than irritated myself. "What are you even doing here? I thought you wanted no part of this!"

"I sure as hell don't!"

"Then why do you keep fucking following me everywhere?"

"Because I don't want to lose the only person I've ever considered a friend!"

There was a pause. I straightened a bit, blinking. Admittedly, I was taken by surprise.

He was breathing heavily by this point, one hand clutching his stomach, the other now bracing himself on the cobblestone wall he'd stumbled in front of. His lavender eyes were unhidden – in fact, they were blaring.

"There you go. You win," he asked, his voice still loud but cracking. "I'm a horrible person because I'm just trying to make sure you don't go and get yourself killed, and that I don't lose you. You get it now? Happy?"

My eyes widened a bit as I watched him tear up. He hastily shook his head and made a distressed sound, hiding his face from mine. He tried to straighten, but instead grimaced once more, his grip on his torso tightening as he folded even tighter.

Despite his best efforts, I could still see the few teardrops that trickled like rain down the side of his cheek and fell on to the cold, stone floor.

I couldn't believe what I was seeing. Never in a million years would I have guessed he would ever associate me with the word 'friend,' or that he would follow in my treacherous foot-steps because of worry. I also would have bet money against ever seeing Felix Clarkson cry. I wasn't sure whether he was crying out of frustration or pain, but either way, the vulnera-bility was raw and present. Those locked doors had finally been forced wide open, but it was clear a key had not been involved. Maybe explosives or a lockpick, but certainly not a key.

I sucked in my lips, approaching him. "Let's get you to a doctor," I said evenly.

CHAPTER 23

NIGHT HAD SETTLED PEACEFULLY over Stignano. Crickets could be heard in the distance, and the air was warm. We sat outside on the cobblestone steps at the entrance of the after-hours urgent care we'd eventually located. The physician had checked Felix out and given him an ice pack, assuring us both that, fortunately, it didn't seem like I'd accidentally broken any of his ribs.

I fumbled with my fingers in a bit of nervousness as I glanced away from the street before me and at Felix instead. He held the ice pack to his stomach still, blinking slowly. He noticed my movement and moved only his eyes to meet mine.

I swallowed. "I'm sorry."

He stared at me for a moment, then turned away. I sighed and looked back down at my fingers.

"I didn't mean to cause you so much worry," I tried again. "Or pain."

I waited a bit, but he didn't say anything.

I sucked in my lips. "What you said back there – I think it's important for you to know that I do consider you a friend, too. Truly."

He shifted a bit. "Charming," he muttered sardonically.

I took a deep breath in. Then I stood and walked a little ways away. There was a large archway that overlooked the rolling hills beneath us. Dots of light from homes and street-lamps were scattered about, faintly illuminating the lush green-ery. I watched one light in particular that seemed to be flickering. It flickered softer, and softer more, and for a moment, it faded to black. But then surprisingly, it returned stronger than before, glowing proudly in the night along with all the rest.

I turned back to face Felix. He was looking down at the ground beneath him, the ice pack still plastered to his torso.

I approached the steps. "Your father told me about your mother," I said.

He hesitated, then lifted his gaze to meet mine.

I cleared my throat. "She didn't want you to become a Phoenix Keeper because she was worried it might do more harm than good," I went on. "But she didn't realize the impact it would have on you becoming who you were meant to be. And she didn't realize the impact it would have if she left, either. Only you truly understand those things, because only you can feel them."

As he listened, I saw a spark in his lavender eyes. They glinted in the dim glow of a nearby streetlight.

"I know I don't have much experience being a Phoenix Keeper," I went on. "Not nearly as much as you. But the expe-rience I've had thus far has taught me that I'm not finished discovering all that lies ahead for me. I understand it might be worrisome. And it could all be a fruitless endeavour, too. But I feel it's something I need to at least try. Just as you becoming a Phoenix Keeper was your true calling, I feel like leaving no stone unturned is mine. Had your mother prevented you from your father's teachings, or been successful in killing Fuego, you wouldn't truly be yourself."

He slowly sat up straight, his back lengthening. Something immediately took over his stature, some wave of understanding and consideration. The embers in his eyes were swirling, a lavender flame flickering in the dark.

I breathed deeply. "I appreciate your concern, but all I ask is that you let me do what I feel I need to do. Whether or not you choose to join me is entirely up to you. You told me you read the stars — I feel like this adventure is me reading mine. I want to read my own stars. I want to write my own legacy. I've always intended to leave a story behind. And you're more than welcome to be a part of it, if you wish."

We stared at each other for a very long time. Had I dipped a finger in his eyes, they would have burned with the fire that danced in his irises. And as his eyes continued to dart rapidly all over my face, he finally spoke.

"You were listening to me," he murmured in a breath of shock.

His words took me by surprise, so much so that I didn't know how to respond. Of all the things he could have said, it was nowhere near what I expected to escape his lips.

"About the stars," he went on. "You were listening to me when I talked about reading them."

A confused frown was struggling not to appear on my face. "Of course I was," I replied. "Weren't you talking to me?"

Those lavender eyes were glued to mine. "Yes. I was. And you didn't just hear me. You...listened."

And then it fell into place, snapping together like magnets.

A lavender sea washed over me, and I drowned in it. And as I did, I allowed myself to dive more deeply than I ever had before, to truly immerse myself in the thoughts I could see painted in him. I could almost feel his strings being strung — the Three Sisters of Fate were hard at work. Clotho kept spinning Felix's thread of life, and Atropos kept her shears closed, but nearby — always accessible, as scary a thought as that was, a permanent reminder of fragility and mortality. But Lachesis, the allocator of fate, was the most frenzied energy I could feel. She was measuring the string, determining the nature of the life before her — deciding his fate for him as my proposition reverberated through the air, through his mind, through his bones and soul. What would the stars say? What was he destined for?

His features eventually smoothed, and he stood up slowly. "All right, friend," he said. "I'm in."

And just like that, his string was measured, his life was written, his fate was sealed — much like my own.

Felix and I both mutually agreed that we were starving, and so naturally, we ended up at a little bistro close to the doctor's office just before they closed — we were their last customers of the night. It was small and seemed to be family owned and operated; we were seated at a small table at the corner of their patio, with a view of the lush foliage on the hills below. We ordered a margarita pizza, a pasta carbonara, and a bottle of wine, as one does in Italy.

"This is the best pizza I've ever had in my entire life," I said as I scarfed down yet another piece in a frenzied manner.

Felix blinked at me. "You do realize it's not going to run away, right?"

"Well, yeah, but you might get to the next piece before me," I explained simply, taking a large forkful of the carbonara. "Gosh — Italian food is the best. Or maybe Greek food. Or, actually, maybe sushi!"

"I think you just like food in general."

I took a long sip of the prosecco we'd ordered. "And wine," I sang cheerily.

He shook his head, but he couldn't hide the amused smile on his face. We were quiet for a moment as we continued eating, and I watched as his amusement waned a bit. He seemed a bit stoic when he looked at me again.

"Why did my father tell you?" he asked.

I swallowed the bite I was chewing. "I asked him."

"About my mother?"

"About Ohên."

He looked down at his plate, nodding after a brief pause. "I see."

"I wanted to know what happened, and you had told me it was his story to share."

"Yes, I remember that. That's fair."

I sipped some wine and cleared my throat. "I'm sorry," I said. "That everything had to happen like that."

He shrugged, not looking at me. "It is what it is."

I gave him a trying smile. "I'm sure she would be proud of you."

"I don't think she cares."

I shook my head quickly. "There's no way a mother wouldn't care about her own child."

"That's what I used to think, too," he replied stagnantly, looking at me. His lavender irises had frozen over. The topic had chilled him to the bone.

I held his gaze. It seemed he was impossible to melt now that we'd opened the conversation. I could see the effects of the past as if they were playing as a film in front of me. It all flashed like movie scenes – the pain, the sadness, the confusion, the frustration. Somehow, it had all etched itself into his features, like an artist who's chiseled stone.

I realized I'd overstepped in an attempt to be positive. "Sorry. I was trying – "

"I know your intentions," he interrupted. "But nothing makes it better." He looked down at his food. "I don't like talking about it."

I took a deep breath in and nodded once. There wasn't anything more I should or could have said.

Suddenly, my phone began buzzing in my bag. I reached for it and realized it was a video call from my parents.

274

"Shoot," I said, looking at Felix. "It's my parents."

He blinked at me. "Not the worst call you could receive, in my opinion."

"Yeah, but – " I motioned all around us " – how do I explain this?"

"Are they familiar with San Diego?"

"Not really."

"Well, then. For all they know, you could be at an Italian-style restaurant somewhere downtown."

I considered this, then shrugged and answered the call. My mom and dad both came into view.

"Hi, honey!" my mom exclaimed. "We haven't heard from you in a while!"

"*Oui*, I know, I know. My bad. I've been ridiculously and stupidly busy with school." Not entirely the truth, but also not entirely a lie.

"That's all right. It's good to hear your voice." She seemed to take notice of the background. "Where are you?"

"Out to eat," I answered.

"Oh. Alone?"

"No," I instinctively replied, glancing at Felix, who met my gaze. "I'm, uh, with a friend. My physics lab partner." I cleared my throat. "Would you like to say hi?"

The question was more directed at Felix, but my mom took the opportunity to answer it before he could even open his mouth. "Sure, of course!"

Felix raised his eyebrows, quickly taking his napkin and wiping his mouth. I then handed him the phone, and he turned it so he would appear on camera. "Good evening, Mr. and Mrs. Pierre," he said.

There was a pause. "Oh," I then heard my dad say, clearly taken by surprise. "Hello, uh…"

"Felix. My name's Felix," he said hurriedly, as if to get that out of the way.

"Nice to meet you, Felix," my dad said. "You know, you look very familiar…"

Felix cleared his throat. "My father is – "

"Luther Clarkson, of Clarkson Corporations! Of course!" my mom interrupted. "You do look a little bit like him, now that I think about it!"

I cringed a bit.

Felix glanced around awkwardly. "…Thanks."

"Well, I sure hope Seraphine isn't causing you too much trouble in your physics lab," my mom said. "We know physics isn't exactly her…strongest subject."

I rolled my eyes, and I could see Felix's mouth twist at the corners. "She's…trying really hard, that's for sure."

"Oh, goodness," my mom said. "You know, we don't quite get it. Her brother's studying mechanical engineering, and we both are pharmacists. Did you know that?"

Felix seemed intrigued. "I did not, no. That's quite impressive."

"Oh, thank you. I only mention it because we thought Seraphine would do something similar. But it turns out being good with numbers doesn't run in the – "

"Well, I think this introduction's been lovely!" I jumped in, yanking my phone from Felix's hands. "It's good to see you, Mom and Dad. We'll talk soon. Love you, bye!"

I then hung up promptly, mumbling under my breath. I heard Felix chuckle and glared at him.

He shrugged. "They seem nice."

"Shut up."

"I like your mom's sense of humour."

I sighed. "I'm going to the restroom."

I got up and left. When I returned, I discovered Felix had paid the bill, and when I offered to pay him back for my share, he waved me off. We met with our Phoenixes in an area shaded by trees, and we took off for San Diego in peaceful silence.

CHAPTER 24

WITH US FLYING backwards in time, we arrived at the cellar in the very early hours of Thursday morning. Felix drove me back to the university, and I retreated to my dorm.

I knew I should have focused on getting some rest, but I had trouble sleeping. I paced around my room, my mind deep in thought. I wanted to figure out where this City of the Sun may be; the lack of knowledge was burning holes in my mind. But an hour or so of this produced nothing, and eventually, I tired myself out from pacing and went to bed.

"So, where do we start?"

Felix and I were sitting across from each other in the cellar Thursday evening, the Phoenixes munching on crushed palms Felix had made with a very necessary replacement bowl beside the sitting area. We had decided to resume our search for the City of the Sun, starting with some much needed research.

"Not really sure," I replied, looking at some of the books we'd gathered on the table. We had a couple of stories written by Phoenix Keepers around the same time as Sedaurea's documented origination, as well as some old atlases, maps, encyclopedias, and my Greek Mythology textbook. I'd figured anything that may be remotely related would be as good a guess as any for finding pertinent information. "Pick whatever appeals most to you, I guess."

Felix looked over all the materials in front of us. With a bit of a sigh, he picked up one of the atlases and began thumbing through it. I opted for a story about Demetrius, an early Phoenix Keeper in Greece, and his Phoenix, Cypress.

But after spending until nightfall scanning books, we had produced nothing but exhaustion. Felix suggested we pause and get back to it on the weekend, when there weren't any classes obstructing our time. I was more than inclined to agree.

On Saturday, Felix picked me up early in the morning. We were back in the cellar as soon as we arrived on his property.

"Shall we pick up where we left off?" he offered.

I plopped a grape into my mouth from the bowl we'd brought with us. "Let's do it."

I had never read so much in succession before. I burned through a few more Phoenix stories, then switched to some atlases. Nothing seemed to be of any relationship to the City of the Sun.

My eyes were burning by midafternoon, and when I shut them for a rest, I ended up falling asleep. I woke up a few hours later and found Felix was flipping through my Greek Mythology textbook.

He glanced up at me as I shifted. "Welcome back. Did you find anything in your dreams?"

I groaned, rubbing my face. "It was an accident."

"How the hell do you nap by accident?"

I sighed, looking at the pile of books we'd gone through. "I can't believe we haven't found anything yet."

Felix heaved a breath as he closed the textbook. "That philosopher you had mentioned – he had a book called the City of the Sun?"

I nodded. Felix took out his phone and, by the way his fingers were typing, I could only assume he was looking him up.

"Hmph. The book's on Amazon." He tapped away on his screen. "I ordered it. Maybe it's worth having a look."

I shrugged. "Couldn't hurt."

He stood from the sofa and stretched. "I don't think I can read anymore for now, though."

I nodded, yawning as I rose as well. "Let's call it a day."

"Same time tomorrow?"

"You bet."

We spent Sunday going through the last of our initial research materials with no further results. The copy of the City of the Sun arrived on Monday, so I went with Felix after classes to pawn through it. It was seventy-six pages of poetic dialogue that I could barely understand, and that certainly had nothing to do with Phoenixes.

"You know, my father once told me that you often find things when you stop looking for them," Felix told me as he shut the philosopher's work.

I sighed, taking in the mess we'd collected on the coffee table in the cellar. Thousands upon thousands of words that got us no further to our destination. It would be a lie to say I wasn't frustrated, but somehow, halting a search in the hopes an answer would come to us didn't seem like the way forward. In fact, it felt almost like admitting defeat.

"Maybe we should take a break for a bit," Felix went on. "Focus on our schoolwork or something."

I pursed my lips, glancing at him. "If you want to take a break, you can. I'd rather not."

Felix let out a breath. "I should have known better," he mumbled, but he made no motion to object to my persistence.

———

The rest of the week went by quicker than I could account for, and although I'd spent most of my evenings probing the internet and checking out more books than I could count at the library, my research had continued to produce nothing but irrelevant information.

I woke up much earlier than I needed to the following Sunday morning. As much as I wanted to spend more time researching the City of the Sun, I needed to catch up on some of the homework I'd put off to the side because of my frequent Phoenix lessons – and admittedly, I was still a little frustrated at the fruitlessness of my search thus far.

I grabbed the books I would need and headed into the lounge. Everly and Hakeem were already in there, eating some breakfast with the TV on some documentary show.

"Morning, guys," I said to them.

"Morning, Seraphine," Everly replied. "There's some extra oatmeal in the pot on the stove."

"I showed Everly how to use dates as a sweetener," Hakeem shared proudly. Everly smiled at him, and I could see Hakeem's eyes melt with a buttery warmth as he met her gaze.

"Thanks so much," I said, helping myself to a heaping scoop. "What are you guys watching?"

Everly shook her head. "Not really watching. Just had it on for background noise. You can change the channel if you want."

I nodded, walking my way over to the sofas and scanning the seating area for the remote. I gathered it was a documentary on Ancient Egypt from the commentary I was listening to as I searched for the elusive device.

"Heliopolis was one of the oldest cities in Ancient Egypt. It was the capital of the 13th Lower Egyptian Nome. The city is now found at the north-east edge of Cairo."

I lifted some pillows, still unable to locate the remote.

"Heliopolis had been occupied since the Predynastic Period and had extensive building campaigns during the Old and Middle Kingdoms," the TV droned on. "Today, it is mostly destroyed; the only surviving remnant of Heliopolis is the Temple of Re-Atum obelisk located in Al-Masalla."

"I think Roscoe was the last person who was watching TV in here, and he was sitting on that chair," Hakeem noted, and I looked up to see him motion to a chair I hadn't searched yet. I approached it, finally finding the remote on the windowsill beside it. I studied the device, looking for the button I would need to change the channel.

"The original name for Heliopolis was Junu, but it was renamed by the Greeks because it was assumed the sun god, Ra, presided there. The word Heliopolis translates to 'City of the Sun,' in Greek, and 'Eye of the Sun' in Arabic."

I stopped, whipping my head around to face the TV. "What did it say?"

I could hear Hakeem's confusion in his voice. "What?"

"What did it say translated to 'City of the Sun?'" I asked, turning to look at him.

He frowned a bit at the screen. "I think it was…Heliopolis?"

"Heliopolis," I repeated. "Heliopolis." I considered this, then fumbled with the remote in my hand. I found a rewind button, and pointed at the TV, bringing myself back to the start of the commentary.

"Heliopolis was one of the oldest cities in Ancient Egypt. It was the capital of the 13th Lower Egyptian Nome. The city is now found at the north-east edge of Cairo. Heliopolis had been occupied since the Predynastic Period and had extensive building campaigns during the Old and Middle Kingdoms. Today, it is mostly destroyed; the only surviving remnant of Heliopolis is the Temple of Re-Atum obelisk located in Al-Masalla…"

I let the TV ramble on as my eyes widened. Had I found it? Had I really found it the moment I'd stopped searching so hard for it?

I reran the sentence several times though my mind: "The word Heliopolis translates to 'City of the Sun…'"

Heliopolis – a city named for its occupant, the God of the Sun, a famous figure in Egyptian Mythology whose Greek counterpart's very name was *Helios*…

I'd been looking for a location named the City of the Sun in plain English, but I'd had completely forgotten that most places were named long ago for their qualities in other languages, just as Heliopolis was. It was not a literal 'City of the Sun,' or a place under that English name – it was named for its historical importance in mythology. Not only that, it also housed an obelisk from ancient Egypt, a civilization that predated Herodotus and the ancient Greeks. That meant it would definitely be an obelisk older than Sedaurea and brought everything together so well I was mad at myself for not figuring it out any sooner.

"You good, Seraphine?" Everly's voice interrupted my thoughts, and I snapped out of my own head to face them.

"Yeah, yeah, all good," I said as I hurried for the door. "Just have to make a phone call." I bolted out of the room before they could ask any more questions.

When I'd nearly slammed the door shut to my dorm, I leapt on to my bed and dialed Felix. He picked up after the second ring, to my surprise. I guessed he must have been up early, too.

"Hello?" came his raspy morning voice.

"Felix, I found it!" I exclaimed excitedly.

He grumbled. "What? Found what?"

"I found the City of the Sun!" I hurried on. "And I know where the sanctuary is!"

"Huh?" he questioned. "Really? Where is it?"

"Heliopolis, in Egypt! The word itself means 'the City of the Sun' in Greek! And the Al-Masalla obelisk, the only remaining part of Ancient Heliopolis – that's the obelisk older than Sedaurea! That's where the sanctuary will be!" I blurted in a rush.

"Okay, okay, hold on a second," I heard him groan. "I'm going to need you to repeat that, but slowly, so that I can actually understand what you're saying."

I sighed, but repeated it slowly so he could actually understand what I was saying.

"Hmph," he said when I was finished. "Interesting. How'd you find this out?"

"It was on some TV show my friends had on in the lounge," I explained. "Maybe we should start watching more documentaries."

"Indeed, it seems that way. I told you we might find it if we stopped looking for it."

"*Oui, oui, oui,* whatever," I said. "So, I'm thinking it'll be best if we leave today. Can I come over and we head out in the next – "

"Whoa, hey, settle down!" Felix interjected. "Leave today?"

I blinked. "Well, yeah."

"Aren't you acting a bit rash?"

I crinkled my nose. "I'm excited. And I want this Phoenix."

"Don't you have classes today?"

"Nobody has classes today. It's Sunday."

I heard him rustle around, then groan. "Oh, you're right. I suppose I lose track of time this early in the morning."

"Well, now you're back on track. Could you stop trying to stall and come get me in an hour or so?"

I heard him sigh. "Yes, I can. I'll be there soon."

"Thank you, Felix!"

I hung up, leapt out of bed, and threw some snacks, toiletries, and other knick-knacks that I thought could be of use to me into my cross-body purse. When it was stuffed to its capacity and I had changed into shorts and a loose-fitting shirt, there was a knock on my door.

I opened it, and Felix greeted me. "Hello," he said, looking me up and down. "Is that all you've got?" he then asked in disbelief, motioning to my purse.

I looked down at it, then back up at him. "Yeah?"

He blinked. "You're going to go to Egypt with nothing but a purse?"

I shrugged. "I've got snacks in there and stuff..."

"*Snacks in there and stuff?*" he repeated. "Oh, heavens..."

I rolled my eyes. "We shouldn't be there very long. All we need to do is get there, get the Phoenix, and get out."

Felix sighed, shaking his head, and stepped aside from the doorway. "Whatever you say, Little Miss Adventure," he said.

His Porsche was waiting in one of the parking stalls. I threw myself into the passenger seat as he plopped himself in the driver's seat, started the car, and pulled out of the parking lot.

Aurora seemed eager to see me when we arrived in the cellar. I hoisted myself on to her back and pushed the button that slowly began parting the overhead skylight. I turned to Felix, who had slung a backpack over his shoulders and mounted Fuego. He nodded at me, and we both took off.

We hadn't been flying for very long before Felix turned to me. "You said you had snacks in your purse, right?"

I threw him some side-eye. "I did."

"Could I...maybe...borrow one?"

I rolled my eyes, reaching into my purse and pulling out a

granola bar. "Here. You're consuming it, by the way, so you're not borrowing it. You're taking it. And I sure as hell don't want it back."

"Right. Thanks," he said.

We flew for several hours, exchanging casual conversation here and there. Eventually, I could feel the warmth flowering on me from the strength of the early evening sunrays above. A glance below me showcased a long, wide river – the Nile – separating cities that were engulfed in a desert landscape.

"We're getting close," I said, a surge of excitement pulsing through me.

"Indeed. The centre of Cairo should be around there," Felix noted, pointing to what seemed to be a highly populated and developed area. "We need to fly a little north-east of here. We'll find a deserted area to land in, and then send the Phoenixes off to go hide until the city quiets. I'll be able to communicate with Fuego and tell him to come find us with Aurora when we're ready."

"And what will we do until then?"

"My family has a hotel in Cairo," he said. "It's early evening right now. We can rest in a room until nightfall, when we'll have more freedom to poke around the obelisk without prying eyes."

I considered this for a moment. "Egyptians are usually up later. They beat the heat by being night owls. We should wait until earlier in the morning if we want the area clear, when they've all gone to bed."

He studied me. "That's quite the background knowledge."

"My mother is Egyptian," I explained. "She grew up here before she immigrated to Canada."

He raised his eyebrows. "How interesting. Full circle, if you ask me. Have you been before?"

"Surprisingly, no. So this is a bit more meaningful in more ways than one."

"I don't doubt it. Do you speak Arabic?"

"Unfortunately, also no. She never taught my brother or me – she was worried it might hinder our English and our ability to integrate."

Felix shrugged. "Might have come in handy, but it is what it is."

We coasted down to the edge of Heliopolis behind a few old-looking and seemingly abandoned buildings, hopping off our Phoenixes quickly before they zipped back up into the air and out of sight. It took me a minute to regain the balance on my two feet after being in the air for so long, but I eventually straightened myself and looked at Felix for instruction.

He motioned towards the road that led to a more populated part of the city. "Come on – let's go find a cab."

We walked for a little while towards the hustle and bustle of Heliopolis, which was a greatly appreciated stretch for my legs, and before we knew it, we had come to a road bursting with foot and road traffic. Palm trees lined the roads that the Arab men and women traversed back and forth upon, and the air was filled with the sound of honking that burst from the cars that were driving a little too close together for comfort. The architecture of the city seemed to be a merging of Greek and Egyptian styling, with tall, columned buildings being decorated with traditional Egyptian and Arabic detailing.

To my left, a small, sandy space opened between the buildings as we walked. I saw a bunch of young boys, maybe about seven or eight years old, kicking a soccer ball around. One of them accidentally kicked it past the worn-down fence, to which they all let out an exclamation of dismay. It rolled past me into the street. Instinctively, I chased after it.

"Miss Pierre, careful!" I heard Felix call after me just as I managed to stop the ball with my foot. I quickly picked it up and brought it back to the sidewalk before I could be hit by any cars, looking up at the boys. They blinked at me, and I smiled as I approached them.

The boys came to a stop before me, but before I could return the ball, I noticed a pair of eyes peer out from behind the other side of the fence. I realized it was a young girl, roughly about the same age, who was watching us curiously. I paused for a moment, and then motioned for her to come out from behind the fence, which caused all the boys to look back at her as well. Shyly and hesitantly, she slowly made her way towards us.

When she arrived at my feet, I bent down so that I was level with her. I handed her the ball, rubbing her shoulder softly, and said, "You can play, too."

I don't think she understood English, but she took the ball from me, giving me a small smile. She turned to the boys, placing the ball on the ground in front of her. After giving it a hard kick, she and the boys became enveloped in their game of soccer.

I turned back to the opening in the fence I had come through where Felix now stood. He was leaning against the side of one of the posts, observing the children and me with an unusually soft look in his lavender eyes. As I made my way back to him, I saw the corners of his mouth lift slightly, but the smile didn't ever take full form. Instead, when I was in front of him, he gave me a single nod and looked away swiftly. We began walking along the street in search of a taxi once more.

Shortly after, Felix spotted a cab amongst the crowd of automobiles and hailed it quickly. The driver pulled over to our side of the road, allowing us to hop in swiftly before he sped back into the chaos of Egyptian traffic.

The driver asked us something in Arabic. Felix and I exchanged a glance, and I shrugged my shoulders. "Clarkson Hotel?" Felix then tried hesitantly.

"Ah, yes, yes, Clarkson Hotel," the driver replied quickly with a nod, making a sudden right turn.

"Thank you," I told him.

It took about ten minutes before the cab pulled up beside a huge, very extravagant looking hotel, with beautiful fountains spewing water beside decorative statues and large, gorgeous glass windows lining the walls of the building. Felix paid the cab driver before we stepped out and entered the Clarkson Hotel.

A petite, Egyptian woman who wore very extravagant makeup stood behind the striking checkout counter that was layered with what looked like expensive granite. Her eyes widened when she saw Felix – I could only assume out of recognition.

"Mr. Felix Clarkson!" she exclaimed. "Oh, my – welcome! I did not know to expect you – " she fumbled with the computer in front of her " – no, it doesn't appear that your name is in our bookings."

Felix frowned at her. "My family owns this place. You don't need to have my name in your bookings."

She laughed nervously. "Well, yes, of course – you're right, you're right! Erm, how is it that I may help you?"

"We need a room," he replied. "A suite, preferably."

"Of course, of course!" she said, and she frantically typed something into her keyboard before producing a key. "Here's the key to room twelve-thirteen, on the twelfth floor. I hope you enjoy your stay!"

Felix took the key before turning to me. "Come on."

I followed him over to the fancy elevators, and we got in one. I pressed the button for the twelfth floor, and the doors shut with a ding before the elevator started moving up slowly. Neither of us said anything, and the elevator spoke to fill the silence, dinging once again as the door opened to the twelfth floor.

We looked at each other, and Felix motioned for me to go

ahead of him, so I began walking as he followed behind me. We came to our suite and Felix opened the door to a breathtaking room that must have been decorated for royalty. The ceilings were high and lined with beautiful, white crown moulding, and the drapes on the windows and the silk sheets on the bed were a deep, ruby red. A red sofa sat opposite the king-sized bed and an extravagant, white armoire that looked bigger than the closet back at my dorm was placed in the corner of the room. Two French doors opened out on to the balcony that boasted a stunning view of the Egyptian city, and a door near the entrance to the suite led to an ornate bathroom filled with white marble. With every detail, it seemed like whoever had furnished the room wanted to outdo the last.

"Wow," was all I could really say. Apart from Felix's villa and Luther's mansion, I wasn't very experienced or well-acquainted with such exquisite rooms.

"Mhm. It's not bad," Felix said matter-of-factly, throwing his backpack on to the sofa lazily.

"Not bad? This place is gorgeous!" I breathed.

Felix shrugged and flopped himself down on the bed. "Matter of opinion, I suppose."

I turned my attention to the balcony, slowly drifting towards it and opening the doors. The heat caressed my skin as the sun kissed the desert city, the sounds of lively Egyptian chatter and dwelling coursing through the air like a chaotic melody. I studied the surroundings, seeing the comfort and warmth of my mother's eyes all around me, recognizing the golden glow of her skin in the way the light melted in the sand.

My warm eyes; my golden skin. They came from here. Half of me stemmed from these very grounds; this place was part of me, a place I could call home.

I shut my eyes as I took a deep breath in, savouring the smell of the air. The scent of a motherland.

"How does it feel?" I heard Felix ask me. "To be here?"

I reopened my eyes, blinking as they adjusted back to the

bright sun. "Like a part of me just woke up from a deep sleep," I replied.

He hummed in acknowledgement.

I turned and threw my bag down on the sofa and headed for the ensuite. "I'm going to shower."

When I'd finished freshening up, I headed back into the suite. Felix had closed the drapes and tucked himself into one side of the bed. He glanced at me as I entered.

I stared at him as he lay on the bed, taking up most of it. I realized, then, that both of us were looking to take a nap, and there was only one bed in the room.

He took notice of my staring. "What?"

I motioned towards him. "There's only one bed."

He looked down at the duvet. "It's a fairly large bed."

I made a bit of a face.

To this, he grew entertained. "Do I smell?" he questioned in a joking manner.

"No."

"Do I scare you?"

"No."

"Are you worried you won't be able to resist such a — " he ran a hand through his hair in a prissy fashion " — *gorgeous* specimen resting beside you?"

I snorted. "Humble yourself."

He rolled his eyes, but patted the spot beside him. "Just lie down. I promise I won't accidentally try to sleep with you again."

I sighed, but the sleepiness had overridden my ability to argue. I threw myself defeatedly on to the mattress.

"I set an alarm for the very early morning, like you said," Felix added.

"Okay," I replied, turning to face away from him and pulling the covers over me.

"You tired?"

"Very."

"Right, then. Have a good sleep."

"You, too," I mumbled into my pillow.

Silence filled the room, beckoning my eyes shut as my breathing softened. I could feel sleep tugging me away from reality and into a realm of dreams.

"You know, I don't mean to brag," he then began, "but I have been told I'm a wonderful lover."

I let out a sleepy breath of amusement. "I'm very happy for you. Save it for the other girls you take to your father's events."

There was quiet again.

"I don't take other girls to my father's events," was his eventual reply.

I could feel my forehead crease a bit as a peculiar emotion spread through my chest. It was a sentiment of…disbelief, mixed perhaps with just a little bit of vanity.

Something about what he'd said had made me feel…special.

I didn't dare turn to look at him.

"Good night, Miss Pierre," he added after a while.

I cleared my throat. "Good night, Felix," I replied softly, and I let the strange hush that followed swallow us both as we slept.

CHAPTER 25

I AWOKE hours later to the sound of the alarm from Felix's phone. Groaning, my eyes fluttered open to reveal much of nothing, as the hotel room was still as dark as it had been when I fell asleep. I rubbed my eyes and glanced at the clock beside the bed. It was four in the morning, Heliopolis time.

The wretched sound was still blaring from the other side of the bed. "Felix," I grumbled. "The alarm."

I waited a few moments, but there was no movement.

I looked over at him. He was facing me and had bundled himself up in a small ball, despite the size of both himself and the bed. His snoring came and went in a steady rhythm that told me he was fast asleep as he remained tightly tucked underneath the covers.

I sucked in my lips, placing my hand on his shoulder and shaking it gently. "Felix, wake up."

He grumbled and stirred, but still did not wake.

I rolled my eyes before taking my other hand and shaking his torso roughly. "Felix, get up!" I demanded loudly.

He immediately responded this time, his eyes popping open as he had what looked like a bit of a startled spasm. "Wh- what?" he exclaimed.

I snorted, amused at the complete lack of understanding that shimmered in his lavender eyes when they met mine. "We're in Heliopolis, remember? We need to go to the Al-Masalla obelisk."

He blinked at me, and then nodded slowly as he groaned and rubbed his eyes. "Oh...yeah...right. What time is it?"

"Four in the morning. Turn the damn alarm off, please."

He finally turned it off, and I let out a sigh of relief.

"I suppose we should get going," he grumbled, sitting up and stretching. As he did, I noticed that a dark, rectangular object was poking out from underneath the pillow. I couldn't make out what it exactly it was in the darkened room.

I frowned and motioned towards it. "Hey, what's – "

Felix, who had immediately turned to look at what I was motioning to, hurriedly shoved the object completely underneath the pillow before I could finish. "Nothing!" he exclaimed very suspiciously. "...It's nothing."

I gave him a weird look. "No, seriously Felix, what is – "

"I told you it's *nothing*, Miss Pierre!" he snapped at me as he met my stare. His lavender eyes were flaring, but even in the dark, I could make out sheepishness hidden in their luminosity.

I put my hands up defensively, a little baffled. "All right, all right."

He scooted up out of bed and stood up straight, huffing a bit. "Come on. Let's get moving," he mumbled.

We gathered our things before I followed him out of the room and then the hotel. Crickets sounded in the warm night sky, and there wasn't a single soul out on the streets of Heliopolis. We walked into a back alley clear from view of the streets, and Felix looked upwards as I assumed he was telepathically calling Fuego. Within moments, I felt a rush of air as both Aurora and Fuego swooped down quickly from the night sky, picking us up on their backs before flying back up into the darkness.

"According to my maps, the obelisk is located in the center of the Al-Matariyyah district," I said, looking up from my phone search and pointing to where we needed to go. "It should be a little ways that way. We'll see the obelisk – that's how we'll know we're there."

Felix nodded, and we mounted. We flew above Heliopolis towards the Al-Matariyyah district, and it wasn't long before I spotted the monument. It was extremely hard to miss – a tall, large, Pharaonic structure standing almost out of place in the middle of its surrounding plaza, which was empty of any people or cars. Fuego and Aurora flew down towards it swiftly and landed right beside it, and Felix and I jumped off, approaching the obelisk.

We stood in front of it for a while, staring at it, wondering where exactly a Phoenix sanctuary could be concealed around it. Sure, it was big, but I doubted there was enough space inside for this so-called sanctuary. Even if there was, there didn't appear to be a door anywhere.

"So…now what?" I asked quietly.

Felix seemed puzzled, too, as he stepped around the obelisk, studying the markings on it. "I…I don't know."

I pursed my lips. Well, this was just stellar.

"Are we missing something?" I asked as I ran a hand over one of the bricks of the obelisk. "Maybe, like, a minute detail?"

Felix shook his head, frowning. "I don't think so. We're in the City of the Sun, and we're at the only remaining part of it that was around in Sedaurea's time…"

Sighing in what seemed like frustration, he leant against the structure with his shoulder, and the brick he leant against was pushed inwards, causing him to jerk backwards in surprise with a slight yelp.

There was a pause, and then the entire structure shifted slowly, the bricks rearranging themselves into some kind of formation. My eyes widened as they pushed themselves to either side of the obelisk and eventually parted into what looked like an entryway.

Felix and I looked at each other, and then he pulled a flashlight out of his backpack and shone it down the newly parted walls. Sure enough, the light revealed a staircase that led downwards into the obelisk and had clearly not been summoned for many, many years.

"Well, this certainly looks interesting," Felix noted.

I stared at the flashlight, and then at him, and I wondered if it was going to click in his mind. When he turned to look at me, he frowned.

"What?" he asked.

I rolled my eyes and snatched the flashlight away from his hands, turning it off. He seemed shocked by my sudden enthusiasm, but as I began making my way down the stairs and using the light powers within me to illuminate the staircase, I saw the lightbulb go off in his head.

"Oh, that's right," he said. "You've got a Light Phoenix."

I giggled. "Well, come on!"

He laughed too, and then followed in my lead with Fuego and Aurora trailing behind him as I bounded my way down the stairs, very much intrigued and curious about what was to come.

It was a long time before we reached the bottom of the stairs, and with the bottom came a large, stone covered room dimly lit by torches. The walls were covered from top to bottom in ancient-looking drawings that were a mix of Greek and Egyptian styling. Upon further inspection I could make out drawings of Phoenixes and humans interacting with them – I guessed they were the interpretations of Phoenixes and their Keepers. Centered at the back of the room, sitting on a stone pedestal that was illuminated by four torches on four pillars that surrounded it in a shrine-like fashion, was a yellow Phoenix egg – a Light Phoenix egg, almost identical to the one Aurora had hatched from.

Felix and I both inhaled sharply when we saw the egg, and my heart was filled with enthusiasm.

"There it is," Felix breathed.

We approached the egg slowly and stopped in front of it. A brief look at each other told me we both knew we'd reached a bit of a conundrum.

Felix cleared his throat and reached into his pocket. He pulled out a quarter, with the familiar head of George Washington engraved on one side and a bald eagle on the other.

"Heads or tails?" he asked me.

It took me a moment to fully accept the fact that we were deciding who would get the Phoenix with a coin toss before I responded. "Heads," I said.

He nodded at me, placed the coin on his thumb, and flicked it upwards. The coin flung off his thumb and on to the stone floor.

He stepped on it to prevent it from spinning or flipping, took a deep breath, and then removed his foot.

George Washington was facing upwards.

A dose of delight shot through me, and I looked at Felix. He glanced at me and gave me a trying smile, a smile of defeat, while motioning to the egg.

I swallowed as I looked him over. "Are you sure?" I asked him.

He shrugged. "You earned it fair and square," he said, but his words didn't shadow his disappointment.

"But you really want it," I countered.

"Of course I do," Felix said, clearing his throat. "But so do you. If the world granted all wants, nobody would ever want anything."

I cocked my head to the side, studying him.

He looked at the egg. "You did most of the work to find this place, anyways. You deserve it. Go ahead, Miss Pierre."

I turned to the egg, hesitating for a moment. It beckoned me like a siren tempts a sailor in murky waters. I could almost hear it whispering my name over and over, a chant in my brain that was hard to ignore.

But I shook my head, stepping away from it. "No," I said, looking back at Felix. "I want you to have it."

He gave me a look of deep puzzlement.

"You taught me how to be a Phoenix Keeper," I explained. "You let my Phoenix stay with yours. You saved me from Alchnost. You joined me all the way over here despite your initial wishes not to. And you've been a Phoenix Keeper for much longer than I have. I think you should have it."

His eyes widened. He opened his mouth, but no words escaped.

I smiled warmly. "Consider it my way of thanking you."

He cleared his throat. "I thought that was supposed to be the apple crumble."

My lips twitched. "Last I recall, we sort of agreed that had morphed into more of an apology for nearly getting us killed the night before." I motioned towards the egg. "This should be the real reimbursement. Please, I insist."

He reflected on this, his gaze flickering from the egg back to mine. "I, um…" he trailed off. "I-I don't know what to say."

I nodded once at him, my eyes softening. "Then don't say anything at all."

I saw a fire ignite in his irises. The lavender swirled and glowed, flames tickling the edges of his pupils like tiny dancers in a circle. And then, as quickly as it had started burning, the fire was doused by the welling of tears in his waterline.

He moved so quickly that it was a blur – not towards the egg, but towards me.

His embrace caught me off guard. I hadn't ever thought that Felix Clarkson would hug me. But when I realized that was exactly what was happening, I wrapped my arms around him, too. He squeezed me tightly, and I felt tiny drops of wetness fall onto the back of my shirt.

"Thank you, Seraphine," he gasped.

I felt a lump in my own throat as my eyes widened; it was their turn to pool with tears. I had concluded long ago that Felix's refusal to call me by my first name had something to do with his difficulty – or his wishes – to remain impersonal with people. But considering all the vulnerability we'd endured together recently, I could only assume that means of remaining detached had vanished.

"Thank *you*," I breathed in response, rubbing his back with my hand.

He pulled away, wiping his face with his hand. I sniffled my own tears back as I motioned to the egg.

"Go on," I encouraged him.

He let out a breathless gasp as he faced his awaiting Phoenix once more. In a matter of seconds, his palm was over top of the egg's surface. His fingers stretched over the metallic yellow surface, and it began to flash a bright array of yellow and white light. The shell cracked quickly, and out popped a fuzzy, white head.

He leaned forwards, offering both of his palms to the newborn Phoenix. It stepped into his hands willingly, its snow-white feathers gleaming in the low light of the sanctuary. Felix looked at me, his expression one of bliss, and gave out a lungful of satisfaction. I smiled just watching how happy he'd become, and came a little closer so I could get a better look at the newborn.

The Phoenix seemed to notice my movement, for it turned towards me. Shimmering, bright, white eyes met mine as it plopped the pendant it held in its tiny beak down into my palms. I opened it.

"It's a girl – Lumina," I announced after revealing the inscription inside.

"Lumina," he breathed, bringing her close into his chest as he stroked the feathers on her head gently. "She's perfect."

With the eggshells split apart, my attention was drawn to writing that had laid underneath what had been the egg. With furrowed brows, I removed the eggshells to reveal an inscription in the stone of the pedestal. Glancing at Felix, who nodded at me in encouragement, I then read it aloud:

"My light has hatched and shall brighten the way
On your journey to the land where a temple lays
In the vastest region of its kind
The temple hides away from the blind
Nestled in fauna with which it blends
Where the trees dance around the river bend
The temple sleeps through sweltering heat
And the cries of the clouds who often weep
Like to each other, this temple will draw
My brothers and sisters in feather and caw
And within it slumbers my wings of Earth
Who awaits your hands to awaken its birth."

"A clue to the next Phoenix. The Earth Phoenix, by the sounds of it. I suppose Sedaurea must have left these clues in all the sanctuaries, to serve as a guide," I concluded pulling my phone out and taking a picture of the inscription. We'd need that for later.

"Hmph. Isn't it frustrating that they all seem to be riddled?" Felix blurted snappily.

I giggled. "I agree it is annoying. But if you think about it, it's also very clever. I would say it protects the Phoenixes from people who don't deserve them."

He considered this. "I suppose. You did put a lot of hard work into deciphering that first riddle. I'd say that's a test of worthiness." He glanced back at the pedestal. "You should be rewarded for that one, when we succeed."

"If we succeed."

"I've no doubts we will."

I smiled to myself. "I'm going to start working on figuring it out right away."

"No," I heard him say.

I turned to him in surprise – I'd thought we'd put all the resistance to rest. But as soon as I got a glimpse the look in his eyes, my mind eased. They were filled with the same determination that I had billowing inside my heart. There was a cunning leer painted on his face, tinted with an almost sinister confidence.

The Three Fates were whirling, reeling, flustered about our strings. Two threads that hadn't known each other very long, that had been spun from very different cloths, that hadn't even fathomed ever being near each other. And now, they were twisted together, interlaced with a need only they truly understood.

I could almost feel our strings tie together in knots as Felix said, "Not without me, kindling."

TO BE CONTINUED

IN

THE PHOENIX KEEPER
AND
THE FIERY WATERS

ABOUT THE AUTHOR

Margarita Artista was born and raised in British Columbia, Canada. She has been writing since she could hold a pen, and as a child, she often found herself scribbling silly little stories in her notebooks. Margarita's lifelong dream has been to write a story that inspires her readers the way her education and favourite books have inspired her. She holds a BA in Sociology and is currently completing a Master's of Public Administration.

Margarita resides with her fiancé, Chris, and their three birds – Iago, Zazu, and Jewel – in British Columbia.

Margarita Artista

www.ingramcontent.com/pod-product-compliance
Lightning Source LLC
Chambersburg PA
CBHW031335020726
47499CB00005B/1279